SHADES of

A Brad Wi'

CH00531401

To PA
HOPE YOU
ENJOY THE BOOK

TOM BOLES
NOV '21

The second book in the Brad Willis
series

ISBN-9798763395334

For my late dad – Joe
Who inspired me to write

Author's Note

Both the South Pole telescope and the IceCube Observatory exist in Antarctica. The SPT investigates the Cosmic Microwave Background, a remnant from the Big Bang and the creation of the Universe. It also played a major role in acquiring the first photograph of a black hole in 2019. The IceCube Observatory detects and observes neutrinos. These are the smallest pieces of anything that can exist. Millions pass through your body undetected every second. Neutrinos are created in supernovae, among other things. Supernovae are massive stars that explode at the ends of their lives. The Amundsen-Scott South Pole Station exists and is managed by the United States. All the other base stations mentioned in this story are also manned over the bitter winter months.

CHAPTER 1

At the Amundsen–Scott South Pole Station, every light went out in the comms room. Even the LEDs on the servers were dark. Communications ceased. The hum of the cooling fans stopped. Time froze on the wall clock at 10:23. It was dark, but a little daylight came through the window. It was summer in Antarctica, and it was always daylight because, in the summer, the sun never sets at the South Pole.

Johnny Ward glanced out of the window and watched a Skibird plane attempting to land. Its wings swayed up and down, out of control. While he watched, he signalled to Andy his colleague. They ran out onto the observation platform, where they saw the aircraft land hard on the ice and bounce back into the air. It crashed down for a second time then careered off the end of the runway and came to an undignified halt, nose down in a wall of snow.

On the base, the lights flashed on then straight off again. All hell broke loose. Klaxons sounded and sirens squealed. Every alarm on the base screamed. Eardrums ached in the deafening cacophony. All logic ceased to exist. It was as though the Universe had temporarily switched off the laws of physics. Nothing made sense.

This shouldn't happen. There should be no way this could happen. There must have been a surge in the electricity supply, but a surge couldn't be the reason either. The units had no common electricity supply; multiple generators were spread throughout the base. Each group had its individual backup supply.

It must have been a huge solar storm that had generated an electrical pulse. That must be the cause. Yes, that must be it. Our nearest star must have expelled a huge coronal mass, propelling ionising gas towards the Earth.

Two hours passed. Everything settled down again, power was restored, but there was no mention of any abnormal Sun activity from any scientific sources. They carried out extensive checks and double-checks on all the generators, and the equipment and the distribution system, but the wiring proved faultless.

Callum McGregor claimed to be in charge of engineering. He shifted in his seat, fidgeted and frowned. Under the pressure, the pencil in his fingers snapped. If he didn't find an explanation for the surge, the same thing could happen again. He had discovered that some circuit-breakers had melted in the surge, so he would need to check that the site engineers had ordered replacements.

When McGregor walked into the maintenance unit, he found the techies in a huddle. He tapped one on the shoulder. The technician turned with a start.

'Hi, Callum.' The senior engineer stepped aside. 'I've called the McMurdo Station. They can't supply us with any replacement breakers. They will have to order them from Christchurch.'

'What? Come on. They're supposed to stock enough breakers for this sort of thing.'

'It's not that. They had the same experience. And it happened at the same time. At 10:23 exactly.'

***

Station Leader Dr John Connor opened the meeting. Above him, the wall clock showed 1 p.m. The long, narrow room, typical of many on the base, had little additional furnishings and a minimum of aesthetic design. Connor sat at one side of a square table with a projector screen behind him and a three-inch wad of papers in front. It was unusual for him to call a meeting of this nature. Slowly he pushed the few hairs he had left back over the crown of his head and took a long, deliberate breath.

'Good afternoon, gentlemen. Callum, you say this happened at McMurdo too?' He didn't wait for McGregor to answer. 'But that's over eight hundred and fifty miles away.'

During the summer months, McMurdo was the principal supply and transport hub for most traffic in Antarctica, and the Amundsen–Scott Station relied on McMurdo for its supplies.

'It also caused problems as far away as the UK's Halley Station. That's on the opposite side of the continent. It's a completely unknown phenomenon – we huvnae seen it afore.' McGregor shrugged, his Scottish accent evident.

'Or else it's man-made,' said one of the techies from the far side of the table.

'The Antarctic Treaty forbids the use of that level of energy. It would need to be weaponised to produce that amount of power,' said another.

'Gentlemen, slow down, let's not jump to conclusions.' Connor was trying to calm their fears. 'First, we need to look for a natural cause. It's still early days. We might still get reports of solar activity. I'll send a report to the National Science Foundation but I imagine every base on the continent will have emailed similar alerts by now.'

'So, what else can we dae apart fae waiting until it happens again?' McGregor gave a cynical laugh. The smile on his face revealed everything he thought.

'Once we finish here, I'd like all you techies to inspect the damage to see if its physical appearance can point us to the cause. For example, did magnetism play a major role, or could it just have been an electrical surge?'

Linda Foreman barged into the room to join the meeting, uninvited. Her cropped spiky hair gave her a manly appearance. Her voice matched. As she dropped into a chair she almost shouted, 'If you ask me, I can confirm the surge was part magnetic and part electrical, because that's what's expected from the bloody physics.'

For the last year, Linda had been the project manager for the South Pole Telescope, or SPT, which observed the sky in microwave frequencies.

'The surge has put the sensors on the telescope out of action for twenty-four hours – we've wasted over two days' work.' She slammed a folder down on the table. 'We cryogenically cool the telescope sensors close to absolute zero. Once we've lost power, we need to restart the cooling process from the beginning.'

'All I can do is report it to the US and see what they advise. As soon as I get any information, I'll call another meeting and give you feedback on what I receive. Hopefully, this is a one-off.' As Connor got to his feet, the others, assuming the meeting closed, stood and followed him out.

***

Connor was wrong. Within twelve hours, the klaxons and sirens had sounded again. The lights in the galley dimmed during dinner. A mass evacuation followed. Meanwhile, scientists left to check on any experiments they had left running, leaving their meals uneaten.

John Connor returned to the square table again. Linda Cross stormed in too. 'I will need to switch the telescope systems off until someone solves this problem. If I keep switching the cooling on and off without cycling it down, it will do permanent damage.' Slapping her plastic folder down on the table for the second time that day, she glowered at Connor, as though her eyes were daggers aimed at his heart.

'If any mair circuit-breakers get fried, we'll have to close the whole base.' It was McGregor. He had a sly grin on his face. It didn't go unnoticed by John Connor.

'Okay,' Connor said. 'We will need to escalate this. As well as our investigation, I will request they send an investigator from the US to look into it. Stop all experiments until we get a handle on this – there's no point putting the instrumentation in danger. First thing in the morning, I'll speak to the NSF.'

McMurdo and the Pole operate on New Zealand time. Since most flights to the continent are from Christchurch on New Zealand's South Island, it made sense to use their system on the base. There was a sixteen- to eighteen-hour time difference between Christchurch and Alexandria, Virginia, where the offices of the National Science

Foundation were, depending on which city was using Daylight Saving Time. Because they were in the northern hemisphere, in early January they lagged eighteen hours behind the base. Since it was past midnight, Connor had less than two hours to wait.

'This meeting is closed. As soon as I hear anything, I will give you an update from the NSF.'

McGregor waited behind, a negative attitude oozing from his pores. 'They should never have put that laddie Connor in charge. He disnae huv a clue.'

The other techies knew him well. They ignored the comment.

CHAPTER 2

The head of MI6 leaned back in his chair and surveyed the paperwork on his desk. He brushed his sparse white hair away from his forehead, gave a deep sigh, and tightened his lips. The last twenty-four hours had been a nightmare. From his office on the third floor of the Secret Intelligence Services Building at Vauxhall Cross, he enjoyed an uninterrupted vista of the Thames. A fine January mist covered the river with a layer of soft candyfloss from the Albert Embankment to the London Eye.

Earlier in the day, another event had been reported on London Bridge. His operatives deemed the incident to be terror-related. Nearly all terror-related events came to his department, and this was no exception. Since the COVID-19 pandemic, there had been an increase in lone terrorists trying to make their mark, with all nationalities competing to see who could cause the most disruption to the public. The lockdown placed a strain on many people's health, mental as well as physical.

Mike Reilly lifted the papers that detailed all the actions he'd put in place resulting from the day's activities, and prepared to walk to his car. He collected another few sheets of paper, slotted them into his briefcase and snapped shut its security lock. Reilly stood and headed for the door. Before he reached it, however, his phone rang. *No, not again.* Reilly gave a resigned sigh, sucked a lungful of air through his teeth, and returned to his chair. 'Hello, Department 33, can I help you?'

'Is that Michael Reilly?'

'Speaking.'

'I'm sorry to bother you this late on a Friday evening, Mr Reilly. My name is Chuck Miller. I'm calling from the National Science Foundation in Alexandria, Virginia. A neighbouring organisation in Langley gave me your details. I hoped that I'd catch you before you packed up and left for the night.'

'Whenever the opportunity arises, I co-operate with the organisation at Langley. How do they imagine I can help you?' Reilly enjoyed a good working relationship with his counterpart in the CIA. Calls like these were routine. But this was the first time that the NSF had called him.

'Recently, I received a recommendation from Brigadier-General Joshua S. Baker. Let me explain. The NSF supports research all over the world on behalf of the US. We manage a base in the Antarctic, at the South Pole. Several incidents have occurred there recently that require scrutiny. I suspect we will need to identify a technical solution or, at least, carry out a scientific investigation to find out what's going on. The US has no legal status in Antarctica – nor does any other country. While we're doing that, we need to handle things discreetly.'

'You must be joking. You need help in Antarctica?'

'I'm afraid so. I realise this is an unusual request, but we need someone who knows what they're doing. He should only need to stay for a couple of weeks at most.'

'Since I assume your contact is Josh Baker, are you thinking of my man, Willis?'

'I am. Josh speaks highly of him following a mission in Kazakhstan last year. Baker described him as a useful guy with a talent for tackling unusual assignments. This situation is certainly unique.'

'That's one way of describing him. Tell me what you require Willis to do, then I will say whether I think the job might fit in with his skills.'

'We've experienced two unexplained EMPs – electromagnetic pulses. They were serious enough to cause disruption and some damage to our equipment. If we allow them to continue, they could disable the entire Amundsen–Scott South Pole Station. People would die if this happened over the winter months. If a surge compromises the electricity supply, they would freeze to death – it would be impossible to get them off the Pole, so we need to investigate these pulses as a matter of urgency.'

'Have you eliminated natural causes?' Reilly asked.

'Not completely. Although a natural explanation is unlikely. That's why we agree with Josh Baker that your man is well suited for the task. Willis has a sound scientific background.'

'I can speak to him – provided you realise that Willis isn't an official operative of our organisation. He operates in a voluntary capacity.'

'Yes, Baker explained that to me. He will get him a pass onto the station and get him an introduction so they recognise him as our official investigator.'

'Okay, do that. Willis might well decide to go undercover. To begin with, at least. He might decide to pass as a visiting scientist for a while.'

'The guy who runs the McMurdo Station is a US Marshal, but he's pretty lightweight for what we need. And he has even less authority with non-US personnel.'

'Okay, I'll contact Willis then ring you with his reaction.'

'Baker told me that Willis suffers from PTSD. Will that be a problem?'

'It's never got in the way of his work before. When he visited St Petersburg at the end of his last assignment, he received treatment for the condition. As far as I am aware, he hasn't experienced a recurrence since. Willis is a good man. If he agrees to this job, he will travel using his own passport. Most of your scientists will recognise him by reputation. Brad will fit in easily. I'll contact him and give you his answer.'

***

Brad Willis was busy preparing his evening meal. Willis lived in a small cottage in Madingley, close to his office at the Institute of Astronomy at Cambridge University. He had moved here, to be closer to work, after he lost his wife, Carole, in a tragic hit-and-run accident. When he removed his microwave meal from the oven, the phone rang. Hot gravy spilled over the edge of its cardboard container and landed on his thumb.

'Bugger, hell and damnation,' Willis yelled. After he'd hastily dropped the meal on the table, he rinsed his hand under the cold tap. With his dry hand, he lifted the receiver. 'Hello?' he shouted into the mouthpiece.

'Take it easy, Brad, this is Mike.'

Willis recognised the voice immediately. There was no need for Mike Reilly to introduce himself. When calling, he never mentioned his family name. Reilly claimed anonymity gave him an extra level of security. To anyone listening in, he might be anyone called Mike.

'Now what problem have you found that needs solving?'

'You'd better sit down for this one.'

'I would be sitting if you hadn't interrupted. And I'm about to eat my evening meal.'

'I'm sorry, Brad. I try to miss your meals but you eat at such irregular times.'

'*Now* where do you want me to go?' Willis concealed his pleasure at speaking to Reilly. His lot in Cambridge bored him. Willis was a professional astronomer. He lived for his work, but no one had allocated him time on any of the world's largest telescopes for weeks. The lack of telescope time got to him. He itched for something new to do.

Reilly told him where he wanted him to go.

'You must be joking.'

Reilly recognised the reply. It was the same reaction Reilly had given when Chuck Miller told him. Willis grinned, but tried to hide the elation in his voice. 'This request is a welcome surprise. What's happening on the other side of the world that might need my talents?'

'They've experienced at least two severe EMPs. Their scientists have eliminated coronal mass ejections from the sun. They've checked out the SOHO and the Parker Solar Probe satellites and others to check if the sun has been misbehaving, but nothing showed up.'

11

'A pretty powerful pulse would be needed to cover a sizeable area in Antarctica. I can't imagine that a man-made pulse could be so powerful.'

'Well, that's what you will need to find out. Are you happy to go?'

'I've always wanted to visit Antarctica, so there's no way I will refuse a once-in-a-lifetime trip like this.'

'Is your visa for Australia still valid?'

'It is. You only need to get me from Australia into New Zealand and onto the Antarctic continent. If you can use your influence and get me assigned to the South Pole Telescope Project, that would be perfect. Then I won't need to say straight away that I'm an investigator.'

'I suggested to Chuck Miller that you might want to take that approach. He offered to arrange it.'

'I'd better start swotting up on whatever research the SPT is working on. The last time I checked, they were searching for galaxy clusters by looking at the strength of two-millimetre radiation.'

'I'll get your flights arranged and the details emailed to you by tomorrow morning.'

***

Reluctantly Willis returned to his microwave meal, which was now cold and looked disgusting. He blasted it for another five minutes. It made the food taste only slightly better. Willis began to fantasise about the trip. The idea made him smile again and forget about the pain in his hand caused by the earlier burn.

He also thought about Sophie and smiled. The last time he'd seen Sophie, she'd cut her mousy brown hair much shorter. Her locks curved around her face and drew his eyes towards her sensual mouth. Sophie was an old friend from his university days, and they had re-established their old relationship last year. But she had to return to CERN in Switzerland to complete her research on the Large Hadron Collider. What Willis hadn't told Reilly was that Sophie was currently working on an offshoot project at the IceCube – an observatory that has its detectors buried under the ice to search for neutrinos. The IceCube Observatory was based at the Amundsen–Scott South Pole Station – in Antarctica. That was the major reason Willis didn't hesitate to accept his new assignment.

While Willis felt unsure about the future of his relationship with Sophie, they certainly enjoyed a strong connection. An image of Carole came into his mind again, which he immediately regretted. Thinking of her always cooled his ardour.

Willis lifted the phone and called Mrs Burns's number. He let it ring twice then replaced the phone. They used this as a code. Two rings meant it was Willis, and she didn't need to answer. Likewise, when she called Willis, she didn't pay for the call. It suited her. Mrs Burns was Willis's elderly Scottish housekeeper. She looked after the house and Ptolemy, Willis's cat, whenever he went away. Willis had called him Ptolemy after the astronomer who had believed the entire Universe revolved around him. The cat shared this belief. He wasn't wrong.

Mrs Burns arrived at the cottage within minutes. 'You're off again, I suppose?'

'I will be, Mrs Burns, but only for a few weeks this time. While I'm gone, can you do the usual? Take care of Ptolemy?'

'That cat is more mine than yours. Ptolemy doesnae ken where his home is. As long as you leave the money in the caddy, I'll be happy.' Mrs Burns acted as a replacement grannie to Willis. She even reminded him of her. She wore her hair in a tight bun behind her head and dressed in a floral pinny that wrapped around her rotund body. The garment tied at the waist with a piece of material covered in the same gaudy floral pattern. She had a heart of gold. Willis would be lost without her.

Ptolemy wound his body around Willis's ankles. The animal always sensed when he was planning a trip. The cat met him first with a show of affection, followed by a disdainful attitude to make his disapproval obvious.

'I'll leave money in the tin. If I get held up, I'll send more to your savings account at the post office.' The tin, a dented tea caddy, sat above the dresser. Willis left Mrs Burns's expenses in the caddy to cover cat food and to pay for her other general duties.

'Time to go, Ptolemy,' she said as she marched out the door. The disgruntled cat followed at her heels, not even looking back.

Willis kept a suitcase packed for occasions like this. He threw a few extras on top of his clothes, added his passport, and left the case by the door. He'd have an early alarm in the morning. He must get some shut-eye. Sleep never came easily to him on long flights, despite his frequent practice. He wanted to sleep soundly tonight.

Willis crawled into bed to dream about meeting Sophie again. The prospect excited him. Did he love her? Doubt swamped his thoughts. He thought he might, but only time would tell. Willis stared at the ceiling, watching a house spider weaving its web in the corner above his head until sleep took over and he fell into a pleasant unconsciousness.

**

At home, Reilly was on the phone with Chuck Miller. 'Our man's on board. He will leave tomorrow.'

14

CHAPTER 3

Willis's head drooped. His eyes closed. The taxi turned into the parking bay at the Departures level of Terminal Two at Heathrow. At last he could relax.

'You're here, guv.' The taxi driver put his cases on the pavement while Willis fumbled in his wallet for money. His ticket was for Qatar Airways Flight QR10 to Sydney, stopping off at Doha. It left at 7.45 a.m. The trip would take over twenty-seven hours, including the stop-off. Sitting in an aircraft seat for over a day did not appeal one bit. Willis planned to use the time to read the latest papers published by the team at the SPT. He'd need to do that if he intended to fit in. Once he was settled in his seat, he ordered some coffee and focused on the task ahead. He felt more tired than he'd imagined he would, and after only half an hour, he fell sound asleep. His research would have to wait.

SHADES of WHITE

When he stepped off the Air New Zealand flight at Christchurch Airport, every bone in Willis's body ached. The final three hours from Sydney had felt like a quick hop after the previous marathon. Before he picked up his baggage, he realised his clothes would be a complete waste of space, as everything he'd packed was for a British winter, not an Antarctica one. The baggage would surely show him up as an amateur. If he'd been more professional, he would have known he'd need specialist cold-weather gear for the temperatures at the Pole.

When he stepped out of the plane, he screwed up his eyes as the natural light assaulted his pupils. The evening rays shone directly into his face. God, he could sleep for a week. He had been popping melatonin tablets since Reilly contacted him, to counter the effects of jet lag. He found it hard to believe that he would soon find himself in temperatures well below zero. Here he stood, in warm sunshine.

His passage through passport control and customs progressed slowly, but – thank goodness – not as slowly as when he'd last visited the USA. If they took that long, he would surely fall asleep on his feet. He answered the banal questions at customs – as though anyone would say, 'Yes, of course, I'm smuggling drugs. Sure. I'm carrying concealed weapons.' A trained sniffer dog paid particular attention to the baggage of an elderly lady in front of him.

'Hello, doggie,' she said and bent to pat the animal. The dog backed away.

'Have you any Terry's Chocolate Oranges in your bag, madam?' the customs officer asked.

'No, I don't. I've brought some sweeties, though.' The customs officer tensed momentarily until she told him she meant sweets. He led her to the next available inspection desk and told his companion, 'This lady has sweeties with her.'

'Oh, has she indeed? I'll take special care of her.'

The old lady walked through, apparently blissfully unaware that 'sweeties' was a code word for drugs in the Antipodes.

When Willis passed out of customs, a tall, fair-haired young man of around twenty-five stood with a card bearing his name. At least, Willis thought it was his name: it was spelled 'Willes'. Below his name was another. The name read Costa.

'Good evening, Dr Willes. I hope you had a pleasant trip.'

Willis grunted in reply.

'My name is Alan. I am here to get you to your hotel tonight. I imagine you're knackered. That trip is a killer. We need to wait for a Dr Costa. Then we can be on our way.'

When Dr Costa finally turned up, she took Willis by surprise. The doctor was about five foot seven inches tall with long auburn hair, and not unattractive. She took Willis's hand and introduced herself.

'My name's Gabriella Costa. I'm pleased to meet you, Dr Willis. I've heard a lot about you and read most of your work, and I'm a great admirer of yours.'

'Ah, Gabi ... Costa? I thought the name sounded familiar. You specialise in clusters of galaxies – excellent work. I know it well. Your team discovered the Phoenix Cluster, if I recall correctly.'

'You've an excellent memory. I believe we will both be working on the ten-metre telescope?'

Willis didn't dare admit that he'd read about it only hours earlier. 'I hope so.' They pushed their baggage trolleys out to the car.

Willis used the ride to quiz Gabi about her latest research. As he did so, he hoped she wouldn't spot that all his questions were open ones. Fortunately, she was happy to talk without asking him any difficult questions – and, fingers crossed, without him revealing the fact that his knowledge of her work was extremely sparse. Gabi summarised the last two years of her research in the forty minutes it took to drive to the hotel. It would have taken Willis hours to read that much information. Finally, he felt more confident that he could pass, if he was careful, as an astronomer experienced in her field of work.

***

The hotel looked basic, but comfortable. Alan left them to eat dinner and rest after saying, 'You will need to come to the CDC to pick up your ECW gear before catching your flight to McMurdo tomorrow morning.'

'Sorry?' Willis asked, confused.

'I'm sorry. I mean, Clothing Distribution Center and Extreme Cold Weather gear.'

Willis was relieved that he was being supplied with the correct clothing.

'Is this the first time you've visited Antarctica, Dr Willis?' Gabi asked.

'Please, Gabi, call me Brad. Yes, it is my first time. I'm excited about the entire trip.'

'That novelty will wear off quickly. Have a good shower before you leave the hotel tomorrow. Showers in Antarctica are restricted to two minutes, twice a week, to preserve water and energy.' Gabi grinned.

Willis wanted to learn more about what would become this novel way of life. 'Alan said a C-17 aircraft would fly us into McMurdo.'

'Yes – they're enormous, and not a very comfortable ride. And don't call the station McMurdo; that's a sure signal you're a newbie.' Gabi smiled. 'The locals call the place MacTown.'

'What about any other tips you can give me, especially anything that stops me from standing out as a newbie?'

'How about midrats? That's the midnight meal for night-shift workers. And don't call the place the Pole. Anyone who's been to the Pole refers to it as Pole. For example, "I'm wintering at Pole this year." The same thing goes for the observatory. "I work at SPT or at IceCube." The term "the Pole" is reserved for the physical poles, either the ceremonial pole or the geographical pole.'

'That'll sound awkward until I get used to it. I can see that I'll need to stay close to you to pick your brains.'

***

That night Willis slept the sleep of the just. He wasn't suffering from jet lag – yet. He awoke the next morning, bright-eyed and bushy-tailed. After rising, he enjoyed an extra-long shower, as Gabi had recommended, then he left to meet her in the restaurant.

'Seriously, I recommend you choose anything other than a fry-up,' she said. 'The food at the base is very calorific. It's mainly meat – and fried meat at that. They serve a lot of fried chicken. That's probably the favourite meal on the base. Everything you eat will be bad for cholesterol, but at least you're young enough not to need tablets to lower your cholesterol. Most of the oldies need to take them. If you winter-over – I mean, if you stay over the winter – you will probably lose weight, at first at least, despite the calorific food, as the cold burns calories like mad. Once you learn the correct clothes to wear outside, this will probably stop. And enjoy fresh vegetables while you can – they become a lot scarcer once the winter starts.'

Willis confided that he had only brought normal clothes with him, that would be unsuitable for life in Antarctica. He was surprised and pleased when Gabi advised him that he would wear those most of the time except when outdoors. The rooms and corridors were all adequately heated. Secretly, he clenched his fists. That should have been obvious too.

Willis and Gabi connected with another few travellers destined for Pole around eight o'clock. They all climbed into a people carrier to go and collect their ECW, as Alan had promised. The bright orange people carrier drove them to a warehouse facility where two heavy duffle bags awaited each of them.

'Open it. Check out the clothes, if possible,' Gabi said.

'How many times have you visited Pole?'

'This will be my third trip. I work with Dr Linda Foreman, as you will. I think you'll like her – she's fun.'

After he'd checked the clothes, Willis was glad he'd done so. 'Nothing in the bags fits me. They seem like loose-fitting clothes, but these must have been intended for a short lady.' He swapped the bags for another set, and tried those clothes on. 'These fit much better.' Willis checked out the inventory list that accompanied the bags. The first line read 'Big Red'. This appeared to be a big down jacket.

'Everyone gets one,' volunteered Gabi. 'You'll find it hard to tell people apart until you get to know them better. I personally recognise people by the way they walk.'

Willis checked out a knitted cap, a balaclava, a neck gator, snow pants – which Gabi told him were called Carhartts – a pair of ski goggles, mittens, gloves, glove liners, thick socks, FX, or 'Bunny' boots, which are well insulated boots, fleeces, long underwear and thick socks.

Willis shook his head. 'The powers-that-be supply enough hand protection.'

'Don't worry, you will use all of it. We also wear hand warmers inside our gloves when we work outdoors. Your hands will quickly chill if you touch anything metal. That includes the telescope. In fact, don't touch any metal with your bare hands when you're outside – the cold will burn your skin off. Gloves on their own can be inadequate at colder times. We'll need more socks. The boots make your feet sweat, so it's better to change your socks regularly. Don't worry, you'll get used to it.'

They embarked directly from the CDC. After they had been processed through security, they dropped off their luggage and it was palleted, ready for shipping. They watched some videos on how to stay safe then donned some of their ECW (big red boots, coveralls, gloves, goggles and hats). They were only allowed to carry a book bag and the rest of their ECW bag with the remainder of their gear, in case of emergencies.

Willis asked himself what he'd got himself into.

CHAPTER 4

When they arrived, the Boeing C-17 stood at the far end of the airport. Even from this far away, the aircraft's four Pratt & Whitney F117-PW-100 turbofan engines filled the sky with sound. This giant would fly them to the Earth's southernmost continent. Willis's heart began to race at the sight of the monster that manoeuvred in the distance.

At 9 a.m., they boarded and braced for take-off. This flight would differ from commercial flights. Willis and Gabi were strapped in along the bulkhead on small seats that swung down from the walls of the cabin. More would fit into the centre space. On this journey, the empty area was filled with cargo. This late in the season, few scientists and staff were travelling to The Ice. The plane's engines exploded into life. The enormous aircraft crept forward. When the plane reached the edge of the airstrip, it did a one-hundred-and-eighty-degree turn. Its jets roared again and surged ahead. As Willis's tiny seat vibrated, his rear end threatened to slide off. He thanked God for his seatbelt. The C-17 accelerated quicker than a civilian plane. The thrust pushed him sideways in his seat, and Willis had to hold on for the first few moments. Within seconds, its nose lifted. The noise from its wheels on the runway disappeared. They were airborne. McMurdo and Ross Island, here we come.

Gabi sat on Willis's right, the duffle bag containing her ECW on the floor beside Willis's, both strapped down safely. Gabi looked at Willis. 'The flight might not be the most comfortable you've ever experienced, but at least we're on our way. A commercial plane from Christchurch to McMurdo takes just under eight hours; the C-17 takes only five.'

'I've never been on a plane this huge. I am amazed it can get off the ground. There's so much room in here, we could hold a party.' Willis inspected the cabin.

'Wait till you get to the base before you consider partying. Parties help keep us sane, so we have several each year to be sociable.'

'I will await them with interest. The whole thing sounds like a lot of fun.'

'Don't be too sure. Before you decide, wait till you've been around for a while.'

During the flight, Willis stood up several times to stretch his legs. He fetched the food bags they had been given by personnel at the CDC. They each contained a sandwich, an apple, some crisps and a bottle of water. Pretty spartan. After all, it was a military plane, not a commercial airliner. The plane's lack of windows might have made Willis feel claustrophobic, but the sheer size of the space stretching in front of them prevented this.

Willis asked himself again why he had wanted to come on this assignment. The answer shouted out to him. Sophie would be there. He wondered what she would do when he walked up to her. Would she welcome him with open arms, or would she think that he was stalking her? Good God, he hadn't considered that. What if she decided he was stalking her? Of course she wouldn't think that. Willis put such thoughts out of his mind. He would startle her, for sure. He hadn't messaged her to say that he was on his way. His lack of a message might upset Sophie. She might be shocked to see him. It would shock him if he travelled to the end of the world, only to find a friend turn up to surprise him. Was that what he was – a friend? Or was he more than that? When they parted they certainly had been more than friends? He hesitated to call them lovers but that was a better description than friends. Willis wished now that he'd warned her. He couldn't help that now. He'd left it too late. Perhaps he would send a note from McMurdo? No, that wouldn't be right. It would be better if he did it in person. Willis was normally so decisive, but something about Sophie screwed up all the logical thinking processes he'd gained as a scientist. He tried to concentrate on more pleasant things. He reflected on their time together in college, how they used to study together. One day they would read in Willis's room, the next they would spend in Sophie's… and then there was the pizza. Willis and Sophie loved pizza. Because they had a tiny food budget, they either bought takeaways or ate at their university halls.

Reminiscing made him regret that he hadn't been more decisive when they'd last met. The bottom line was, he couldn't wait to see her again, no matter how she reacted when they met.

24

But there were even more serious matters to consider. Was the phenomenon of the EMP the sort of problem he could resolve? It would take all the ingenuity that he could muster. What could lead to a magnetic discharge of the energy reported? The reason eluded him. Nature might generate something of that strength but they had ruled that out. Willis wanted to keep his options open, to avoid eliminating any possibility at this point. The winter close-down at Pole approached fast. Soon the temperature would drop. All transport in and out of the base would be suspended. If he didn't find the cause before mid-February, he might be trapped on the Ice. It all depended on the weather. If he missed the last flight, he wouldn't be able to get off until after the base reopened, perhaps at the end of October, weather permitting. He must find the solution before the weather cut the base off from civilisation.

Even though he tried hard to stay awake, Willis got sleepy. He closed his eyes. The natural rocking of the plane lulled him into a state of somnolence. At least two hours passed while Willis dozed. A bout of turbulence woke him. Despite its size, the C-17 still shook and vibrated in storms. Willis tightened his seatbelt then turned to see if Gabi was okay. He found her staring at him, grinning.

'Hello, are you back in the world of the living again? Had a good sleep? You were out for the count for a couple of hours.'

'No, I wasn't,' Willis insisted. 'I only dozed.'

'You did not.' Gabi was equally insistent. 'This storm has been going on for at least an hour. I thought you would fall off your seat at one stage.'

'I'm sorry, I thought I was dozing.'

'Oh, you more than dozed. And who is the young lady that you're fearful of upsetting?'

'Don't tell me I talked as well?'

'You did. At one point, you got quite upset. I toyed with waking you but decided against it. At least you didn't snore.'

'I'm so embarrassed. I apologise.'

'Don't worry, I'm the soul of discretion. Your secrets are safe with me.' Giggling, Gabi handed him a bottle of water.

'Where are we?' he asked.

'I'm not sure. We can hardly look out of the window.' Gabi grinned. 'Looking at my watch, I imagine we're still over the Ross Sea, about an hour from MacTown.'

Five minutes later, the PA system crackled. A voice from the cockpit announced, 'Ladies and gentlemen, we are over the Ross Sea. We expect to land in about sixty minutes.'

'Well estimated.' Willis gave a thumbs-up to Gabi. He lifted his bottle of water into the air and pretended to toast Gabi. 'What will the South Pole Telescope be doing in January while the sun is still above the horizon?'

'The telescope works normally, even in full daylight. The sunlight doesn't disturb the frequencies that the detectors use.'

Drat, Willis thought. I knew the sunlight didn't affect the telescope, but I forgot. I need to be more careful.

'At this time of year, a lot of maintenance will have taken place. The team will have taken the opportunity to oil the motor drives and check the refrigeration system to make sure it's working at maximum efficiency. A full test takes about thirty hours. The telescope works in thirty-six-hour shifts. That's how long the cooling process can work without refreshing the coolants. After that, it becomes less efficient.'

'I can see that I have a lot to catch up on before I will be any use on the telescope.' Willis attempted to keep up the pretence that his visit was for research, but he doubted if Gabi was convinced.

'Linda also does upgrades; she has recently completed an upgrade to the detectors. I missed helping since I took a trip home, but I would have liked to assist.'

They sat in silence for a while. Willis's head nodded again, in readiness for sleep. He allowed a warm glow to envelop him for a second time. His eyes closed. His chin came to rest on his chest.

Then Willis awoke with a start. The entire plane was vibrating. The jet engines squealed. A novel that Gabi was reading flew across the cabin. The straps of Willis's seat belts dug into his hips and rib cage as his body catapulted sideways.

Gabi gave a short wheeze as the plane lurched sideways. Its floor tilted at an acute angle. The plane's nose pointed downwards. Its tail lifted into the sky. The jets continued to scream as the plane hurtled down towards the Ross Sea. Above the roar of the engine, they heard shouts coming from the cockpit. Loud, panicking voices.

Willis's heart thumped.

Gabi turned around and grasped the bulkhead behind her seat with both hands to steady herself. Her body shook. She made a retching sound and threw up. The contents of her stomach sprayed over the duffle bags on the floor.

Willis swallowed hard, just in time to stop himself from doing the same. He looked at the other passengers. Their faces were drained of blood and their eyes opened wide. Their heads turned left and right enquiring from their neighbours what the hell was happening. The deafening noise increased until the cabin was filled with a symphony of twisting and straining metal.

Then, as quickly as the racket had begun, the noise stopped. The plane fell silent. Even the engines went quiet. The C-17 levelled off then began to climb, and they continued on their original smooth course.

'Bloody hell.' The blood had drained from Gabi's face. 'What the fuck caused that?'

The PA cut in. 'I'm sorry for the scare, folks. We don't have a clue what caused that temporary loss of control, but everything seems to work fine now. We are on schedule for landing at McMurdo at 1430 hours.'

'Maybe they don't have an idea what caused that, but I do.' Without meaning to, Willis said the words out loud. He unfastened his belt and walked to the cockpit. 'Hi, I'm Dr Brad Willis. I'm a scientist at the Amundsen–Scott Station. Would you describe what just happened to me?'

'No problem, Doctor.' The co-pilot pointed to a green display on his console. 'The instrument panel turned off for about thirty seconds then switched back on. We lost control when the panel switched off. I've never experienced anything like this in my fifteen years as a captain.'

'Do you have an accurate time for the dropout?'

'The time was exactly 13:16. The LCD clock displayed the time throughout. And it lasted about half a minute.'

'Thanks. This is the second time this has happened. Can I have a copy of your report when it's finished?'

'I'm sorry, Doctor. When you touch down, you will need to request that from McMurdo. I'm afraid I won't be able to let you have a copy, except through them. We're praying that it doesn't happen again while we are attempting to land.'

'I am close to certain that it won't. An external influence caused the problem.'

'I sure hope you're right.' The pilot winked. The American's Texan drawl left Willis in no doubt about where he came from.

'Thanks, guys. I won't bother you any more. Good luck with the landing.' Willis returned to Gabi's side.

She gave him a puzzled stare. 'Are you sure you're an astronomer?'

'I can assure you that I'm an astronomer.'

***

The C-17 banked sharply to begin its steep descent into McMurdo. Willis watched the clenched knuckles of the other passengers. At the last moment, the jet levelled off and its wheels made almost silent contact with the ice field as it touched down softly on the well-manicured ice runway. As the engines stopped and the giant beast slithered to a halt, a spontaneous round of applause erupted from Willis and his fellow travellers. Willis turned to face Gabi as he unfastened his seat belt. 'We made a safe landing. We're in one piece.' Gabi smiled back as they picked up their soiled duffle bags and headed for the exit.

CHAPTER 5

The runway was right on McMurdo Sound. As Willis alighted from the plane he looked in awe at the amazing views of glaciers and mountains, with Mount Erebus magnificent on the horizon.

Sharp little pieces of dust attacked Willis's eyes every time he faced the gusty breeze. They scraped the surface of his eyeballs. 'Shit,' he murmured. He had to put on his goggles to protect himself.

Gabi introduced him to Ivan, the Terra Bus. Ivan, a huge rectangular orange and white transporter, moved people around the town. Equally spaced around the vehicle, Willis counted six wheels, each the height of a man and about half that wide. The bus was as tall as two men. Before they climbed the steps to reach its elevated deck, they stacked their duffle bags in the side storage units. Their luggage was taken separately to the station. Once aboard, they sat several feet above the snow.

McMurdo looked nothing like Willis had imagined it. The settlement comprised sprawling sheds and warehouses. Four large gas or oil tanks dominated the area, while smaller green tanks were scattered randomly around the base. Cargo containers lay in rows, stacked two high. Boxes were piled high, presumably holding more stores. Three small helicopters stood together. Everything looked boring, grey, dirty, and covered in mud. It looked like a rundown mining township. The earth was a brownish black, made up of crushed volcanic rock, not unlike the black beaches Willis had seen on Tenerife, but coarser and muddier. The drab buildings made everywhere look sad and tatty. In summer, the base was home to over one thousand people. The idea of being stranded here if he missed the last flight before the airfield closed for the winter did not appeal to Willis in the least. He understood why the town needed to be utilitarian: all supplies for the Amundsen–Scott South Pole Station entered via McMurdo.

Once he had recovered from the shock of seeing the town, Willis took a few minutes to absorb the views surrounding MacTown. Observation Hill stood proud in front of him, between him and where he knew New Zealand's Scott Base lay, while magnificent mountains decorated the horizon leading down to the sea.

Much new building was taking place. A new station was in the process of being constructed.

Willis and Gabi attended the mandatory orientation briefing for new arrivals an hour after they landed. It was almost 3:30 p.m. They listened to the talk, which was about safety, where their rooms were, and arrangements for meals.

Afterwards, they collected bed linen from the laundry and headed for their rooms.

His room was comfortable and warm. But he would only be there for a night. When he'd unpacked, a messenger came with a note asking him to visit the Station Leader. The messenger, Matthew, offered to show Willis where to find him. Once he'd dressed in some of his ECW, Willis followed his guide.

At the Station Leader's office, Willis walked in and introduced himself. Glen Mason was a short, rotund man, at least forty pounds overweight. Willis considered his completely bald head might be a considerable disadvantage in these temperatures. His office, neat and tidy to a fault, was no doubt similar, if not identical, to every other room on the site. The complete lack of any personal items stood out. Willis saw no family photographs or mementoes to remind the owner of home. That should say something about the guy. On the wall was displayed a certificate that Willis was unable to read from where he stood. Another framed item with a US crest hung close by. They must relate to his position on the base, Willis thought.

'Welcome to McMurdo. I bet the site isn't as you expected. New arrivals always seem disappointed.'

Willis offered his hand. 'A little disappointing describes my first impression well. I didn't think that McMurdo would be so industrial. They obviously work hard here to distribute things around the continent, but I didn't expect it. I'm glad to meet you, Glen.'

Mason got straight down to business. 'I've received an update on why you're here. I will give you as much help as I can. You wanted to be kept informed about the C-17 incident? I have a copy of the papers for you to read.'

Willis thanked him, and took the file Mason offered him. 'Did you read the entire thing?' he asked.

'The report describes the EMP we experienced here. The same pulse happened at Amundsen–Scott at the same time – exactly 13:16. We're still checking things out but, other than a few more circuit-breakers blown, nothing much got damaged because the disturbance didn't last for as long as the first one.'

'That's amazing,' Willis said. 'It requires enormous power to affect the base and the C-17 at the same time – they are hundreds of miles apart.'

'The previous pulse affected us considerably more. That blew a lot of the circuits. Our techies tell us the damage happened because they melted before they tripped out. The same thing at Pole. They requested a load of replacement breakers that we can't provide. We're out of them. We've ordered more, but we won't get them anytime soon.'

'May I take a photocopy of the C-17 report?'

'Of course. They instructed me to give you the fullest support. Why you're going to Pole puzzles me. If you stayed here at McMurdo, that might be more effective. We're closer to any action here than the polar base is.'

As much as Willis longed to meet Sophie, he had considered that too, but not for long. 'They use a lot more equipment at Pole. I will need that to collect evidence. I also want to stay undercover. At Pole, that will be easier for me.'

'Good point,' Mason said. 'If the information will help, I'm a deputised US Marshal but, at the moment, I can't imagine how.'

Neither can I. Willis didn't say the words out loud. Instead he said, 'Thanks for the offer. I'll keep it in mind. If I need to get in touch, how can I contact you?'

'When you arrive, speak to John Connor. He's in charge of the base and can set everything up for you. Can I take you for something to eat?'

Willis declined. 'I'm trying to stay discreet for as long as possible. I'm supposed to be here as an astronomer on the South Pole Telescope. If I am seen dining with you, then that might make people suspicious about why I'm really here.'

'I understand. I hope I haven't done that already by inviting you to my office.'

'I doubt they noticed. I have met so few people so far. Anyone who will have seen me hopefully won't remember my face.'

***

When he left Mason, Willis headed back towards his room.

'Hi, Brad.' Gabi came up alongside him. 'Have you eaten yet?'

'Not yet. The briefing said we were to head for the galley.'

'Follow me. I'm going now. It's that large blue building directly in front, but I think they might be building a new one as they rebuild the station.'

They turned a corner, then entered the galley. Inside, everything shone bright and colourful; the galley didn't reflect the image that its exterior portrayed.

Willis followed Gabi, took a tray, and sat down at a table near a window.

'I'm glad we aren't staying at McMurdo,' Willis said.

'Living here has its compensations. There's a bit more to do in the evenings. The social life is better, but only just.'

'I chose this meal because it looked good, and I'm not disappointed. This goulash is cooked to perfection and it has just the right amount of paprika. It's excellent.'

'You'll get used to that. As I said, you need to eat a lot of calories to keep you warm on the ice. Don't worry. Even with insufficient exercise, you will lose some pounds before you get home. The low temperature has a way of burning your fat away, especially if you go outdoors often and don't dress properly, not to mention the physical work you need to do.'

'What happened to Mason?' Willis was visualising the bulk of the little man.

'I suspect he might be the exception, or he might spend all his time in the galley.'

'Thank you for the warning. I will take care. Our flight out to the Amundsen–Scott Station is at 9 a.m., isn't it?'

'That's right. I'll meet you for breakfast. We can walk over here together.'

Willis left most of the gravy on his plate, but watched as Gabi soaked her bread enthusiastically in it, then stuffed the mixture into her mouth.

'I suppose that's something I will get used to.'

***

After dinner, Willis crashed out on his bed. It seemed so soft after the past few days of discomfort. He felt good for another reason. He had survived the stress of the incident on the C-17 with no ill effects. The tension should have brought on a bout of his PTSD, but it hadn't.

Ever since he'd witnessed the hit-and-run accident that had killed his beautiful wife Carole, Willis had suffered from post-traumatic stress disorder. He'd received treatment for it in St Petersburg last year. From the evidence so far, it might have been successful. He smiled.

Willis rolled over and closed his eyes. As ever, he dreamed of Carole and the night that the driver of the red car had stolen her away from him. But this dream was different. This time, the images of Carole faded. The smiling face of Sophie Fenwick took their place. Sophie, whom he'd soon see again.

***

The alarm woke him at seven. He showered with difficulty, trying to keep to the two minutes maximum that Gabi had advised him about. Willis estimated he took at least four and a half minutes. That will improve with practice, he promised himself. Willis dried off briskly, then headed for the galley. Gabi was already at the table. He chose a fry-up. They finished their bacon and eggs in fifteen minutes flat, then went outside to wait for the bus. Ivan the Terra Bus dropped them off at the airfield, where an LC-130 Skibird sat ready to board.

They stood at the bottom of the ramp, ready to board the plane. 'Look at them,' Gabi said. 'Bumbling around like nervous pupils on their first day at a new school. Now just watch the fourteen other "Big Reds" move their luggage around, waiting to be told they can get on.'

The Skibird's three hydraulically adjusted skis had left track marks in the snow from its landing.

The plane needed no taxiing, as it sat at the end of the airstrip facing the right direction for take-off. When everyone was on board, it fired up its four prop engines and raced along the runway. The skis skimmed along the ice, and a swishing sound filled the cabin. Then all went quiet. They were airborne.

The thought that another EMP might interrupt their flight crossed Willis's mind. His knuckles were tight and white, gripping the edge of his seat. He took a deep breath and relaxed. If it happened, it happened. He tried to think no more about it.

At least this plane had windows, so he could admire the ice and mountains during the trip, but the plane was noisy. It was packed with people and cargo. As expected, the trip was uneventful, but not particularly pleasant.

Willis's first sight of the Amundsen–Scott Station would remain in his memory forever. The snow sparkled. The sun, low on the horizon, made the multi-coloured sparkles move and shimmer. Ice crunched underfoot. The landscape was virginal, untrodden, unspoiled, apart from the trails left by vehicles driving to and from the airstrip. Behind the station, the ice had been groomed to prevent blowing snow from burying the buildings. Willis stopped in his tracks to absorb the beauty of the panorama. The view spread out endlessly in all directions. The enormity of the sky took his breath away. His imagination filled it with shining stars and the band of the Milky Way.

He had never imagined that so many shades of white could exist. He sighed.

By the time they reached the base, all that had changed. Yes, lots of fresh snow still lay all around, but the magic was no more. Well-trodden pathways led between the buildings. Lines of coloured flags marked out the less-used paths. Still, Willis preferred it to McMurdo. He would enjoy being here – for a while, at least. The station was elevated on stilts to allow snow to blow underneath it and to delay it being swallowed by the ice.

Gabi guided him to the main entrance, which she called Destination Alpha. Above it stood an observation platform. Willis and Gabi entered at level one and climbed the stairs to the upper floor. They strolled along a long corridor to the galley.

'Let's get a bite to eat here, then I'll show you around. You will have been allocated a room. There's no need to check in yet.'

They put their duffle bags on the floor then Gabi walked to the serving hatch and bought food for both of them. 'I've bought fried chicken – that's what's on the menu today. We might as well kick off with the most popular dish. You can experience the rest another time.'

After eating, they had to watch another video. This one warned of the dangers of altitude sickness on the Antarctic Plateau, and discussed how best to protect yourself from the cold.

Willis shuddered. The environment was even more hazardous than he imagined. The task he had accepted seemed more difficult the more he learned.

CHAPTER 6

'… and the pulse hit here, too. It didn't cause any damage this time, though. Just as well, as we're low on spare parts. They'll need to send circuit-breakers soon.' John Connor, the tall, broad-shouldered Station Leader at the South Pole, stood, approached a map of the base that was tacked to the wall, and pointed to a small square shape to the left of its centre. 'This is one of the switching units that supply power to the living areas. If any more circuits fail here, we'll be in the proverbial. If we enter the polar winter unprepared, it will be a disaster.' Connor looked at Willis. 'In an emergency, we have a "lifeboat" installed in section B1. It has its own power system and life support facilities. But if the surge can take out the main supply, then…'

'When did the pulse happen here?' Willis asked.

'At 13:16. We checked with McMurdo – that's the same time it hit there. We're sure it was the same pulse.'

'I'd like to look around and call on some of the research facilities to see how it's affected them. I'd like, if possible, to visit SPT first, if that is okay?'

'The site is at your disposal. You may visit anywhere you like.'

'How many guys on the base know that I'm visiting?'

'Only the guy I've asked to cover security, and me.'

'Good. I'd like to keep it that way for a while. It's not that I suspect anyone on the base, but people will relax more about telling me information if they don't know that I have an official investigation in progress. When can I meet your security manager?'

'I can arrange that now, if you like.'

Willis nodded, and Connor shouted through to the outer room. Willis heard some movement as someone stood and walked out.

'Callum will be here in about five minutes.'

Willis looked around Connor's office. It was more like a room than an office. Several family photos decorated the walls and covered the table in front of them. There were also a couple of photos of a middle-aged woman, much the same age as Connor. Willis assumed she was his wife. He did a mental comparison between this room and that used by Glen Mason at McMurdo. The difference stood out.

The door behind Willis slammed, making him jump. 'This is Callum McGregor. He's in charge of security. He's also the chief engineer. Callum, this is Dr Brad Willis – he's come to see what's at the bottom of all these surges.'

'Hello.' The short man had a strong Glaswegian accent. 'I'm pleased tae meet you.' McGregor took Willis's hand and squeezed it like he was taking part in an arm-

40

wrestling contest. When he let it go, Willis let his arm drop to let its circulation return to normal.

'You're a powerful guy.' Willis bent and straightened his fingers several times. 'I bet you must work out a good bit.'

'Aye, that I do. We enjoy a decent gym here on the base. I can take you and show you it when you have time.'

Willis nodded his agreement. 'What security features do you use on site?'

'We dinnae have any at all. There's nae need here for cameras and the like. We dinnae get any crime on the base. We dinnae even lock our doors. Everybody is all good friends here.'

'That's a pity. I wisnae – I wasn't asking because I suspected anybody, but it would have been useful to record what was happening and where,' Willis explained. 'Never mind, we'll discover other ways of finding out. Have you any ideas yourself, Callum?'

'I've racked my brains. But I cannae think of anything. I'm no' even confident that a pulse that strong, and covering such a big area, is even possible.'

'It sure is.' Willis told him about their near-death experience on the flight to McMurdo. 'The pulse affected an area from the Ross Sea to the South Pole, and that must use a lot of energy. There's no way somebody could generate it at McMurdo or here.'

'Well, I cannae figure it out either.'

'I've explained to Mr Connor that I'd like my investigation to stay under wraps for a while. Have you mentioned to anyone that I was coming?'

McGregor was a lousy liar. His gaze darted around the room and settled on the floor before he said, 'Naw, I huvnae told a soul.' His accent got stronger when he lied.

41

'That's good.' Willis stared at him. 'If you had, I would have asked you to have a word with them, to tell them to keep shtum, but it's fine that no one else knows.'

'Is that all, Mr Connor?' McGregor looked keen to get away to right his wrongdoing.

***

Willis decided that it was time to learn his way around the base. He set off towards SPT. The walk was strenuous, even although the path was smooth. He had to concentrate on each step. The more he walked, the easier it became. The observatory was a kilometre from Connor's office. As even microwave ovens could cause havoc with its sensitive detectors, it had to be well clear of other buildings to avoid any radio interference. When he reached the telescope, he found Gabi helping to pull a heavy box of electronics off its shelf to lay it on a bench.

'This is Dr Linda Foreman,' she said, pointing to a tall woman who was assisting her. 'Linda is in charge of the SPT projects for this winter. Linda and I have started on the last bit of the maintenance schedule. This needs to be completed before the sun sets for the winter. It's almost finished.'

'Hi, Dr Willis. I'm pleased to meet you.' Linda's husky, masculine voice caught Willis off guard. 'Your reputation goes before you.' She waved a heavy mitten in the air to infer that there was no point in shaking hands.

'I must have been a surprise to you, joining your team at short notice.'

'Yes, all the winter teams are usually in place by midsummer, but the NSF warned me to expect you. You must know people in high places.'

'Not me. But my chief does. Mike, my boss, was desperate for me to get my project done.' Willis wasn't lying.

Reilly had set everything up. But Willis didn't need to volunteer that he was only his temporary boss.

'One can, of course, use SPT when the sun is still up?' Willis was showing off his newly won information.

'All the detector frequencies work well even in daylight, but we must keep it pointing at least ten degrees away from the sun, for safety reasons. There is some extra noise created by the atmosphere, but we can live with that.'

'This maintenance looks like hard labour.'

'It's not just maintenance.' Linda explained that the surge had caused the cooling system to crash, and it would take days to recover it safely. 'Before we turn the instrument on again, we will need to examine everything. Waste heat from the electronics warms the telescope's main motors. If we switch them on before they warm up, they will seize. There'll be irreparable damage. Without warmth, the telescope would be dead in the water, as would everything else – *and* everybody else.' Linda laughed. 'Let's get out of the cold and into the DSL – our Dark Sector Laboratory. C'mon, Gabi. Let's get a cappuccino.'

The coffee was delicious. It wasn't Willis's favourite Brazilian blend, but for now, it tasted ten times better. 'So, tell me about the pulse. What did it do to the telescope?'

'The damn thing turned off all the coolers. We use cryocoolers, which work like an icebox to remove heat. It switched them off. Next, the sorption fridge turned off too – that's a lot more serious. The sorption fridge is more complicated. It uses helium 3 to help suck out the heat, but we shouldn't switch the bloody thing off abruptly as it can cause permanent damage. It works the same way as sweat cools you down by evaporating. The chilled liquid circulates behind the detectors to cool them.'

'Hell. That would be an expensive accident if it happened in midwinter.'

Linda nodded and sipped her coffee. Its warmth spread a smile over her face. 'Luckily, we were aware as soon as it occurred. We took immediate action to save the day.'

Willis removed a high-energy bar from his pocket and took a bite. 'The cold is getting to me already.'

'The galley doesn't stock those on-site – not that brand, anyway.' Gabi read the English brand name on the bar's wrapper.

'I brought this from England. We need these for the bitter winters we get,' Willis joked as he treated himself to another bite. He grinned. 'Tell me about the SPT's role as part of the Event Horizon Telescope.'

'That was one of our big successes,' Linda said. 'You will have seen in the news that we helped take the first picture of a black hole in 2019. We got a lot of positive publicity from that.'

'That means you must operate an atomic clock on site?'

'We run a hydrogen maser clock. It's accurate to a few nanosec— What's the matter, Dr Willis? You look awful.'

Willis's face had distorted into an ugly grimace. He threw his energy bar on the floor. 'I've been…' He spat out the words as he vomited. 'I've been poisoned.' He bent double, and rolled off his seat, in agony. His eyes opened wide and his pupils dilated. Soon his eyes rolled upwards and nothing was visible in his eye sockets other than the naked whites of his eyeballs. Within seconds, he was unconscious.

Linda screamed at Gabi, 'Get some warm salty water!' Then she ran over to the maintenance cupboard and removed the equipment they used to service the telescope's refrigeration system: a length of plastic tubing, a 400cl syringe and a tin of petroleum jelly. Linda rolled Willis into the recovery position, and carefully inserted the lubricated elastic tube down his throat. 'Hurry with that water!' she yelled at Gabi. Squeezing the syringe, which she had attached to the end of the elastic tube, she deliberately forced some air into Willis's stomach to make sure the tube wasn't in his lungs. When Gabi returned, Linda grabbed the bowl of warm saline water, then filled the syringe with it. Carefully, she pushed down the syringe plunger, forcing the water into Willis's stomach. At the end of the stroke, she reversed the direction of the syringe and drew out the contents of Willis's stomach. Linda emptied the syringe, refilled it with salty water, and repeated the process until the fluid she withdrew from his stomach ran clear.

***

Three hours later, Willis woke in the medical unit. The lights hurt his eyes. Everything was blurred. His throat felt like he had been eating sand. His gut was in immense pain. Straining his eyes, he could make out three silhouettes. The image focused and defocused a few times. Eventually, he could identify the outlines of Linda, Gabi and Connor, standing at the side of his bed.

'You are very lucky, Dr Willis.' It was Connor's voice. 'Lucky that Linda knew what to do. In another few minutes, you would have been a goner.'

Willis turned to Linda and tried to speak. Nothing came out but a couple of groans.

'Don't talk yet,' Linda said. 'Your throat is bruised. It will take a few days to return to normal. It was quite an effort to bring you back from the DSL to the medical centre.'

'We've saved the remains of your energy bar, complete with its wrapper.' Connor waved a plastic bag containing the offending bar. 'We have no way to analyse it here, but we've kept it in case we can later. There are no police or forensics experts at the station. But I doubt it was the energy bar. Very few poisons work that fast. So you were probably poisoned earlier. You're lucky that Linda is a trained nurse. We all play dual roles here.'

Willis nodded. He was desperate to continue the conversation he had started with Linda when he collapsed, but that would have to wait.

***

It took over two days before Willis's voice had recovered enough for him to speak without discomfort. He had worried so much about keeping the purpose of his presence a secret, but someone sure as hell knew why he was there. He would need to be doubly careful in future. He tried to think who might have doctored his energy bar, or his food, but it could have been anyone from London, who added something to his energy bar or someone who added an unwelcome supplement to his food at the South Pole. Willis's money was on the fact that someone on the ice wished him ill. He was forming a weak strategy for how to proceed, but he needed a few things to fall into place first.

CHAPTER 7

The IceCube is an odd observatory because its detectors are underground – at least, under the ice. Its thousands of sensors are out of sight and cover a cubic kilometre. Their purpose is to detect neutrinos, the smallest pieces of anything that can exist. One hundred trillion pass through your body every second without you being aware of them.

The IceCube was a recognised outpost of CERN, Sophie's employer, and why she was here. Willis found the IceCube facility about a kilometre from SPT. It stood out against the horizon, its pair of white vertical towers joined to the main laboratory building with two structures bridging them. He clambered up the metal-framed staircase that led to the elevated levels of the laboratories. The steel rungs clanged with each step.

Willis wanted to surprise Sophie, but he couldn't be sure that the surprise would succeed, given the noise he was making. A warm feeling flushed over him as he opened the door and stepped into one of the biggest neutrino observatories on Earth. No way would Sophie expect to see him at the bottom of the world, he thought.

He was wrong.

'Hello, Star Man,' Sophie said as he entered. That was her usual greeting when they hadn't met for some time. She didn't even bother to turn around. 'You thought that you'd come to my world and I wouldn't notice? There are not so many people here that a newcomer isn't spotted.'

Sophie's lab was huge, with desks stretching from one end to the other. Pieces of scientific apparatus littered their surfaces. Most of the instruments Willis didn't recognise. There were seven oval windows on each side of the building, four on the upper floor and three on the lower. It was clear that the laboratory was being shared by many researchers. The benches at the centre of the room were reserved for a row of desk computers, and those were the only tidy ones.

'I assumed that with over twenty newcomers arriving, I would get away unnoticed.'

'No way, Star Man. You're the only newbie who got poisoned. Didn't you think I'd notice? You were in good hands, otherwise I would have visited. I also worked out your visit was meant to be a surprise, so I didn't want to spoil your boyish fun.'

Willis stepped forward and kissed her on the cheek, then moved to her lips. But she backed off. 'Woah there. You can't expect to walk in here and take over from where you left off. I haven't seen you for ages. You failed to come to Switzerland to visit me … *again*.'

'Yes, I'm sorry. Things have been hectic, but when I heard you'd disappeared to the South Pole—'

'That's all the more reason you should have called me before I left. The excuse you'll give, I suppose, is that your "intelligence work" kept you away?' She made parentheses in the air with her fingers.

After Willis's last assignment, he had been forced to confide in Sophie about Reilly and his 'other' activities. Willis knew he was wrong. He should have visited Sophie. But when he was busy with astronomy, nothing could interrupt him – apart from Mike Reilly, that was. By the time he had enough free time, Sophie had already moved to Antarctica. 'I'm sorry. Will you forgive me?'

'There's nothing to forgive. We both have our careers to follow.'

Willis considered it wise to let the subject drop – for the meantime, at least. Sophie had left to investigate a strange subatomic particle she had discovered on their last adventure. One that had indirectly caused the deaths of some of her colleagues and friends.

'What is the up-to-date information with the mysterious new particle you observed?' he asked. 'I know we spoke on the phone but that's not the same.'

Sophie explained that they were still investigating, but finding the particle was proving tricky. Her bosses had pressurised her to come to Pole to help with the neutrino experiment at IceCube. Sophie enjoyed the work. She'd flown in with the over-summer groups, settled in well with her new team, and had successfully detected high-energy neutrinos on several occasions.

'Coffee?' Sophie asked.

'Yes, please, I'd love some. I seem to drink more of the stuff here than I did at home,' Willis said.

'The cold will do that to you – just wait until the weather gets worse.'

'Anyway, tell me about the experiment. How did the surge affect it?' Willis asked.

'When the surge hit, we believed we'd struck the mother lode. Our instruments went wild. Our sensors activated down to a depth of six metres. That's the opposite to what we'd have expected from neutrinos, but the excitement got us going for a while, I can tell you.'

'Can I see the results? I'd like to check the time at the start of the interference.'

Sophie opened a screen on her computer. A list of numbers flashed up. She explained to Willis what the table represented.

'So, the code in the leftmost column shows the sensor that detected the radio noise, and the right-hand list shows the time recorded for the event?' he asked.

'That's correct.'

'This is brilliant. You measure the difference in nanoseconds? You must use an atomic clock to resolve the interval to this precision, like Linda at SPT?'

'The resolution must be at least two nanoseconds, as the exact recording of results is critical.'

'Can you sketch out where these detectors are on a piece of paper for me?'

When Sophie pressed a key, the screen displayed a layout of the sensors. Then she printed out a copy of their layout for him. Willis took the printout and wrote down the time the pulse had registered at selected detectors. When he finished, he sat back, satisfied. 'Using the times that the signal passed over each sensor, I've worked out where the pulse came from. It's a narrow area in the Ross Sea. The signal triggered each of the detectors at different times as the interference passed over them, so I can work out its direction and distance from those times.' He scribbled some more, finally developing a set of co-ordinates. 'The pulse originated approximately here.' Willis put a circle on an outline map of Antarctica that Sophie found for him. 'I must contact Reilly. I need to send a confidential email to him. How do I do that? Is there a secure email system?'

'John Connor can do that for you, but I can't say how long sending an email might take. As soon as the broadband satellite comes over, John will connect you, but you might need to wait a while. The SPTR satellite is accessible between twelve and fourteen hours per day.'

'I'm going back to Connor's office. When does your shift end?'

'I never finish. Everything is informal here; I work until I feel tired. Then I sleep.'

'Surely you can get away so we can have lunch together?'

'Okay, I'll see you in two hours. I'll find you in the galley.' The galley was the large communal dining area that Gabi had introduced him to, and where everyone met at the end of their shifts.

'I'll meet you at noon.' Willis checked his watch, then left.

***

He went straight to Connor's office. When he opened the door, Connor was speaking to someone on a hand-held radio, so Willis waited until the conversation was finished. 'I need to transmit an urgent but confidential email to London. How do I go about that?'

'Follow me.' Connor swung his arm over his shoulder like he was leading a platoon of men. He led Willis along the corridor from his office. 'This is the central communications

51

room. You can send routine emails elsewhere, but Johnny is the best person to speak to if you want anything private sent.'

Johnny, a thin, spindly man, appeared to have been on the ice for some time: his skin looked pale, with most of its elasticity gone.

'Johnny, Brad has an important email that needs to go to London ASAP. Will you take care of it?'

'I'll set Brad up with a USAP email account so he can email from his room, but if this is urgent, I can email on the military channel,' Johnny said.

'Do that. And if it's an emergency, you have my authority to use the protected channels on the Iridium System for anything that Brad needs to send.'

Johnny's eyes opened wide in surprise.

Connor leaned over and entered a password on the keyboard. Then he vanished out of the door.

'I'll set up the comms screen for you, Brad,' Johnny said. 'The screen's like an ordinary email program. Once you've added your note, close the window. Your message will stay on the server but it will be encrypted. No one will have access to it without Connor's password.'

Johnny discreetly left the office, and Willis took his chair. The wall behind the computer was covered with yellow and orange sticky notes. Johnny clearly used them as reminders to look out for replies to previous emails and tell him who to notify when they arrived. Willis composed an email to Reilly, telling him about the surge he experienced on the C-17 flight and how he'd triangulated its source. He input the co-ordinates of the location in the Ross Sea where he calculated the origin lay. Then Willis encrypted the memo using a basic code that he used whenever he needed to communicate with Reilly in secret. Although the message would also be encrypted by the system, another layer of security would do no harm. He confirmed the information, paying particular attention to the co-ordinates. After he'd double-checked the wording, he pressed the Send button. The screen changed colour. A new window cut in. The notification read:

Message successfully logged. Estimated time of transmission - 45 minutes.

Willis closed the dialogue box and stood to leave. When Johnny returned, he thanked him for his help.

'John Connor has authorised me to send any future emails that you might need with no extra clearance from him,' Johnny said.

Willis shook Johnny's hand, thanked him for a second time, and left.

***

The time was 11:45. Willis stepped out of the building to stretch his legs. He still took care walking, taking his time, even on the well-trodden tracks. His walk took him around the main building then back to Destination Alpha. He wanted to map out the layout of the base. When he'd done this, Willis headed for the galley to meet Sophie. When he entered, Sophie was already there. He collected a plate piled high with beef and potatoes from the self-service counter and joined her. The food looked delicious. He glanced at Sophie's plate, which was piled high. She began her meal without looking up.

'How long did it take you to get used to this high calorific food?'

'No time at all.' She continued to chew.

'You're eating with relish. It looks as though you're thoroughly enjoying every bite.'

'Food is one thing that you look forward to – eating is one of the more pleasurable pastimes out here. The folk who cook for us consider food to be one of the most important things to help us stay sane. Good food means good morale.' Sophie came up for air long enough to answer his question.

Willis looked around at the huge room. It was by far the largest communal room he'd been in up to now. Presumably they called it 'the galley' to give the place some characteristics of a ship. He remembered Gabi referring to the inhabitants of the base as 'the crew'. From the ceiling hung three enormous video screens. They didn't show television programmes; instead they displayed the weather outside and gave safety-first advice, such as how to use a microwave oven, which Willis found annoying. *Be careful. The plate and food will be hot.* The one useful piece of information he spotted was the times when the SPTR, or 'spitter' satellite, would be available to allow internet access. As Sophie had said, it would be available for between twelve and fourteen hours each day, and each day it appeared four minutes earlier. After a year, Willis mused, it would appear a whole day earlier.

'Nothing worthwhile is showing on the screens.'

'What do you expect? Sky TV?' Sophie grinned. 'Sometimes we get the odd movie downloaded from the internet. But films take ages for Johnny, the comms guy, to download. He only gets them if someone requests a movie and if the satellite has enough idle capacity to cope with the extra load. Even then, he only does it in the winter when there's no NSF supervisor on site.'

'That must be a big event,' Willis said.

'A new film sure is, but they show the movie several times until everyone has had the chance to see it, and everybody's sick of it. The walls are not normally as bare as this either. All the nations' flags that fly around the striped post that represents the ceremonial South Pole are brought in and hung on the walls as soon as the sun gets close to setting.'

'What do you do to pass the time?'

'We work. What else can we do? Everybody here has at least two jobs. I back up a squad when they carry out fire drills, and two of my research team do likewise.' She looked at him and grinned. 'They will find you another job to do soon. But it's not all work. One of the best parts of life here is the community spirit and culture. There's a lot of focus on working, but after their contracted hours, people aren't expected to work unless there's an emergency that falls within their area of expertise.' Sophie took another mouthful of food and quickly chewed and swallowed it. 'Science groups definitely have a lot more freedom to work when they want, as defined by their project's requirements, but the maintenance people or cooks work six days a week during normal business hours. A lot of people focus on hobbies – starting a band, learning a new instrument, crafting, watching DVDs playing video games, reading, playing a sport, or just hanging out.' She put her hand on Willis's. 'And we have social events to mix things up. In the winter, if someone doesn't pick up a hobby in their off-work time, they're more likely to get homesick, bored or depressed. In both seasons, everyone is supposed to help to clean the station. It's called housemouse. When I first arrived, everyone got together in their groups and did housemouse at the end of a Saturday. Each group rotated responsibilities weekly. For example, in week 1 group A would take the downstairs bathrooms and hallway while group B cleaned the gym and weight room. In week 2, they'd swap. And in the winter, everyone has an extra emergency response job: fire team, medical, etc., and everyone takes turns washing dishes. That's called dish pit. Everything outside what's included in your contract is

55

voluntary. If a winter-over is also doing a summer here beforehand, they will probably take on the same emergency response position during the summer – I was on the fire team in the summer and winter.'

'I know. I've missed you. It's been the longest year I've ever experienced. Even our emails didn't help me feel any better.' Willis took a deep breath. 'I guess they will find me something to do as well as astronomy.' Willis grinned. He stared at the pile of food on his plate. He stuck a fork into a sausage and winked at Sophie. The meat tasted good. He devoured each morsel as fast as Sophie did.

Sophie rose, apologised, and said that she had to go back to IceCube. She was in the middle of a project she had to finish. Willis finished his meal, then left.

***

Willis managed the walk to SPT easier this time – he'd found his 'snow legs'. He would soon learn the knack of living on this continent. He was glad he'd come: he was finding the experience better than he could ever have imagined. The memory of being poisoned and nearly dying had been pushed to the back of his mind.

When he reached the telescope, he opened the door and walked in, then reeled back in surprise. Linda and Gabi were embracing, sharing a long, lingering kiss. They parted abruptly when they heard him. Although he was surprised, Willis didn't shock easily and soon recovered his composure. 'Can I join in?' he joked.

'No, you certainly cannot.' Gabi gave a wide-eyed grin. 'We don't think Sophie would approve of that.'

'You've spoken to Sophie, have you? What did she tell you?'

'Sophie told us everything.' Linda let out a coarse laugh and tapped her temple with her forefinger. 'We girls chat a lot. We can recall everything about Sophie's Star Man.'

Willis flushed.

'The doctor's blushing,' Gabi said. 'Sophie told us all about you two, but I bet she didn't expect you to turn up on her doorstep in Antarctica.'

'Don't worry,' Linda said. 'We're the height of discretion. We won't whisper a word to a soul.'

Willis changed the subject. 'Did you get an exact time for when the pulse hit the telescope?'

'Accurate to a second, if that is close enough.'

Willis explained that he was hoping for more accuracy. He was trying to measure a signal moving at the speed of light. He would need to measure the time in nanoseconds.

'I wish we could give you the time as accurately as you need. The clock we use is correct to a few nanoseconds, but the clock wasn't connected when the pulse happened.'

'Why don't you keep the damn thing connected all the time if it's more accurate?'

'The clock uses power.' Linda's eyes narrowed. 'We don't need to be so exact for a lot of the things that we do.'

'Would it be possible to run the clock for a few days? So if the pulse happens again, we can get an exact fix on the time that it reaches the telescope? If I can get that and also the time from Sophie from when it passes the IceCube observatory then some simple trigonometry will let me work out its position more accurately.'

'I don't see why not,' Gabi said. 'We will connect it this afternoon.'

'Great, thanks. I'll see you guys later.' Willis turned to leave.

Linda called out jeeringly, her coarse voice unmistakable, 'We know about Sophie. She told us all about you two.'

'And I know about you two.'

'But we don't care.'

CHAPTER 8

As Willis walked back to the galley he appreciated his Big Red and face-covering. As soon as he'd stepped outside the air bit at his throat as he breathed in its icy cold. His forehead hurt with the pain he remembered as a youngster when eating freezing ice cream. He lowered his head to protect his face from the chilling breeze that enveloped his hood. Willis strode on towards the main building. He'd arranged to meet Sophie for dinner. He sat at the top of the long table nearest the entrance, so she would spot him as she walked in. As he waited, he practised identifying people as they walked in from outside, even though they all wore 'Big Reds', the traditional down parkas everyone wore. Although hoods and goggles covered their faces, he could identify people by their beanies. Sophie wore a green and yellow striped beanie, Linda a dark blue, Gabi a deep pink. Willis's beanie was navy. Whenever he met someone he expected to see again, he added another 'beanie ID'. He was also learning to recognise the way people walked.

Even though her face was still partly covered, he spotted Gabi as soon as she entered. She sat down on Willis's right-hand side, then shuffled on her chair. Her eyes looked serious. She didn't smile. 'I need to have a word with you.' She leaned over until her mouth was level with Willis's ear and lowered her voice. 'There's a problem with Linda that needs sorting.'

Gabi whispered in his ear, 'Your status is worrying Linda, because you've been assigned to Pole with no reference to her. She was, after all, the current team leader for the SPT project and you've challenged her authority by suggesting she change the clock on the telescope. Linda was worried in case they'd sent you to replace her on the project. Were the powers-that-be unhappy with her results?' Gabi looked at Willis. 'I realise she's silly. I told her so. But I know that you're here for some other reason. I guessed that much on the plane into McMurdo, but I have no idea what that might be, so I haven't said anything to Linda. Would you speak to her, please? Put her mind to rest?'

'Of course I will. I didn't realise I was overstepping the mark.'

'Here she is.' Gabi made a zipping motion over her lips. 'Change the subject.'

Linda came and sat down beside them, her plate piled high with stodge.

'You're hungry, obviously?' Willis stared at the mountain of food on her plate.

'Wait till you've been here a few weeks. You'll start to look forward to the meals too.'

'I'm not planning to be here that long, if I can help it.'

Linda glanced questioningly at Willis. 'Why not? People rarely come here on a flying visit – the trip costs too much for that.'

'I'm really here for a non-astronomical project. Then I'll be flying home again.'

'Better hurry and finish the job then,' Linda said. 'If you're not off The Ice before the station shuts in a week, you'll have to join the winter-overs.'

Winter-overs have to remain on The Ice until after the sun rises again, around the 21st of September.

'Soon, depending on the weather, the station will close to all air traffic and you'll be stranded here for months. That's before the sun sets.'

'Well, I'm hoping to be far away by then.' Willis crossed his fingers and held them up.

Gabi smiled at Willis and waited until Linda had bent to shovel in another spoonful of food, then mouthed, 'Thanks.'

'I've connected the atomic clock to SPT,' Linda said after she had swallowed the mouthful. 'Before you came over, Brad, I tried to coerce that snide McGregor into letting me order a spare circuit-breaker from the sparkies, because the surge damaged one. The swine tried to block my request because there are more critical things needing it. McGregor has no authority over what gets and doesn't get fixed. After I promised that nice Roy Elms a drink as a reward, he let me replace it.' She smiled as she wiped up the last bit of gravy with a chunk of home-baked bread.

Willis assumed that Roy Elms was one of the electrical engineers.

'Sorry I'm late, everyone.' Sophie walked in. Willis hadn't noticed her absence; the conversation had been so engaging. 'The computer recorded a positive signal on a neutrino counter so I needed to carry out an inspection to make sure the alert was a false hit before I left.'

'You have such an exciting time,' Linda said.

'Maybe, but *I* didn't get to take the world's first picture of a black hole. And before you say anything, everyone collaborated, but SPT is an essential link in the network. They wouldn't have succeeded without you.'

Linda smiled. 'I'm going for some cake before my head gets too large for my beanie.'

Willis had half eaten his dessert when an alert sounded on Linda's personal radio. Linda jumped to her feet. 'That's the telescope alarm!' She dashed towards the door, pulling her Big Red on as she ran. Willis raced after her.

'It will take too long to get transport sorted,' she said. 'If I walk, it'll be quicker.'

Walk? She was all but running. Linda left Willis well behind – her skill on the snow outshone his. She covered the kilometre to SPT twice as fast as Willis did. When he eventually turned up, Linda was adjusting the heater for the ten-metre dish of the telescope.

'An electric switch has tripped out,' she said. 'I hope I've reset the damn thing soon enough. If the temperature of the dish drops, ice will form on its surface and disable it.'

'Is it the same breaker you replaced earlier?'

'That one was part of the clock circuit. This is for the heater. I've put a resistance meter on the circuit, but it tests okay, so I can't see why it tripped.'

'Could it be that the power supply is ready to give up?'

'I've tested that too – it's fine. I've also checked out the cooling fans for the supply. All of them are fine. I can't find why it switched off.'

'That's a bugger,' Willis said. 'You'll have no confidence in the system until it's been running faultlessly for a while.'

'I won't sleep tonight worrying about whether the alarm will go off again.'

Willis wasn't concentrating on Linda's words. He touched the floor inside the housing that covered the stairs leading up to the roof. Water had pooled on the wooden surface. Someone had left damp footprints between the circuit and the steps. Willis checked his boots. They were dry. He looked for any prints Linda might have made, but found none. Somebody had been in the lab and manually tripped the breaker. He pretended that he hadn't seen the wet boot prints.

'I might as well spend the night here,' Linda said. 'If I go back to the station, I won't sleep anyway.'

'I'll stay here with you.'

'There's no need for that. I'll ask Gabi to stay.' Linda took an adjustable wrench out of a cabinet, and dumped the heavy tool on the bench. 'I suspect that someone is trying to screw up this project. I have no idea who it is or why they are doing it but if they come back, I'll be ready.' She pointed to the wet footprints. 'Pity they're smudged. They might have given us a clue as to who owned them.'

A few seconds later, the noise of an arriving skidoo interrupted their conversation. It was Gabi, being dropped off. The two women ganged up on Willis. 'Go to the base. Have a drink, we'll be fine. Go. We'll see you at seven tomorrow.'

Willis returned to the station, but his mind raced, his thoughts focused on the evening's events.

Might someone at the station be involved with the surges? There was little chance that anyone would try to damage the telescope again soon. It would be too risky. Yet Willis daren't risk leaving the women alone at SPT overnight. So he headed for his room, took out a thermos flask, filled the flask with hot chocolate from the galley, then lifted a couple of sandwiches the cooks had kindly provided. Willis complained that he had to spend a while on the telescope tonight instead of going to bed.

He trudged back along the track towards the observatory. As he walked, he thought about the two-plus kilometres of ice that lay beneath his feet. The depth of the ice fascinated him. Rarely did snow fall at the South Pole; all this ice had been snow blown from other quarters of the continent or had accumulated from 'diamond dust', the precipitation that comes from clear air.

**

When he arrived at the telescope, he heard Linda and Gabi chatting. Willis opened the door quietly, then sneaked into the control room.

The wind from earlier had subsided – otherwise, the blast of cool air from the door opening would have given his presence away.

Both women were working close to the far wall on the right. The room was quite small: three or four good paces would take him to the rear wall. He eased his way to the left, where a crate sat at an angle in the corner. A flip-chart stand, complete with flip-chart, stood in front of the crate.

Willis edged around the back of the box, found a comfortable position on the floor, put his flask down beside him, and waited. The girls were at least twenty feet away. They would neither see nor hear him. Likewise, he couldn't hear or see them. He didn't want to be accused of spying on them.

Linda and Gabi worked hard, using the time to catch up on routine tasks. Willis closed his eyes and allowed himself to relax. It was eight o'clock in the evening. He nodded off a few times but he woke whenever his head fell forward, or when one of the women dropped something or, as happened on one occasion, when someone banged on the wall with a hammer.

Around midnight, all went silent. The women huddled down at the far end of the control room, in the opposite corner to the one he had chosen.

About 3 a.m., Willis woke. All was quiet, but he needed the loo. However, he didn't know if the laboratory even housed a toilet. He hadn't noticed one earlier. Willis sighed and nodded off again.

Another hour passed, he woke again. The situation had become urgent. He must get to a loo – and quickly. Gingerly, he got up. The silence in the control room exaggerated every sound that he made. He kicked an empty box, which scraped across the floor. He froze, waiting for a sign of movement from the sleeping pair, but none came. Willis took short, deliberate steps as he worked his way to the door. When he reached the corner, he pressed the bar on the door to open it.

The bar felt stiff at first, but then it moved and the door unlatched. He edged the door outwards.

And all hell broke loose.

A siren filled the room with a deafening blare. All the lights came on.

He swung around in surprise. Linda stood over him, holding a heavy wrench above his head. 'God, Brad, what are you doing here?' Linda didn't lower the weapon. 'Well, explain yourself.'

'I'm going for a pee. I held on as long as possible.'

'There's no loo in the control room.' Linda spat out the words, raising her voice above the din of the siren. Gabi touched something at the other end of the room. The wailing stopped.

'Oops. I planned to spend the night here, as backup,' Willis said. 'I'm sorry I woke you.'

'You've been here all night?'

'Yes – in the corner behind the flip-chart.'

'I'm not happy that you are here at all.'

'Okay. Okay, don't jump to conclusions. I'm not the saboteur. I'd better come clean on a few things.'

'I'm all ears,' came the curt reply.

'I'm here at the invite of the National Science Foundation to investigate the electromagnetic surges that have happened over the past few days. Other than professionally, I have no interest in your telescope.'

Linda looked relieved. 'But I thought…'

'I know. I wanted to tell you, but I also needed to stay undercover for as long as possible.'

'There's no reason you can't remain undercover. Your secret is safe with us, isn't it, Gabi?'

'I did wonder why you were really here, but I wasn't absolutely sure.' Gabi touched the side of her nose. 'We won't say a word.'

'So why were you hammering in the middle of the night?'

'We connected a micro-switch to the door to trap intruders. You tested the alarm for us.' Linda stood on her toes and tapped the micro-switch on the top of the door.

Then the door crashed open, and McGregor forced his way in. 'What's going on here? Why has the telescope alarm gone off?'

Willis noticed that his accent was a tad weaker.

'We carried out some maintenance on the temperature sensors. The alarm triggered accidentally.' Linda shrugged unapologetically. 'I'm sorry we disturbed you.'

'I should say so too.' McGregor stomped out, slamming the door behind him.

Willis opened the door and looked out. McGregor was trudging back towards the station.

'That's odd,' Willis said. 'McGregor's on foot. How did he get here so quickly? Only a few minutes have passed since the alarm went off. And it's the middle of the night. He should have been in bed and the dorms are a kilometre away.

,

CHAPTER 9

Willis decided to keep an eye on McGregor: he didn't like that he'd turned up so soon after the observatory alarm had gone off. Willis fell asleep thinking about the issue and woke up late the next day to Linda hammering on his bedroom door. 'What the hell?' He needed more sleep.

'Come quickly!' her voice was strained. 'Someone has sabotaged the telescope.'

'How is that possible?' Willis swung the door open while he pulled on his trousers.

'I don't know. The alarm must be disabled; it never went off. Come. Look. See for yourself.'

Willis finished dressing as fast as he could, and was in the corridor in three minutes flat.

When they entered the telescope area, everything looked normal. The switch on the door was in one piece, the wires still attached.

'I can't explain it. The door opening should have triggered the klaxon – the door's been forced but the signal didn't sound.' Linda was near hysterics.

'Calm down. The power to the building must have been cut. That would disable your alarm.'

'Don't tell me to calm down.' Tears were flowing down Linda's cheeks. 'The telescope is broken; it's been bloody sabotaged. We only left it for an hour to get some breakfast. Someone has damaged the SQUIDs – this is serious.'

'The SQUIDs?' Willis asked.

'The SQUIDs are the detectors that sense the signals that the telescope receives. Stands for Superconducting Quantum Interference Devices. Without them, the instrument is blind. It's useless. It's a heap of scrap metal.'

Gabi came up and put her arm around Linda's shoulders. Linda shrugged and backed away, wiping her eyes. 'It will take months to get replacements. With the winter coming, it could be next year before the telescope is operational again.'

'Show me where they are. What do they look like?' Willis was handling the open casing on the telescope.

'Leave it alone,' Linda slapped his hand and pushed him aside. She swung open a panel. Inside was a distribution board covered by a mass of cables. 'Someone has taken a knife and sliced through the main harness.'

'The good news is that the damage must only be physical, it's got to be, since the power was cut.' Willis said. 'The sensors themselves are undamaged. Only the harness is damaged, and that will take hours to fix. But we can repair it

69

in situ. They cut the wires when the power was off, so the detectors won't be damaged.'

Linda sat down, cradling her head in her hands. 'Who would want to do this?' Her voice was muffled. 'What will they gain by ruining such a wonderful instrument?'

'I don't think it was the telescope they wanted to disable; it was the atomic clock.' Willis paused then added, 'With the telescope out of operation, there would be no need for you to run the clock. The clock could help time the electromagnetic pulses accurately. It could help us locate where they came from.'

Linda looked out between her fingers, which covered her face. 'Well, we'd better get on with reconnecting the cut wires so that we can put the power back on to run your damn clock, Dr Willis.' She got up. 'Bring the crimping tool from the bench, Gabi, sweetheart. There's a lot of work ahead of us.'

Since the sun never set, it was difficult to keep track of the time, but when Linda finished connecting the last wire, it was late afternoon. The task had taken almost the entire day.

'The only thing left to do is insulate the crimps, add some new mesh shielding and we're done.'

'I'll go for fresh coffee and food,' volunteered Willis. 'Until we understand what's going on, we'd better stand guard around the clock.'

When Willis returned with the snack and drinks, Linda had finished insulating and protecting the harness.

'Let's enjoy a cappuccino and a sarnie before we put on the power to the system, in case I've made a mistake and I blow everything up.'

Gabi and Willis agreed. 'Good idea.'

'I am fully confident in your ability,' Gabi added.

'... and you're completely unbiased. Right?'

Gabi didn't answer. She just smiled and sipped her coffee.

***

'Okay. Now for the moment of truth – we've procrastinated long enough.' Linda opened the electrical panel, closed her eyes, mouthed a count of three and flipped the switch.

Nothing.

'I had forgotten, the power to the building has been switched off.' Linda put the switch back off on the control panel. 'Thank God we have some windows in here.' She opened the door, stepped outside and opened a cover beneath the stairs. The icy air cut into her face in the few minutes she was outside. She threw the mains switch back on. Then she looked down. 'The mains connection has been cut.'

Willis said. 'Not only did he disconnect the power he cut through the cables to disable it. We might as well relax for a bit. Let the base sparkies come and repair it.'

Within two hours, they had restored the power. Once again, Linda opened the distribution panel. 'Now for the moment of truth for a second time.' She didn't hesitate. She threw the switch. As the fans cut in and the control lights for the telescope burst into life, everyone breathed a sigh of relief. Linda threw another switch. A row of green LEDs lit up the panel. 'The repair's worked.' The relief in her voice was palpable. 'It'll take forty-eight hours for the SQUIDs to run up to operational status. The atomic clock is already running – it will automatically synchronise with the clock at IceCube. We're back in action.'

Gabi came over, put her arms around her and gave her a slow kiss on the lips.

'Right, who's going on the first shift? Gabi, you get something to eat at the galley. Then grab a few hours' sleep.

Brad and I will stay here to check on the panel to make sure it behaves itself, and I created no short-circuits when I rewired it.'

Once Gabi had gone, Linda turned to Willis. 'It must be Callum McGregor who did this. Since we met, he has been openly hostile.'

Willis had suspected McGregor for some time, but there was something that didn't fit with him being the culprit. Whoever sabotaged the telescope didn't have access to the laboratory. They'd had to force an entry. Although few doors were usually locked in Antarctica, recent events had made everyone take extra care. This included Linda. She had locked the telescope building before leaving. Since he was in charge of security, McGregor would have a set of keys. He wouldn't have needed to force the door. And Willis couldn't imagine him being so crude as simply to cut through the harness and the power cables. McGregor would have been more sophisticated. He would have done more damage to the telescope. Whoever did this had been in a hurry. They'd been afraid that somebody might spot them. McGregor would have an excuse for being in the building. He could have relaxed and taken things more slowly.

'I dislike him,' Linda said, shaking her head. 'Just looking at him winds me up.'

'You're not alone. He has that effect on everybody. Listen, if we're going to do around-the-clock shifts, we should do them in pairs.'

'Well, there's no problem if Gabi and I do a shift together, but who will you partner with? Sorry, that was a stupid question.'

'I'll ask Sophie if she will stay with me, but she might not. She and I aren't on the best of terms since I didn't visit her at CERN.'

'Ask her now. I'll be safe here. No one will come so soon after the last attempt. Go and speak to her.'

***

'God, you look as though you haven't slept – you're like a zombie. Has jet lag finally caught up with you?'

'No, I haven't had enough sleep yet. They sabotaged SPT.' Willis told Sophie of the events of the previous twenty-four hours, and how they might relate to the electromagnetic pulses that were disrupting Antarctica.

Sophie let out a long, slow whistle. 'You think it's the atomic clock that they wanted to disable? Then that could happen here at IceCube as well – our clock will be a target.'

'Of course – I hadn't considered that. I had planned to ask you to partner me on a night shift – we're going to guard the telescope in case there's a second attempt made to sabotage it, but I guess you'd better stay here to help set up your team's system of shifts.'

'There are four of us here, but we work around the clock, so I couldn't be sure of being free to help you.'

'That's alright, we'll manage. I'll ask one of the men to stand in. Before I go back to the telescope, do you fancy going for a bite to eat? If we leave right away we'll have time for dinner before everything closes down. I need to go back to the base anyway to see who is available to help.'

'Yes, okay. Give me a couple of minutes to hand over what I'm working on. I'll be right with you.'

'I'll call Linda to tell her what I'm doing.'

***

'Have you got used to this high-calorie food yet? You certainly ladled enough of it onto your plate.' Sophie smiled as she pushed another scoop of mashed potato into her mouth.

73

'I've adjusted to it. The temperature isn't too low yet. I'm sure I'm putting the pounds on.' Willis patted his stomach.

'I can't say that I've noticed. You're quite slim. Any weight change will take some time to show.'

Willis stared down at his plate. He was half lying. This food was different to everything his taste buds were used to. At home, Willis was partly vegetarian. He stuck his fork into a piece of lamb and let the gravy run off its fatty rind before putting the chunk in his mouth. The meat was tender enough, but the fat took some chewing. Willis glanced at Sophie. She seemed to be really enjoying her food. Even though she was chewing, she looked stunning. Sophie's hazel eyes sparkled. He stared at her, but she wasn't paying attention to him. She had lowered her head as she concentrated on her meal. She looked up momentarily, and the green flecks that mingled with the gold of her eyes caught the light. Sophie's short, mousy hair framed her face perfectly. God, she was beautiful. How could he have let her go back to CERN alone?

But he knew the reason. They were both dedicated to their careers – his astronomy, her particle physics. There must be some way that they could get their relationship to work, he mused. But he didn't know how yet.

'Brad, you've stopped chewing. You're staring.' Sophie was looking right at him.

'I'm sorry. I have told you that you're beautiful, haven't I?'

'Several times. The isolation at Pole is getting to you. It gets to everyone eventually. Eat your food and shut up.' The words sounded harsh, but she was smiling. 'You're doing pretty well for someone who is supposedly a vegetarian.'

'I'm not a serious vegetarian. I eat meat once or twice a month at home.'

'Think about it this way. If you eat it all the time, it only counts as once a month.'

Willis sprayed the contents of his mouth back onto the plate. 'That was the wrong time to say that.'

Willis walked Sophie back to IceCube. Even although they were walking through snow, it felt like a warm spring day. Although it was well below zero, there was no wind and the low sun shone directly on their faces. He let his mind drift. How should he handle the current problem? Asking Sophie to help with the shifts was one thing, but it was another matter to ask any of the men on the site for help. He was still unsure who to trust. The decision was straightforward. Willis would trust no one – at least, for the foreseeable future. He would do the shift on his own in the observatory. Willis was fit, so he felt confident that he could tackle anyone who tried to enter – as long as they came alone.

He collected some of his belongings then returned to the DSL – the Dark Sector Lab. When he got there, Linda was making a pot of coffee. He explained the situation, saying that Sophie could not help to guard the telescope. Willis would carry out the shift on his own, but requested that he do the night shift. That way, he could carry on the investigation during his working day.

CHAPTER 10

Willis bundled his blankets into a corner of the room at SPT then selected the place he had hidden previously, when he'd tried to protect Linda and Gabi. A flask of cocoa sat at his side as he settled down and allowed his brain to wander. Makeshift blackout sheets covered the windows to keep out the rays of the never-setting sun. Willis listened for any noises, but all was peaceful and silent. Gradually his eyes closed and he fell into a gentle sleep. Each time he woke, he checked his watch: 1 a.m., 3 a.m. and 5 a.m. passed without incident. He was having a much better night than he had expected.

Willis's dream took a diversion. He dreamed that he and Sophie were lying in bed in a hotel room when a maid visited to make up the bed. The maid knocked on the door. The banging persisted. It got louder. Slowly he awoke to sunlight escaping into his darkened world through the gaps around the blackout blinds. As the sleep fell from his eyes and he grew fully awake, the tapping became more distinct. The clamour increased. Was someone knocking on or hammering on the laboratory door? Willis reached out to one side and groped for the big adjustable wrench he'd dropped by the flip-chart as a precaution. As he rose, he stretched. Willis's fist tightened around the wrench. A dozen silent steps carried him to the metal door. The noise changed to a metallic sound, as something solid repeatedly hit the door. Willis grabbed the locking bar, raised the heavy tool high above his head, drew a deep breath, threw the handle down, then swung the door wide open.

Sophie stood there holding a can of soda. Her hazel eyes were worried. 'I imagined you'd been attacked in the night.' The tension left his body. He gently lowered the wrench.

'I thought you'd be pleased to see me. It's 7 a.m.' Sophie gazed up at him with a wide grin. 'Aren't you going to invite me in?'

'I could have killed you.' Willis waved the would-be weapon in front of her. He stepped back to let her pass. Dropping the metal implement on the floor, he shut the door. 'You told me you'd have to do shifts at the IceCube. How did you get away?'

'I've finished my shift. The idea just occurred to me to come along. I wanted to see how you were doing.'

'Of course I'm pleased you're here, but what a pity your shift didn't end earlier. Linda and Gabi are due back soon to take up their shift.'

'Now, now, my reason for visiting is nothing like that. I'm here to check how you're—'

Before she could finish, he took her into his arms then landed a long, passionate kiss on her lips.

'Let's take things a little slower. I still haven't forgiven you for not coming to CERN to see me.'

'You didn't come to Cambridge either, so we're equal. We both have reasons why we didn't visit.'

'I forgive you, but I'm a woman. I'm entitled to be illogical,' Sophie joked. She put her hands on his ears and pulled him close, returning his kiss with increased passion. Willis looked at her and shook his head. Sophie was never illogical.

'We need to think about how things might work. I know we're meant to be together; we just haven't worked out a plan that suits us both yet.'

'How's your PTSD been?'

'Great. I haven't had any symptoms since I returned from Kazakhstan.'

'So, you've had no recurrence since you returned from St Petersburg? Then, Professor Alek Sidorov's sessions must have helped you?'

'I think they did. But it's too soon to be sure although I'm feeling optimistic that they did. Do you remember the disk that he gave me that he recorded while I was under hypnosis? It recorded me recalling the number plate of the red sports car that hit our car and killed my wife, Carole.'

Sophie put her hand on his. 'I was worried that since the number recorded was indistinct that it might have caused you even more concern than no knowing it at all.'

'It is the exact opposite. It gives me something to concentrate on when I'm home. Until I find the culprit of the hit-and-run, I'll never be able to be really content. I asked Reilly, as an unofficial favour, to investigate the plate and see if he could find out what car the number belonged to.

Reilly said the DVLA have no record of a car of that type having that partial plate. Perhaps I imagined the whole thing, maybe the memory was false. These things can happen, but there can't be too many old red sports cars around for Reilly to search through. I had hoped the number was correct,' he said.

Sophie hugged him in sympathy. Why don't you have another look at the registration, then try substituting some numbers and letters for some that you might have misread?

He kissed the top of her head. 'Thanks.' He pulled her close to his chest. 'The situation is getting dangerous. Whoever tried to kill me, and who successfully sabotaged the telescope, might well come after you. You need to be careful. If the same person wants to damage the IceCube clock, you will be a target, especially if they identify you as an associate of mine.'

'We've never shrunk from danger before,' she said. 'Don't start now. Finding out who's doing this is too important.'

'I know, but this is such a closed community. It makes it difficult to recognise who's a friend and who's an enemy.'

Willis made some coffee. They sat at Linda's workbench and chatted. After thirty minutes the door swung open. In came Linda and Gabi. As they entered, the wind picked up and a burst of icy air blew into the room. It caught a piece of cardboard which in turn caught on a rack of tools and knocked it off the nearest bench.

Linda spoke first. 'Ah, you've found a way to while away the hours on night shift.' She grinned. Sophie opened her mouth to reply, but Willis put his hand on her thigh.

'Linda's teasing you – don't rise to the bait.'

'Yes, I'm only teasing.' Linda grinned again.

'No, she isn't,' Gabi said. 'Linda can be such a bitch. Ignore her.'

'If you'll let me, I'll walk you back to the rooms?' Willis looked at Sophie. She smiled then headed for the door.

The winds that drive all the snow that arrives at the Pole pounded them as they walked back to the residences. These winds are gravity-fed, as the cold air runs down from higher ground on the plateau in a flow that is the reverse of convection. Now this wind drove snow particles into their faces as they walked. The flakes aren't real, fluffy snow, but small ice crystals that formed high in the atmosphere. The particles stung their faces as they pressed forward.

Half way back they stopped and marvelled at the halo surrounding the sun created by the interaction of the crystals with the sunlight. The wind was only eight miles per hour. When winter came, what would the weather be like? Willis appreciated the thick down jacket that gave him much-needed protection. He put his arm around Sophie to steer her into the cold breeze. She twisted to speak to him. Willis saw her lips moving, but her face-covering smothered her words. Both looked down at their boots to protect their faces. The outline of their feet was barely visible through the haze of crystals. They went to the galley. Inside, Sophie brushed the particles of ice from their parkas. She burst out laughing because ice had encrusted Willis's eyebrows and eyelashes. He had prematurely removed his goggles, allowing the crystals to form. She wiped her fingers across his eyebrows to dislodge what she called his 'Santa' face. After he'd recovered, they grabbed two mugs, added a packet of cocoa and hot water to each, then held the warm mugs against their cheeks.

'Boy, that wind came on quickly.'

'It always does. We need to put on our face coverings and goggles every time before we go out. Even after a few seconds, ice crystals can form, and eight miles per hour isn't exactly a blizzard. I didn't expect much wind this early in the season.'

'Before the mini-hurricane blew your words away outside, what did you try to say to me?' Willis asked.

'Oh, it's nothing. It isn't important.'

'Yes, it is. Tell me.'

Sophie's cheeks turned bright pink. And the wind wasn't the cause. 'I'd rather be in bed.' Her face reddened even further.

'So would I. Your place or mine?' Willis looked straight into her eyes. 'I'm deadly serious. Better make it yours. Someone might interrupt us at mine.'

Sophie gulped the rest of her cocoa. She stood up. 'Well? What's keeping you?' She almost ran to the door.

Willis got to his feet and followed her. He looked around nervously to see if anyone had overheard their brief conversation, then smiled to himself. If they did, so what? Would I care?

***

In Sophie's room, they tore off each other's clothes. Sophie started to giggle. 'We will need to adjust; this little bed isn't intended for two.'

'We'll manage, but I don't suppose they deliver pizzas here?' Willis was alluding to the habit they'd got into at university of ordering a pizza when they needed a break after making love.

'I'm not sure I'd want someone to come here with pizza, that would be too—'

Before she'd finished, Willis pushed her onto the bed, kissing her neck and shoulders. Sophie lay back, her eyes closed, and sighed, enjoying every second. Sophie gave a deep, lingering sigh as he licked her ear. After they'd kissed, Willis moved across her body. Their lips met. She curved her back to arch closer to him, then grabbed his hair and pulled. Although his eyes watered, he didn't ask her to stop. This was too good. This was heaven. Sophie tasted perfect – as perfect as the last time they'd met. The touch of her soft, moist mouth was ingrained into his memory. He entered her too soon, too fast. Within seconds, she had screamed and stretched her arms towards the sky, shuddering. Once more, she arched her back, this time much higher. Willis let his orgasm release into her. After a low whimper, she collapsed onto the bed, motionless, her warm breath brushing his cheek and ear. The smell of her hair invaded his nostrils.

Sophie pushed Willis's shoulder to move him onto his back. As he moved, she climbed astride him. When he felt her take him in her hands then slip him inside her warm wetness, his eyes rolled back. Sophie looked down at him, holding her hands above her head. The movement accentuated her pert breasts.

'You don't think you're getting away with only once, do you?' She tightened her thighs around him, rocking backwards and forwards. The pleasure became almost unbearable. Willis's mouth moved, but no sound came out. He didn't want her to stop. Sophie raised and lowered herself, letting her bottom slap down on Willis's thighs. She gave a whimper, then a silent scream and Sophie collapsed onto Willis's chest, letting her lips graze his. She held the position for what felt like an eternity, then rolled off, breathless and satisfied.

'Now you can consider ordering pizza.' Sophie could hardly speak for giggling.

'I wish.'

'You can't have two wishes come true at the same time. Don't be greedy.'

Willis snuggled up to her so closely that he was unable to focus on her eyes. He rested his hand on her hip, as though to hold her in place. 'I love you. I never want us to become separated again. Let's work on a plan, as a couple, to make that happen.'

'You're a romantic, Brad Willis. That's easier said than done. And you are well aware of that. We have separate lives... we live apart by necessity... we have chosen different professions.'

'You're right, but we're scientists. If we put our minds to it. we'll come up with a solution. Promise me, when this is over we'll sit down and see what we can come up with.'

Sophie smiled, but shook her head. 'I promise we'll give it a try. If we succeed, we will get the Nobel Prize.'

'We have already been nominated for the Nobel Prize for lovemaking.'

'By whom, dare I ask?'

'Well, me, for a start.'

'I second that.'

CHAPTER 11

John Connor lounged back in his chair, his boots on the edge of his desk. The low sun shone through the window behind him and reflected off his almost bald head. The Station Leader's bulk might easily have overcome the strength of the fragile chair, which creaked in an effort to support him.

'Come,' he called in reply to Willis's knock on the door. Willis disliked people who used 'come' when they meant 'come in'; he considered the habit lazy and authoritarian.

'Did you make any progress with your investigation?'

'Very little. I worked out an approximate location for the source of the last surge. The interference came from the Ross Sea. I emailed the information to London after you arranged a secure internet connection for me.'

'Because the military server doesn't notify you when you receive a reply, you will need to log on to read it.'

'That's useful to know. When I leave you, I'll log on.'

'I'll come with you. Johnny won't be able to get into the system without my password. Now, about this incident in the Dark Sector Laboratory? What do you want me to do about it?'

'Nothing. At the moment. And I'd rather that you didn't mention it to anyone on the base. Although the word will get around on its own. I'd also rather that included McGregor.' He looked Connor straight in the eyes while he made the request. John Connor gave him a nod that suggested he understood Willis's reasoning. That was not the result Willis had expected. Because McGregor was effectively Connor's security officer, they should be close colleagues. But Connor's reaction pleased Willis, as he hadn't been looking forward to arguing with him over McGregor. Connor offered to double with Willis on his shifts guarding the telescope. He declined, using the excuse that people would readily notice Connor's absence – which was true. The real reason was that he wanted nothing to interfere with Sophie visiting him after she'd finished her shift.

Willis was just suggesting that they check his email when the office door burst open. In marched McGregor, his features red with rage. 'Connor asked me tae tighten up security here. I demand tae know what's going on. I insist ye keep me in the loop – this is no' acceptable.'

'Whether or not you need to be in the loop is my decision.' Willis glowered at him. 'Has something happened that I'm not aware of?'

McGregor's face turned pale. He obviously realised he had pre-empted the information about SPT. 'The telescope's broken and I wasnae told about it.'

'Then how did you find out about the damage?' Willis stared into his eyes.

McGregor paused. 'Everybody knows about it – everyone's goin' on aboot it.' McGregor's accent got stronger the more stressed he became.

It was logical that word would get around, but Willis should have anticipated it would happen this quickly. 'I haven't heard a single soul chatting about it. If you'd been doing your job, the damage wouldn't have happened. I'd be pleased if you would deny any rumours that you hear. I want you to tell me who you heard talking about this so-called incident. Well?'

'I cannae think who told me.'

'Surely you recall someone?'

'I cannae say I remember anybody. They all talked at the same time. I'm the security officer here. I need to be involved in any investigations that are going on.'

'I'll keep you in the picture if you also keep me notified.' Willis swung his back towards Connor to let him see his fingers crossed behind his back. He twisted his head to look at Connor, who was suppressing a smile.

Willis turned to face Connor. 'Now can we check my email messages?'

The men headed for the door, leaving McGregor standing there.

'I've set up a personal USAP email address for you. You can send and receive non-urgent emails using your laptop,' Johnny said, before connecting Willis to the secure military email system then discreetly exiting before Connor entered his password. The Station Leader also stood to leave, but Willis waved his arm, indicating that he should stay. Willis opened the mail and studied it, then swivelled the screen so Connor could see it. The message read:

Located suspect vessel by radar. Ship on way to intercept. Will advise when we establish contact — Mike R.

'That's short and to the point.' Connor stood up then called Johnny back from the hallway. 'This could turn into a major international incident. We'll wait until the fireworks begin.'

***

The fireworks indeed began, but not in the manner Connor had expected. At 3.30 p.m., alarm bells and klaxons began to sound. People scurried around like ants.

'Where's the fire?' Sophie asked.

'I don't know.' Willis touched a rushing passer-by on the arm. It turned out to be McGregor.

'A fire has started in a bedroom on the upper floor.' McGregor didn't stop, but hurried on.

'That's extremely serious.' Sophie walked away fast. 'I'm a member of the emergency unit, so I need to go.' She headed towards the nearest stairs, Willis following closely behind. As she ran, she explained. 'Everything on the base is tinder-dry because of the dryness of the atmosphere. The low temperatures cause moisture to condense out of the air. That makes everything dry out, making a fire spread rapidly. We've set up emergency teams who are trained to act in these situations.'

By the time they reached the bedroom, which lay at the end of the second spur leading off from the top corridor, fire teams were already tending the blaze with extinguishers. They quickly put the flames out. The stench of smoke and burnt bed coverings caught Willis's throat, making cough and cover his mouth.

Somebody said, 'I can smell accelerant.'

'Here it is,' said another, pointing to a dark greasy patch on the wooden floor. Willis moved discreetly into the room to inspect the stain. The black stain outlined the bed. Willis dipped his finger into what remained, then put it to his nose. Without a doubt, it was machine oil used as an accelerant. Someone had deliberately set the room alight.

Then the obvious dawned on Willis. How could he be so naïve? Of course someone had started the fire on purpose – that made perfect sense.

He turned and raced for his room and his Big Red, also picking up his gloves and goggles. Willis ran out of the dormitory and sped the kilometre to the telescope. With his boots constantly slithering on the compacted ice, he ran as quickly as he dared. Then he lost balance. He fell against one of the guide flags that had been used to mark the route. Its pole pushed under his goggles. He felt warm blood running down his cheek. The blood didn't run for long; it congealed immediately in the freezing air. He got to his feet and continued to rush onward. The kilometre between the base and the telescope had never seemed so far before.

Willis arrived to find the door ajar. With an impatient pull, he forced the door wide. Once inside his heart sank. Someone had taken an axe to the line that fed the cooler pumps. Without these, the cryogenic coolers would be inoperable. The sensors would overheat. Willis pulled open the cover to the distribution panel and threw the master switch. Switching off the power would protect the sensors from overheating, but the motors depending on the waste heat from the other circuits would freeze. He'd protected a piece of equipment while endangering another.

Then Linda, Gabi and Sophie arrived. Taking one glance at the damage, Linda fell onto a workbench chair. Her eyes filled with tears. She was inconsolable. Gabi turned to

Willis. 'Did you throw the switch? You might just have been in time, but we won't know for sure until we power everything back up. If the detectors overheated, the heat will have irreparably damaged them. We will be out of action for the entire winter; it will be impossible to get replacements before the base closes for the season.'

Willis walked over and put his arm around Linda. 'The coolers might be okay; the power was only off for a short while.'

'I can't be sure. We attended to the fire when the klaxons sounded, so we didn't arrive here for at least twenty minutes. That's more than long enough to cook the detectors.'

Willis placed his hand on her back to comfort her. Linda looked at him through her tears. 'We're idiots. We should have expected a distraction like this. It got us to leave the telescope unprotected. It worked.'

Willis wandered off towards the door. He saw something propped against a workbench, in the lab adjacent to the door but partly hidden in the shadows. An axe, leaning against the woodwork. He put his hand out to pick it up, then stopped himself in time. Fingerprints, he thought. A long shot. But the intruder might have failed to wipe it. The culprit would have been in a hurry. If so, he would have likely kept his gloves on.

At that moment, McGregor came to the door. He appeared genuinely saddened by what he saw. Willis was certain at least this incident didn't involve McGregor. Willis had spoken to him as the klaxons went off. Willis was a witness to McGregor's whereabouts.

'I hae plenty o' heavy duty crimps to reconnect the cooler lines, if ye need them? I'll fetch them.' McGregor nodded then walked towards the door. 'I'll be back in an hour then we'll get going, lass.'

'If you give me instructions, I'll stay here and help,' Willis said. 'Unlike the wires to the SQUIDs, these have no colours or marks. Before we can reconnect them, you'll need to trace them back to their origin.'

Linda collected a sheet of sticky labels from her desk. 'When we've traced it, I will attach a label to each wire. Gabi will sit near the power source with a walkie-talkie and an electrical continuity meter. When I've finished working, from left to right, through half the wires, there will be room for you to get in to do the crimping while I continue with the rest of the labelling.'

'At least the DSL furnace is still working. That will stop the lab from getting cold. I'll make some coffee. And I'll radio John Connor to tell him what's happened. He'll need to know.'

Within the hour, Callum McGregor had returned, carrying a half-kilogram bag of mixed-size crimps. He looked at the cut wires, then sorted the connectors into the correct sizes for the job.

Willis wondered why McGregor was being so helpful. After Willis had thanked him, he got to work as soon as Linda had labelled and cleared the first thirty centimetres of the lines.

'Seeing as you guys huvnae eaten yet, I'll bring ye something fae the galley. You'll be needing some sustenance before too long.' McGregor produced paper and pen, then wrote out food orders from the three of them.

'We're making good time.' Linda held up her crossed fingers and twisted them in the air so everyone could see. 'The wires are thicker than the previous ones we repaired, but there aren't as many, so the reconnection of the wires is proceeding swiftly.'

McGregor soon returned with the food. They rested while they ate. Linda brightened up. She seemed in much better spirits than before.

After they finished, McGregor tidied away the dirty plates. He washed up and returned the other dishes to the galley. He was back an hour later, with three bottles of wine: a red Malbec and two white Sancerres. Under his arm he carried a big bowl of popcorn wrapped in a duvet cover. It was straight from the machine and still warm.

'Ah'm sorry for the Sancerre. It's a wee bit dry to drink on its own, but it's awe I could get my hands on quickly. There's never a shortage of alcohol on the base because it helps to keep oor morale high.'

Willis called another quick thirty-minute break. That was fine, as they'd got on much better than they'd expected to. They would finish this stage in an hour, barring any problems. McGregor poured them each a plastic beaker of wine. That wouldn't do any harm. The five had cheered up immensely by the time they finished their break. Even McGregor had become a part of the friendly group. He volunteered to return the empty bottles as they were finishing the popcorn and set off to the galley to do so.

Finally, when they had finished, Linda said, 'I'll turn the electricity supply on but keep the motors and the detectors isolated until the heat from the electronics warms the motors. This will prevent them seizing up because of the cold. We can't do anything for seventy-two hours. It will take that long for the motors to warm up.'

They sat around, feeling pleased with themselves.

Willis's gaze wandered over to the door.

The axe was gone.

SHADES of WHITE

The only person who'd left the lab was McGregor.

CHAPTER 12

Willis crashed into McGregor's room. As he pushed past his cabinet, everything on it scattered onto the floor. McGregor backed off instinctively, but Willis followed him and pinned him against the wall. His hands gripped McGregor around his neck, choking the life out of him. Slowly McGregor slipped down the wall. Willis let go. The limp frame landed on the floor. McGregor grasped his throat and made gulping sounds as he tried to suck air into his starved lungs. Willis took a swipe with his boot that made contact with McGregor's jaw. McGregor's head shot back and bounced off the desk. Blood splattered from his mouth and sprayed down the front of his shirt. Willis was preparing to kick him once more when a massive hand caught him by the shoulder. The grip belonged to John Connor; he pulled Willis away. Connor bent to check on McGregor.

'McGregor's been sabotaging the telescope.' Willis, eager to get to his quarry again, pushed forward.

Connor heaved McGregor to his feet. 'Right, tell me your version of what happened.'

Before he answered, Willis shouted a reply. 'He used an axe to destroy the cables on SPT. The bastard has been incapacitating the observatory for days. Why are you doing this?'

'Let me...' McGregor coughed up a mouthful of blood. 'Explain.'

'You better had.' Willis took a step forward, but Connor blocked his path.

'May I sit down?' All remnants of McGregor's Scottish accent had vanished.

Connor pulled up a chair. McGregor collapsed clumsily onto it and looked up. A bruise was already forming on his right cheek. He held out his hand, signalling patience, while he caught his breath. 'I am CIA.' He swallowed hard. 'Because the CIA shouldn't be on this continent at all, they sent me to investigate undercover, for political reasons.'

'Why did you remove the axe?' Willis looked unconvinced.

'I didn't think you'd noticed that. I needed to collect fingerprints off the handle before someone contaminated it by moving it.' McGregor shook another splash of blood from his mouth.

'And did you? Did you get any prints?'

'Yes. I found a clear one and a few partials. I will need to exclude everyone who might have touched it. I also took the beakers that we drank out of to eliminate the women and you.'

Connor said, 'You should have identified yourself.'

'Would you have? I have a Station Leader who's relatively new to the base and an astronomer who seemed to have pulled strings to get here at short notice. You're both under suspicion and you will remain so until I can prove otherwise.' He arched his back to relieve the stiffness and pain. 'My name really is McGregor. My father immigrated from Scotland over forty years ago. We detected some weaker pulses about three months ago – long before the powerful ones. The smaller ones attracted the attention of the authorities, so they assigned me to investigate.'

'If you are CIA, you might know Brigadier-General Joshua S. Baker or Admiral Jamie Wilson. Both are my CIA contacts.' As though he was firing two pistols, Willis aimed his forefingers in McGregor's direction. He intended it as a challenge, not for information.

'Yes…' McGregor drew the word out slowly. 'Jamie and I have met. When I trained as a recruit, he was an instructor at Langley. Is he still drinking Martinis as though they're going out of fashion?' McGregor stared at Willis, his brows raised.

'Jamie still drinks a lot, but he drinks malt whisky, not Martinis.'

'You're my man,' McGregor said. He held out his hand. 'I'm sorry I mistrusted you.' His accent sounded Texan. Willis guessed he might be from Dallas.

Willis took his hand. 'That's okay – no need. You're just doing your job. I apologise for attacking you. We have a lot to catch up on.' Willis sat down on the bed. McGregor drew his chair nearer. Connor made an excuse and left to allow them to talk. McGregor kicked off. 'Although I don't know who the other prints came from, I eliminated the women and you from the fingerprints I took from the axe.'

Willis shared his idea about using the DSL clock, and that by measuring time delays, he could locate the source of the pulses. 'That's why I believe the saboteur has targeted the telescope. So that the clock would be inoperable,' Willis said to his new friend. 'I have tracked the location of the last surge to somewhere in the Ross Sea – a military ship is on its way to investigate. I'm waiting for an update from my boss in the UK.'

Between them, they made some decisions. They were that McGregor would keep his Scottish accent; he would say that he'd fallen on the ice to explain his bruises; they would let the women know his actual role but swear them to secrecy; he would keep up his cantankerous manner.

***

Willis, McGregor and the women met at the DSL and repeated everything from their previous conversation. McGregor volunteered for the shifts to protect the instruments. Willis objected for the usual reason – because of Sophie's visits – but used the excuse that doing so would blow McGregor's cover if anyone noticed. Willis felt more comfortable knowing that there was someone else he could bounce his ideas and theories off.

'So far, I have eliminated only four members of the base from suspicion, and we're all in this room. I am not proud of that performance.' Willis glowered and slapped his palm on the desk.

Finally, power had begun to return to the electronics, as Linda had said. It would now take a while for the motors to warm up sufficiently to prevent them from seizing and burning out. 'Powering up the instruments isn't straightforward,' Linda said. 'Metal conductors can reduce their resistance in cold conditions. That makes them draw too much current. The system needed to be switched on for short periods, at first, to allow the circuits to heat and avoid damage. Eventually, things stabilised so I left the electricity on continuously. The good news is that the atomic timing clock is working and ready to time the next surge, in case anything happens again.'

***

The following three days passed without incident. All the motors ran. The detectors were fully functional. Thankfully, the delicate circuitry of the instruments had suffered no damage. Everything appeared so good, in fact, that Linda, Gabi and Sophie decided to arrange a minor celebration and to invite Willis and McGregor. The women bought some real fizzy wine glasses from the station's store. As the store's crew had so far failed to get their hands on the new season's delivery of champagne, they secured half a dozen bottles of cava to take its place.

Sophie produced a lemon drizzle cake and a chocolate gateau to accompany the wine. 'I didn't make either, but I convinced the chefs to supply them for us.' The cabin's loudspeaker played soft ballads in the background. For a while, at least, things were perfect.

McGregor offered to dance with Gabi, apparently unaware of her relationship with Linda. Gabi accepted. Linda smiled at Willis as she listened to McGregor's futile chat-up lines. After a few songs, Gabi thanked him, then walked over and kissed Linda full on the mouth.

'Oh shit.' McGregor covered his eyes with his hands and winced. 'I've made a right fool of myself.'

'No problem.' Gabi smiled. 'I like to make her a little jealous every so often. It keeps her on her toes.'

'Well, thank you anyway,' McGregor said. 'I very much enjoyed the dance. But I feel like a spare doodah at a wedding.' He looked at Willis and Sophie. 'You two make a fine pair.'

'Sophie and I didn't realise we'd made it that obvious.' Willis pulled Sophie towards him and gave her a quick peck on the cheek.

Together they cleared a workbench, then spread some tissues on its surface. The drink tasted delicious. Willis used a mouthful to wash down a slice of lemon drizzle cake. The cake was his favourite; Sophie had remembered that from their days at university. McGregor enjoyed a glass too, but had decided not to drink too much, as alcohol would make him forget about the Glaswegian accent he had affected. Laughter filled the lab. All five were friends. They were enjoying themselves. Three hours raced by – it would soon be time to get back to work. While Willis was still deciding what to do, Linda and Gabi opted to take the first shift, leaving the second for him. He and Sophie walked McGregor back to the base, then said their goodbyes. They intended to go to the galley for a quick cocoa, but they never arrived. Sophie looked at Willis through her steamed-up goggles. Her eyes said 'pizza'. Willis recognised the look. He nodded. They hurried to the end of the upper corridor and vanished into Sophie's room. Willis tasted the cava on her lips as they kissed.

***

Willis woke early the next morning. He dressed before Sophie stirred. 'Come back to bed,' she mumbled. 'It's too early.'

'I can't. I need to check if I have a reply to my email. The military satellite is due to be overhead soon.'

'Suit yourself.' Sophie turned over, pulled the duvet over her head and dropped back to sleep. Willis went to the door and opened it a couple of inches. Because he reckoned he should be discreet, he slipped out quietly, walked along the corridor, and headed for the galley.

John Connor sat at a table close to the door. His fry-up looked delicious. Willis chose the same and joined him.

'You seem to be becoming accustomed to the cooking here.' John chewed on a bit of crispy bacon.

'Why not? The food's delicious and of the highest quality. I hoped to check if I've received a reply to my email yet.'

'Johnny is always early. He likes to imagine he's keeping normal office hours, despite the perpetual sunshine. We can go together when you've finished and check.'

***

Connor's office sat on the upper floor of the main building. A big cardboard box sat on his desk. 'That's the base's supply of vitamin D. The pills are necessary when the sun sets after March. Your body doesn't produce the vitamin without sunlight.' He removed the box and put it in one corner of the room. 'Let's visit Johnny.'

As Connor had promised, Johnny sat in situ. 'Good morning, Dr Willis. Give me a few seconds. I will open up the email server.' As soon as the email page flashed on, Johnny made his usual discreet exit. Connor leaned over and entered his password. He didn't offer to leave this time, but stood behind Willis as he opened the reply.

The message was in code. The words looked like gobbledygook. But Willis understood Reilly's cipher.

'Shit, I have no idea how to decode this,' he lied. 'Do you have a printer I can use? I'll need to take this away to work out how to read the damn thing.'

Connor pointed to a printer against the wall behind Willis. Willis pressed Print and waited for his message to be spat out. He handed the printout to Connor. 'Does this look like a substitution code?' He was keeping up the pretence that the code was unknown to him.

After studying it Connor said, 'I doubt it. The pattern is quite complicated but there's no sign of a high count of a particular letter that might reveal an "e", which is the most frequently used letter in the English alphabet.'

'I agree. But I'll let you know once I've cracked the cipher.'

***

Back in his room, Willis took his copy of *The Handbook of Astronomical Statistics*. He divided the code into sets of three numbers. The code was an old favourite: the first number gave the page, the second the line, and the third the word. Without a copy of the book, the code was unbreakable. He set about deciphering Reilly's message.

CHAPTER 13

Willis finished decoding the message. He sat and read it a second time. He placed the sheet on his desk, then leaned back in his chair. Then he let out a long, low whistle. This was serious, but it was only part of the story. He lifted the paper to read it a third time:

Ship intercepted in Ross Sea is flying Chinese flag. Unable to board without causing an international incident. Transmitted message to captain to desist, or action would be considered hostile. Captain did not reply. Will continue to shadow suspect ship and monitor. Strong objection sent to Chinese government. Awaiting response. More to follow. M.R.

'Bloody hell, this is already an international incident,' he said out loud. 'What does it take to get some action?' He tossed the paper onto the desk in disgust.

Willis marched into Connor's office and slumped into the chair in front of his desk. 'A bloody Chinese vessel is the source of the interference, and London doesn't even say if it's military. Would you believe it? They've sent a strongly worded complaint to Beijing. While this goes on, *we* need to put up with all this crap.' He emphasised the 'we'. Ashamed to look Connor in the eye, he turned and stared out the window. Willis's lower lip trembled with rage.

After Willis's rant, Connor linked his hands behind his head. He shook his head in disapproval. 'If they shadow the vessel, they will be the first to know if a second pulse occurs. After that, they will have the excuse they need – then all hell will break loose.'

'Not necessarily. If the ship can focus the beam so that it misses them, they won't detect it. And it would need to be focused, otherwise the Chinese ship would knock itself out.'

'We're in the hands of the politicians and the military. We'll just have to wait and see.'

'There are no Chinese on the base, are there?'

Connor thought for a moment. 'There might be some Americans with Chinese origins working here, especially in the galley. Although I doubt they will even have Chinese names.'

'Until we can get this mess cleared up, I'm going back to put the observatory in lockdown to protect it.'

***

Willis called a meeting of the women and McGregor in the lab to tell them what Reilly's email contained. 'Until we resolve this, I recommended switching off the telescope and its instruments.'

Linda opposed closing everything down. 'No bloody way will I do that. Even that might cause harm.'

'If another surge occurs, it will cripple the equipment more,' Willis argued.

They sat and discussed it for over an hour. They agreed, albeit reluctantly, that closing down was marginally the better option, so Linda triggered the shutdown process. It would take several hours before they could switch off all power, but at least they knew it would come up again when needed. Sophie did likewise for the IceCube Observatory. Willis wasn't happy, because this mean losing the use of the clocks. But what must be, must be. If a subsequent event happened, the lack of timings would handicap him from tracing its source. They made it known on the base that they were powering down. Their logic was that, with the telescopes out of action, there would be no incentive to damage them.

Once the shutdown process had begun, they returned in four hours for stage two. Linda set off to email the National Science Foundation in the USA to tell them of her decision, since it enabled and supported the science projects on the base.

'Until I get a reply from Reilly, we'll need to wait. Unless he confirms that the danger is over, it won't be safe to power up again.' Willis decided that coffee was in order.

A sad Sophie came and sat at his side. 'Although I've switched off the IceCube Observatory, I can still leave the IceCube detectors and clock running. Since they're deep below the ice, they will be better protected from a surge than any of the equipment in the other observatory.'

'Better?' Willis asked. 'But is "better" good enough?'

'I can turn off everything except the sensors and the timer. If there's another burst, we will get a bearing on where it's come from – and because we won't need to let anyone on the base know it's still running, it will be safe.'

Willis's eyes lit up. 'I'll have at least one weapon in my armoury.' He leaned back and drank his coffee with new relish.

By 5 p.m., everything that was due to be powered down had been. They could relax, but relaxing hadn't been in the plan. The team had lots of spare time, and nothing to fill it.

'I suggest we socialise with the other crew members.' Willis got to his feet. 'Something might turn up in conversation that will shine a light on who the bad guy is. Doing so will also give us the chance to get the grapevine going, to let as many people as possible know that we've powered off the observatories. If we keep our eyes and ears open, who knows what we might uncover?'

They locked up then set off for the store, then the galley. They brought drinks with them that they had purchased from the store, spoke loudly so people might hear, and made themselves conspicuous.

Groups of workers came and went. The team sat through all the meal sessions: that way, everybody would notice them. The plan was to take note of anyone who showed an interest in knowing the labs were closed. Though it shouldn't have surprised them that everyone was interested. There wasn't much news around in such a tiny community, so everybody was keen to learn about the power surges. They told them they were being investigated, and left it at that. By 8 p.m., they had downed quite a lot of alcohol. They tried to ration what they drank, but even with their best efforts, they were feeling a little groggy. They kept reminding McGregor that he was a Glaswegian and not to forget his accent. Never mind, it was all in a good cause, they convinced themselves. Since they had decided it was better than working, they poured yet another round. Willis gritted his teeth. Normally drinking this much on the base would be a disciplinary offence, there were strict rules on drinking for safety reasons, but he decided that it was all for a good cause.

***

The next morning, their heads throbbed. They were all in the same room. Gabi and Linda were on their bed; Sophie and Willis sat propped up in one corner; McGregor lay spreadeagled across what remained of the floor. Groans and moans filled the room. Willis forced them to wake and get up. Sophie moved away from the wall and nearly fell as she stepped on an empty wine bottle. It skidded away, clinking against another four that were lying under the bed. Plates with half-eaten food littered the floor, energy bars with bites out of them sat on the desk. Fortunately, there was no evidence of anyone throwing up after their booze fest.

Sophie held the door open. 'Okay, Brad, you take McGregor, go for breakfast. Leave Linda, Gabi and me to tidy up. We need to recover.'

The men staggered down the long corridor leading to the stairs. It was a slow process as they bounced off the walls and tried to walk with their eyes half closed.

Once in the galley, they formed a rotating queue for coffee. They swallowed each mug with a single gulp, but it didn't make them feel better. The throbbing in their heads persisted. The galley emptied. The last stragglers from breakfast left. As a group passed their table, they giggled. Willis and McGregor could hear odd phrases as they passed. The words sounded disjointed but were describing what they had witnessed the night before.

Willis felt guilty. Not only had he drunk too much last night, but he had also been negligent in his duty. What would have happened if a surge had occurred during their drunken frolic? He sat, embarrassed, self-critical. Nothing had happened, or so he assumed. There was no sign of anything disrupting business this morning. He sank his head into his arms and closed his eyes, not even sure how much time had passed.

He awoke to Sophie tugging on his sleeve. 'C'mon, let's get you back to bed. The sooner you have a decent sleep, the sooner you will recover.' He grunted. Finally, he gave in to Sophie's constant tug on his collar.

When he woke, he was lying beside Sophie in the spoons position, his arm around her, holding one of her breasts. He cuddled up closer, not wanting to spoil the moment. But Sophie turned to face him. 'Good afternoon, Star Man. Shall we get up and see if we can get something to eat?'

'In half an hour.' He rolled over. He lay with his weight across her chest. 'I'm not too heavy?' He kissed her before she had time to shake her head.

'I see you're feeling better...'

'Just a tad,' he said, nipping her neck. He heard her sigh. Her body felt relaxed, pliant, and submissive.

Lunch would have to wait.

***

When they reached the galley, Linda, Gabi and McGregor were already eating. They gave them a knowing smile. McGregor mumbled something that sounded like 'I'm jealous.'

'We've been out to check the observatory, and everything is fine. There aren't any problems.' Linda was speaking but kept on chewing.

'No thanks to me,' Willis said, then added, 'Great, we must have done a convincing job last evening.'

'We sure as hell did.' It was Gabi who made the observation. 'But let's not repeat it for some time.'

All five ate ravenously – there's nothing like alcohol to improve the appetite. Lunch was over in ten minutes flat.

They decided that some cold air might help. They ventured outside and headed for the lab. There was little to do there, but getting out of the base would clear their heads. The snow that had arrived over the previous forty-eight hours had not yet compacted or been groomed, and no fresh ice crystals had been deposited, so the boot marks they had left on their last trip were still visible. Gabi called out each print as she attempted to recognise whose boot had made it. Since everybody wore the same boots, this was nigh-on impossible. She tried to guess the person's weight, judging by the boot size and the depth of the tread. She started carefully, then got more and more confident: 'Linda, Brad, me, Callum, Linda, me, Brad, Callum...'

'Oh, for heaven's sake, Gabi, give it a rest.' Linda was the only one who could tell her off without triggering an argument.

Gabi ignored her. She continued, 'Me, Linda, Brad, Callum, me – hey, wait a bit. Whose boots are those?' She stopped and pointed to several huge treads. 'They're fresher than the others. I'd guess they're a size twelve. What do you think?'

Willis put his boot into the clearest one. There was a gap of an inch beyond his toe. 'I'm a size ten,' he volunteered. 'These must be about a twelve – you're right.'

'Callum, how would you like to trace these back to see if you can find where they originated from? The women and I will walk ahead. We'll investigate where they go.'

They followed the footprints, but it was a slow process. There were gaps, so they had to interpolate where the prints were missing or indistinct. One thing was clear: they were heading for the telescope. They tracked them right up to the laboratory door. As they ascended the steps, ellipses of snow that had dropped off the walker's boots replaced the white smudges. Willis tried the door, but it was still securely locked. Linda unlocked the door and they stepped inside. Nothing was out of order. Willis checked for wet marks on the lab floor near the door. There was none. Whoever had left the boot prints had checked out the lab, and had apparently satisfied themselves that it was no longer a threat.

'Let's try to follow them.' Willis headed off to find the return path of the footprints. They picked up the trail of footprints going in the opposite direction. 'These are easier to track, as they take a different route on virgin ice to return to the base.' As they neared the building, they spotted McGregor approaching. He was heading straight for them. If he didn't stop, he would destroy the tracks. Willis held up his hand. McGregor halted. Willis explained what they were doing and together, they followed the path around the rear of the base. The footprints stopped at the top of the stairs, in front of an emergency fire door. They were now at the back end of the building. Willis tried the door, but it was locked. He threw a questioning glance at McGregor. 'This door would normally be securely closed. Whoever went in had planned to return this way so left it ajar.'

'Nae joy,' McGregor said. 'The trail led from the main door. It could have been anyone who left it.'

Willis walked back to Destination Alpha. He ran up the stairs and headed straight to the internal side of the fire door. The damp prints continued from the fire door into the corridor. He tracked them along the passageway until the prints faded in the heat of the base.

Willis returned. 'Whoever left these tracks works – or lives – at least halfway along this corridor. It isn't much, but it's more than we knew before.'

CHAPTER 14

Willis wondered what it might be like to feel being toasted. That's the polies' equivalent of cabin fever. Polies is the name given to people who will stay over the winter. Symptoms included getting short-tempered. *And* he had been abrupt with Connor the previous day. *And* he'd started to develop 'a thousand-mile stare', or so he thought. Willis dismissed the idea. Symptoms were less likely to appear with the modern design of the base. He daydreamed a lot, which was also a symptom. But as most of his daydreams involved Sophie, he convinced himself that they didn't count. No, he was certain he hadn't been toasted. Yet. But he would need to be careful – he didn't want to become any crankier than usual. He had been perfectly justified in losing his cool yesterday – the British government can be such a wimp when making important decisions.

Reilly should have sent a follow-up mail by now; he would check.

When he approached, Johnny's door was closed. That was odd. He pushed on the handle but it wouldn't open. That was even more unusual. Not too worried, he walked two doors along to John Connor's office, where he found Connor on a walkie-talkie. When Connor finished his conversation, he placed the unit on his desk and looked up. 'Good day, my friend, and what can I do for you on this lovely morning?'

Willis thought the morning had struck him as fine too, with crystal-clear air and very little wind. Indeed, the weather seemed so pleasant that Willis had taken a walk after breakfast.

'I intended to check my email, but Johnny has locked his office,' Willis said.

'That's not like Johnny – he usually keeps his door open because he doesn't enjoy being in confined spaces. Let's give him ten minutes then go along to see what he's up to.'

Willis glanced at the bookshelf behind Connor. 'Is that your wife?' He asked, studying a framed picture that sat on the top shelf. Connor turned and looked at the photo. He nodded.

'Doesn't she mind you spending so much time away from home?'

Connor swallowed. 'Maria … died a year ago.'

Willis wished the ground would open up and swallow him whole. 'I'm so sorry, that was a clumsy thing to ask.'

The two men sat in silence for some minutes. Willis cast his eyes over the range of books in the bookcase. The top couple of shelves were full of ledgers and official-looking folders. Crime and detective novels stacked the lower levels. Connor caught Willis studying the titles.

'They belonged to my wife. She loved anything like that. I brought them with me to read – I hoped she might feel closer if we shared something that she'd read.'

'That's a lovely idea.'

'It doesn't work.' The comment was abrupt. Angry. Connor got to his feet. 'Let's walk along and visit Johnny. He will be back by now.' He pushed past Willis, rushing towards Johnny's room. Willis had upset him again. Feeling guilty about his clumsiness, he shook his head.

Connor tried the handle, but it was still locked. He shrugged dismissively and made a turning movement with his hand, showing that he intended to get the key. When he returned, Willis stepped to the side. The door swung open, but the opening door hid their view of Johnny's desk. They entered the room and immediately froze. Johnny lay across his desk, his head crushed uncomfortably against his computer screen. Willis pushed forward. He put his fingers against Johnny's neck to search for a pulse. Then he drew his hand back. Blood dripped from his fingers.

Johnny's throat had been cut.

'Touch nothing,' Willis said. 'I'll get McGregor to test for fingerprints. Lock the door to prevent anyone else getting in.'

***

McGregor looked around and shook his head. 'I hae nae idea where to start.' He unpacked his kit and laid it on the desk. 'I'll dust everything.' He loaded his brush with powder then got to work searching for fingerprints.

At that point, Willis noticed the screen flashing. It displayed an email page. 'Shit. My email is visible. Although the message isn't open, I can see the email title. It's no longer in bold, which means that someone has read the contents. We must ask everyone on the base to let us take their fingerprints. Can you arrange that?' He faced Connor. 'Now it's a murder enquiry.'

'I will sort the fingerprints out. Most of last winter's personnel have flown home already and will be sitting on a beach somewhere, but that still means the number remaining is still over ninety.'

'Are any flights scheduled to leave today?'

'The last flight took off two days ago and none is due off today so, whoever did this is still on the base.'

Before McGregor finished lifting every fingerprint he could find, an hour had passed. It took another sixty minutes for Connor to get permission from Glen Mason, the deputy US Marshal at McMurdo, to move the body. They would freeze it to keep it fresh. Ironic, thought Willis: even with all this ice about, they still had to refrigerate a corpse.

After about three hours, Willis got to check his email. Quickly he transcribed the message onto a scrap of paper then disappeared back to his room to decode it. After several minutes, he read:

Reaction from Beijing: they deny all knowledge of ship in Ross Sea. Ship hailed again, no reply. A brief burst of radio frequency detected. The burst temporarily disabled power supplies on HM ship. Said ship opened fire. Suspect vessel exploded. Intelligence suggests something like a large Tesla coil visible on deck before ship sank. Immediate problem resolved. Now await international ramifications from wherever.

Willis wrote a reply to Reilly. This time he typed it without encryption, as it contained nothing of consequence, merely an acknowledgement. Then he hit Send, closed the email program and went to give McGregor a set of his prints.

***

Willis joined Linda, Gabi and Sophie in the queue. The queue moved quickly, even though over forty people were waiting. When he got to the front, and had his prints duly taken, he stepped aside to chat to Connor, who was supervising the process.

'Has everyone agreed to give their fingerprints?'

'A few people protested, as some always do, but reason prevailed. I told them I would send them home for refusing to assist with a murder enquiry. That did the trick.' Connor gave Willis a broad smile and a wink.

Willis gave him a friendly pat on the back then went to join the women on their way to lunch.

All four sat staring at their food, but had no inclination to eat. They played with their forks without talking. McGregor busied himself elsewhere, cataloguing the prints he'd lifted from Johnny's office. Willis spoke first. 'A word of advice: don't mention Connor's wife if you speak to him. She died less than a year ago and he's still very sensitive about mentioning her, so take care.'

Three heads nodded. But the silence continued.

Willis cut into his fried chicken. Fat oozed from beneath the bird's skin. Although his stomach demanded food, he needed to get out. The icy breeze would do him good.

After he excused himself, he aimed for the double doors that kept the cold air at bay. He fastened his parka, protected his eyes and face, then stepped out. The chill hit Willis immediately, but he enjoyed the experience. The weather remained fine and the wind slight. He decided to walk around the compound in a circle. He could still feel the heat from the sun, but it was getting lower and lower each day. After another three weeks at most, twilight would begin.

Long before then, every non-essential person, including him, would need to be off The Ice. Once the sun set, the temperature would drop precipitously. After a few weeks, dusk would give way to complete darkness, then to absolute blackness. So absolutely dark that nothing similar existed anywhere else on Earth. Willis hoped he would finish his investigations before then. In a way, he was disappointed about not being on the continent after the sun set, as he wanted to see Antarctica with the sky moonless. Dancing aurorae would fill the vista to disrupt the inky blackness and the southern Milky Way would mimic a long thin cloud as the white ribbon crept across the heavens.

The crunching of footsteps on the virgin snow attracted Willis's attention. He swung around, to find Sophie almost running to catch him up.

'Now what are you fantasising about?' she asked. She took his arm, matching him stride for stride.

'I've been dreaming of Antarctica. The place is so beautiful. I never imagined so many shades of white existed until I witnessed them for myself.' He shared his other dreams with her: about the sky, about his investigations, and about his notion that he would like to spend the winter with her in this wonderland.

'Antarctica's not always so pretty, but the landscape is beautiful when the weather allows. You can winter-over if you choose. One of the research staff for the telescope has taken ill. He's called off, and it's much too late to find a replacement. I'm sure I can get you to take his place. If you want.' She smiled, but he couldn't make out the expression in her eyes.

'You told me everyone here needed to have two jobs. What would I do? I'm an astronomer – that's the limit of my talents.'

'I'm positive we can find you something. Supposing you're willing, you can always do some dishwashing in the galley.' The sound of her sexy giggle escaped through the protective layers that covered her face. Willis glanced at her, wanting to kiss her at that instant. Sophie squeezed his arm and pulled him closer. They continued to walk around the section of the building that housed the accommodation blocks.

'The window in Johnny's room is uncovered,' he said. All the dorm rooms had triwall – a form of triple-layered cardboard used for cargo or food transport cases covering the windows. It blocked their windows to keep out the summer sunlight, enabling them to sleep at night. It also acted as an excellent heat insulator in both the summer and winter. But it had been removed from Johnny's room.

Willis climbed the emergency stairs to get to the upper floor, and looked across at the exposed window of Johnny's room. He noticed the dark shape of a man sitting at Johnny's computer. He peered through the window, straining to see more details. Willis could see the man rummaging through Johnny's papers. Dust particles stuck to the window and the low sun reflected off the glass. The indoor light was on, as was a bright reading light. The visitor was busily photographing something in front of the window. When Willis moved, the sun's rays cast his shadow against the opposite wall of the office, and the movement attracted the intruder's attention. He grabbed something from the desk and ran out of the room. Willis leaned away from Sophie, who stood beside him on the stairs, and screwed his eyes up to see the door through which the intruder had left. He could see the outline of the intruder running along the corridor to the left.

He hurried back to the main entrance, towards Johnny's office. The door was open. Curious, Willis thought.

After I checked the email from Reilly, I'm sure that Connor locked the bloody thing. He did a quick recce of the desk, he found nothing out of place or, more importantly, anything missing. He visited Johnny's bedroom but nothing seemed out of place there either, other than the door being left open. Willis would have to ask Connor. He ran along the corridor to Connor's office. Drat! His room was empty. As Willis turned to leave, Connor entered. 'What can I do for you now?'

Willis told him about the man he had seen. They both went back to Johnny's office. Connor found nothing missing or out of place either. He moved a folder that lay to the left of the computer screen. 'Hold on. Where's Johnny's notepad? It's usually here on the left-hand side. Johnny was left-handed. He used the notepad to jot down the emails he received, so he could notify the recipients. But the pad's gone. Johnny always kept the notebook on his desk. He never removed it.'

'I've learned something,' Willis said. 'Whoever I saw has a room further along the passage from Johnny's. I also know that his room is in this half of the corridor. It was up to here that we tracked the previous footprints. Can you get me a list of the people who have rooms in this half of the corridor?'

'Of course I can.' Connor disappeared along to his office.

At that moment Sophie turned up, disrupting Willis's concentration.

'Anything disturbed?' She leaned over the desk.

'Only a pad.'

'Where's Johnny's stylus?'

'Stylus?' He cocked his head to one side and looked at Sophie.

'Yes – Johnny always used a stylus. This screen is touch-sensitive. He was always careful not to get greasy marks on it.'

'Of course. Let's grab Callum. Now!'

CHAPTER 15

It took Sophie no more than five minutes to return with McGregor. No, he hadn't taken fingerprints from the screen. He'd done everything else, but not the screen... He quickly did so, but everywhere checked out fine. There were no unexpected prints on the desk or computer.

McGregor lifted several finger-marks from the monitor, paying particular attention to the area pointed out by Willis: the small window that needed to be touched to open the email program. That's where he suspected the most suspicious print might be. McGregor explained that, as soon as he got the full set of base personnel fingerprints from Connor, he would give Willis a report. But not to hold his breath, as it would take a few hours.

Willis met Sophie, Linda and Gabi to fill them in on the sinking of the Chinese vessel in the Ross Sea. 'The intercepting ship was the target of one of the weaker pulses –

they could definitely confirm that the pulse came from the craft displaying the Chinese flag before they sank it. It seems logical, therefore, that it's now safe to power up the instruments in both observatories.'

The women sighed with relief.

'We can start the switch-on sequences for the telescopes as soon as possible,' Linda said. 'They will need a full seventy-two hours to get fully operational again.'

Willis left them to continue with their tasks. He went to see Connor.

***

Connor's pine desk was overflowing with cards containing both the fingerprints and details of their owners. Multi-coloured pieces of card were scattered over every inch of the desk. For that reason, Connor had brought in a second table to handle the overflow from the desk.

'This is Paul.' Connor pointed to the man helping him to count the sheets and sort them into alphabetical order. Paul was slender, sported a thick bushy beard and stood over six feet three inches in height, but his bulky Arran jumper gave him the illusion of being bigger and broader. Each time they completed a collection relating to a letter of the alphabet, Paul ticked off the name on each card on the staff manifest. This ensured that every member in the organisation had a record showing their details. Willis, to assist, lifted a batch of cards. He marked off names on a page from the crew list. With his help, the work was complete in about twenty minutes.

'Great, we can take these over to McGregor so he can get his part of the process going,' Connor said. After Paul had left with the box under his arm, Connor looked quizzically at Willis. 'Have you detected an improvement in

McGregor's attitude? Callum seems to be a lot more helpful and amiable recently.'

'I have noticed that, but I can't think what caused it. Let's not complain – long may it last.' He continued, 'The latest message from London said that a ship flying a Chinese flag has been identified as the source of the surges. They have sunk it, so we can all relax again. There should be no more power outages. We only have a murder to solve now. Only!' He repeated the 'only' with a touch of sarcasm. 'I'm off to see if I can be of any help to McGregor, since he's being very helpful to us.' Willis grinned. He sketched a salute and headed for the door.

**

'We could have saved a lot of effort if we'd just taken the prints of the people who were allowed to go into Johnny's office, because your prints, mine and Connor's were the only ones I found. Taking everyone's fingerprints was a waste of time.' McGregor sat with his feet up on his desk. He shook his head. A half-empty carton of steaming coffee sat to his right, alongside a bundle of sheets containing fingerprints.

'Not necessarily.' Willis shrugged. 'Now we have everyone's prints. They might come in useful in the future – we can check them without alerting anyone to the fact that we are doing so.'

'They will be a valuable resource, so I'd better lock them in my safe just in case someone has the intention of nicking or destroying them.'

'Great idea.' Willis paused, then added, 'I forgot to tell you. When I looked into Johnny's office from outside earlier, I noticed that the intruder had a two-inch tear on the left shoulder of his parka. That's something we can look out for – he won't be able to get a replacement. If we see it, we've got him. Let's go for a sherbet before dinner. We can keep our eyes open.'

'A sherbet?'

'Sorry, a beer. I forgot you weren't English.' Willis waved his hand over the pile of sheets. 'After you've locked this lot away, that is.'

***

'So, this is a sherbet? When I was a boy, it used to be a powder that fizzed in your mouth once it got wet.' McGregor looked around the galley. 'Very few people bring their parkas in here. Those who do, carry them over their arms.'

'Some beers do that too, especially American ones.'

'Stop taking the piss out of American beers. They're better than the warm crap that you English like.'

'Touché.' Willis held up his can of Bud and clinked it against McGregor's in a toast. 'This stuff tastes okay. I usually drink this and eat popcorn while I'm watching the Super Bowl. It helps create the right atmosphere.' Willis drew a long, slow sip of the amber liquid, then rested the can on the table.

'Who do—'

Willis interrupted. 'Before you ask, the 49ers. Because they've been a skilled team and consistent over the years. I've followed them ever since Joe Montana took over in '79. No, I haven't. I lie. I'm too young for that. But I've watched all Joe's back games.'

'What about Tom Brady?'

'Yeah, Tom's good. He was my era, but he wasn't up to the level of Joe Cool, the comeback kid.' Willis smiled, enjoying showing off his knowledge of American football. But Willis knew Tom Brady was terrific, even better than Joe Montana, especially after he won Super Bowl LV in 2021. That win gave him seven to his collection, more than any other quarterback in history, including Joe, but Willis enjoyed being controversial. 'And who do you support?'

'Ah! That would be the Dallas Cowboys, from my home town. I go to Jerry World in Arlington to support them whenever they play at home.'

McGregor jumped to his feet. 'There he is!'

A rotund fair-haired man was crossing the floor of the galley, carrying a tray of food. Willis could see the tear on the left shoulder of his parka. They waited until he'd sat down, then they picked up their beers and walked over to join him. Willis sat on his left and McGregor on his right.

'Good evening.' Willis spoke first.

'And good evening from me.' McGregor leaned forward and stared at the man.

'Hello, what is this about?' He spoke with an accent that Willis thought was Norwegian, or at least from one of the Scandinavian counties.

'We were admiring the tear in your jacket. How did that happen?' Willis leaned in closer to the man's face.

'Bah, this isn't my parka. This parka doesn't even fit. Look, it's two sizes too big – I drown in it.'

'Whose coat is it?'

'I don't know. Why do you ask? Someone took my coat after lunch. He left this damaged one in its place.'

'Can I ask your name?'

'Is this to do with the murder? I am Dr Franz Franck; I am the physician on the base.'

'It could very well be relevant to the murder.' Willis realised that this might be a mistake. 'Can you give us your movements from early this morning?'

'Of course I can. I've been in the medical unit checking the records to ensure that everyone who is planning to stay over the winter is fit enough to do so. Ask my nurse –

she will confirm that. The only time I am away from my office is to get some lunch. And to get my jacket stolen.'

'Thank you very much, Dr Franck. We won't be bothering you again.' Willis got up to leave. McGregor followed.

'Please, please, speak to my assistant. I want you to be sure.'

'We will, thank you.' Willis paused. 'Do you recall who you sat next to at lunch?'

The physician hesitated for a few seconds, then his gaze flashed from side to side. 'A tall man was sitting on my right-hand side, on the same side as I laid my coat.'

Willis asked, 'Did you know him? What did he look like?'

Again, the doctor paused. He stared at Willis while he concentrated. 'I can remember that he was tall and well built. He was big enough to fill this parka.' While he spoke, he tugged the loosely fitting jacket. 'Whoever he was, he sat down but brought no food, just a coffee. As he took up a lot of room, I had to move to give him more space. Now, I recall, I might have accidentally picked up the larger jacket myself rather than the other man swapping it. Yes...' He was thinking again. 'That's what might have happened. As I moved to the left, I took a coat and shifted it to my left-hand side. It would have been the one sitting on top. God, I must have lifted the wrong parka.'

Since whoever the tall man was wouldn't have been aware that the tear in his jacket had been spotted, this theory fitted better with Willis's thinking. What a weird coincidence.

Willis pressed the good doctor further. Was there anything else that stood out? The doctor thought again, then he jumped with excitement. 'The guy was reading. I'm not sure what he read, but it was small, not as big as a regular work folder.' Franz held his fingers about seven or eight inches apart to show its size. 'The man spread his elbows out, taking up even more room as he turned the pages.' The physician shook his head. 'That's definitely all I can remember. I'm sorry.'

'You've done well. What you've told us is very useful.'

'Well, that's a bummer,' McGregor said as they rose to leave. 'That would have been a great clue.'

'We still have a great clue.' McGregor stared at Willis. He didn't seem to understand. 'We're now looking for a six-foot-four man with a jacket at least two sizes smaller than he needs.'

***

Willis couldn't get his conversation with the doctor out of his head. Something gnawed away at his brain but it was just out of reach; he couldn't put his finger on it. Willis met McGregor and the women for dinner, then afterwards they hung around in the galley and drank a couple of glasses of wine.

'Your thoughts are somewhere else.' Sophie pulled on his sleeve. 'You've hardly uttered a word since we sat down.'

Willis apologised, and told her about the conversation that he had with the base doctor. 'Something is niggling me, but I have no idea what it is.'

'Stop thinking about it. It will come when you least expect it.'

'I've heard of that theory, but it never seems to work for me.' He was playing with his food again. Willis was pushing a pea around his plate, but it didn't want to go onto his fork. He lost patience and stabbed it. It seemed the best

125

way to lift it, but it was overkill. Overkill was maybe what he needed to shake him into remembering what was niggling at his brain. 'After dinner, I think I'll go for a stroll around the base. I'll try to retrace where I walked earlier. Hopefully, something will jog my memory. Fancy going for a walk with me? I could do with the company.'

The four sat chatting for a while. They suggested another bottle of Malbec, but Willis wanted to keep his mind clear. Two glasses were more than enough, he told himself. Otherwise, his brain would become anaesthetised. Willis was keen to get going. He made an excuse, then he and Sophie set off.

They walked the kilometre to the telescope, then they turned and came back to the central building. He moved around the back and looked at the fire door they had stopped at earlier. The footprints were still undisturbed in the loose ice. Willis and Sophie walked around the front, passed the entrance door, continued to the back then climbed the stairs, from where he had looked into Johnny's office window. All was quiet; nothing jogged his memory. They went inside and visited Johnny's office. Still, nothing.

'It isn't working.'

'Sleep on it. Something might come to you while you are sleeping. I hate to see you torturing yourself like this.'

'It's too early for bed. Anyway, I won't sleep – my brain is too active.'

Sophie smiled and kissed him. 'Some exercise might help you remember.'

'That might work.' Willis was grinning from ear to ear.

Sophie took him by the hand and led him to her room. He followed like a little boy being taken to a sweetshop. Two hours later, he was fast asleep.

***

Sophie played with his long brown hair. 'You need a haircut, Star Man.' She felt the warmth of his body next to her and the smell of his hair. As she fell asleep, she dreamed of a future with Willis that, in her waking moments, she knew was impossible.

CHAPTER 16

Willis jumped up from the bed. 'I've got it! I know what's been bothering me.'

'Shit,' Sophie complained. 'You nearly gave me a damn heart attack.' She looked at the clock: it was 3 a.m. 'Go back to sleep. Whatever it is, can wait till morning.'

'I'm not sure that it can. It's critical.'

'Of course it bloody well can. Everyone's asleep except those on shift. No one will want to see you, so go back to sleep.' She turned around and closed her eyes. 'Call me at eight.'

But he couldn't relax. He tossed and turned. Although Willis knew she was right, he couldn't put it out of his thoughts. Lying in bed, staring at the ceiling, he ran over everything that had happened the previous day. He tried to sleep, but sleep eluded him. The hours passed slowly.

Finally, Willis decided what he was going to do. He would first contact Glen Mason, the deputised Marshal at McMurdo. Glen would need to fly to the base on the next flight, bringing some men with him. But it might take Mason some time to travel here, so Willis would have to act sooner. The more he struggled to concentrate, the blurrier his mind became. He had to think rationally. Without intending to do so, his eyes closed and he fell into a deep sleep.

***

When he opened his eyes for the second time, he was facing Sophie, but she was still sound asleep. He glanced over at the clock. It read 8:45. He jumped out of bed.

'I thought you had set the alarm. How do you ever get up on time?'

'It's easy when I'm not exhausted. Then woken at three in the morning by a workaholic.'

'Get up. We need to bring the team together, it's going to be a rough day.' He dressed quickly, without showering or even washing. It wasn't his day for a shower, but he told Sophie that she had to do likewise. When he was on his way to visit McGregor, Sophie rounded up Linda and Gabi. Willis found McGregor in the galley, eating muesli. He had to coerce him to empty his plate and come with him.

'Have you recovered my jacket yet?' Dr Franck called from two tables away.

'I might have,' Willis called back. 'I'll let you know later.'

Willis headed out of the galley. McGregor trailed behind. 'Where are we going?' McGregor sounded irritated.

'To my room,' Willis snapped. They got there with perfect timing, as they met the three women as they came down the stairs behind them. Five people were too many for such a small room, but Linda sat on the only chair, Willis,

Sophie and Gabi on the bed, and McGregor plonked himself down on the floor in front of the window.

'This is like an Agatha Christie novel where Poirot brings all the suspects together and confronts them.' Gabi was joking.

Willis wasn't. 'It's closer to that than you might think. It came back to me last night that earlier, when I visited Connor's office to brief him about the Chinese ship, he said that if they shadowed the ship, they would be the first to learn if any additional surges happened.' Willis paused while he caught his breath. His heart was racing. 'The problem is, I said nothing to him about the vessel being shadowed – Connor must have accessed my mail without telling me. Also, in his office, he has rows of Alistair Maclean novels and other crime novels his wife used to read. Connor read her books, so he told me, to bring her nearer to him. Ring any bells?' But he didn't wait for anyone to comment. 'I made a call to Glen Mason, the deputised Marshal at McMurdo, early this morning. Mason confirmed that Connor's spouse, Maria, was a member of the Antarctic team – she worked on the telescope before you did.' Willis looked at Linda. 'She died making adjustments to the equipment in the receiver cabin – the room-sized box that's held on the end of the boom. As Linda and Gabi already know, a three-tonne part of the roof can roll back to allow the cab to dock against the main control area.' He was explaining for McGregor's benefit. 'But they only partially docked it. While she was in there working, her assistant pulled a manual pulley to close it fully. As a result, it crushed her. Connor tried to sue the NSF, but they ruled that she had ignored safety instructions. Connor still holds the base responsible for her death. In some kind of sick revenge for his wife's awful accident, he sabotaged the telescope. I think Connor killed Johnny to stop him from telling anyone that Connor had been intercepting my emails. That Callum found no prints other than mine and Connor's on Johnny's screen and only Connor's on the email window supports this. Dr Franck said the man who had sat down beside him had been reading something small. A novel is small, so that also points to him.'

McGregor spoke first. 'This is all circumstantial. It proves nothing.'

'That's why I need your help, Callum. We have to confront him, demand that he shows us his jacket, and ask him to put it on. If it fits, I'm wrong. If it doesn't…'

'And if it doesn't, you'll have a fight on your hands, as you will have to overpower him.' Sophie was looking worried.

'Maybe not. In my experience as a nurse, I've seen this sort of thing before. If we approach him, he might fold and give himself up. He's a sick man and he needs treatment.' Linda cocked her head to one side.

'But we can't guarantee that,' warned Willis. 'We will need several powerful men to back us up. That's where you come in, Callum. There must be men you've identified to help you run security on the base. Could you get three or four to assist us?'

'That will be easy.' McGregor nodded enthusiastically but said, 'I hope you've got this wrong, because most folk on the base believe he's a good man.'

***

After an hour, all was ready for Willis and McGregor to confront Connor. The other men would wait in the corridor. As usual, Connor's door was open. With McGregor at his heels, Willis took a deep breath and marched in.

'Hello, friends.' It was Connor's normal greeting. 'What can I do for you today?'

'Good morning, John, please bear with us,' Willis said, hoping that the nervousness he felt wasn't evident in his voice. 'Could we have a look at your parka?'

Connor looked puzzled. 'Whatever for?' He didn't sound as though he was aware of any reason to be concerned.

'Please, bear with us,' Willis said again. 'Is that it hanging behind the door?'

The Big Red obviously couldn't belong to anyone else, but Willis was trying to make his point as quickly as possible.

'Of course it is.'

'Could you try it on? I suspect you might have lifted the wrong jacket, in error, yesterday in the galley.'

'Sure.' When Connor reached the door, he lifted the red parka off its hook, swung it around his shoulders and tried to put his arms through its sleeves. While the right arm fitted snugly, he couldn't get his left arm in at all.

'You're correct, Brad, it doesn't fit.'

McGregor stepped forward. 'As the security officer on the base, I am arresting you for the murder of Johnny Ward. Anything you say will be taken down and may be used against you.' It was the first time that McGregor had made an arrest. He looked at Willis to confirm that this caution was enough. Willis had heard it repeated many times on television police dramas, but had taken no close heed. Anyway, US Law was in force at the station and this sounded more like a UK caution. Willis shrugged his shoulders. It would do.

But neither he nor Willis needed to be concerned. Connor removed the parka, dropped it on the floor and flopped in his chair, grasping his head in his hands. 'I'm glad it's over and I'm pleased you've stopped me. I know it was wrong, but I had to avenge my poor wife's death because everyone was blaming her.'

'How did you read my code?' This puzzled Willis. 'I assumed it was fool-proof.'

'That wasn't too difficult. After the first message I saw you going to your room, so I followed you. You rarely close your door, so I could watch you read the manual. As soon as I realised the statistics book was the key, everything else was easy.'

'How did you poison my energy bar? What did you put in it?'

'I added nothing to your energy bar; I swear that wasn't me.'

Willis took a deep breath. He believed Connor. He had no reason to lie. The ramifications of his statement were dire.

'I must ask you to accompany me.' It was another phrase that McGregor had heard on television. 'We will need to confine you to your room until we can send you home.'

'I understand. I won't cause any trouble.'

Willis and McGregor led him to his bedroom. It was exactly where Willis had calculated it would be – almost a quarter of the way along the ground-floor corridor. They searched Connor's room, looking for things he might use to injure himself. They removed his laces, his belt and any other items he might use for nefarious reasons. When they had satisfied themselves he was unable to injure himself, and they were about to lock the door, Willis turned and said, 'I'll need your password for the system.'

Connor's eyes filled with tears. He picked up a piece of paper, then asked for the return of his pen. He wrote the password down then handed the paper to Willis. It read 'marlac0nn0r' – Connor's wife's name, with the 'o' and 'i' substituted by numbers. Willis's stomach heaved, and he felt sick.

***

Willis had found the culprit, but it didn't give him the least feeling of satisfaction. Although he rarely drank Scotch, today he decided to make an exception. He wandered into the galley and poured himself a large whisky from an open bottle. Willis threw back the fiery liquid and poured a second.

'Can I join you?' McGregor asked. Willis nodded. McGregor dispensed another double malt, and dropped into the seat beside Willis. The two men sat in silence.

After they had sunk another two glasses, McGregor said, 'Glen Mason will be here tomorrow to take him back. He's ordered a special flight to pick him up.'

But Willis didn't reply. He stared into his drink, his thoughts elsewhere.

Connor's story was so reminiscent of Willis's own. After the death of Carole, he too had suffered. Willis had witnessed her death. He clearly saw the red car hitting them. Then it had reversed and left the scene. As he held her in his arms, he kissed her limp body. He couldn't forget Carole's empty eyes.

The last day had been an excellent test of his PTSD, he thought. Perhaps he was finally cured? He hadn't lost the plot once. Willis smiled to himself, then admonished himself for doing so.

He thought of Connor. Willis had loved Carole no less than Connor had loved Maria. When he found the man who murdered his wife, what would Willis's reaction be? Would it be the same as Connor's? He imagined it might be, and that worried him.

***

134

While they ate dinner that evening, Willis chewed his food lethargically, mainly in silence. Each mouthful took longer than the previous one until he could eat no more. He pushed his plate away. Sophie, Linda, Gabi and McGregor fared no better. Five half-eaten meals sat on the table.

A neon tube flickered in the ceiling above Willis's head. It irritated him to the point of distraction. If he stayed here much longer, he would develop a headache, so he rose to his feet.

'We need to cheer up,' Sophie said. 'Nothing's changed from this afternoon. Snap out of it, let's play some darts.' She led the way to the B1 lounge and the dartboard.

CHAPTER 17

Glen Mason was due to arrive by noon. The LC-130 Skibird would land a short distance from the base. Willis and the team wanted to have an early breakfast. He and McGregor planned to check on the prisoner first, then meet the others in the galley.

Outside, it was another calm day. The sky was eggshell blue and contrasted against the dazzling snow. There would be no problem for Mason to make the flight from Ross Island to Pole. The plane would arrive from the left, as seen from the observation platform, and would come to rest close to Destination Alpha, the building's main entrance. It would drop its passengers off two hundred yards from the entrance.

McGregor knocked on Willis's door as he passed. Both men walked to Connor's room. While they slept,

McGregor had left a man on patrol outside his door, with instructions to call him if there were any issues. The officer on duty had acquired a chair and was sitting reading a magazine when they arrived.

As McGregor approached, the guard, a guy called Steve, stood. 'No, there were no problems during the night,' he said in reply to a question from McGregor. 'And Connor hardly made a sound all night. He's been the perfect prisoner.' After producing his key, the officer swung the door open for McGregor and Willis to enter.

The men froze on the spot.

Connor had been quiet all night. Because he had been dead all night. He lay on the bed, a ball pen protruding from the left side of his throat. Blood spray spattered the wall to his side. It had saturated the bedclothes and pillow, and dripped down the paintwork. John Connor wore green pyjamas. Where the red stains had soaked into the fabric, it had turned black. The metallic smell of blood wafted towards their nostrils. McGregor leaned forward and touched Connor's forehead. The skin was cold. 'He must have died a while ago.'

Willis fell into the chair and placed his elbows on the table. 'This is my fucking fault.' His face was white and his lips trembled. He lowered his gaze to the floor and shook his head. To ensure everyone within earshot heard, he repeated the phrase louder. 'This is my fucking fault.'

His brow furrowed, McGregor looked at him, waiting for Willis's explanation.

'It's my pen – my fucking pen. After he gave me his security password last night, I forgot to take it back.'

There was a long silence. Neither man spoke for several minutes. Eventually McGregor broke the silence. 'As neither of us has any experience with a prisoner in his state of mind, what happened can't be helped. It was an easy mistake to make.' He paused and drew in a deep breath. 'Connor's death was my fault. It's mine more than yours. I'm the security officer. I should have placed him on twenty-four-hour suicide watch, but I failed to.'

They left Connor's body in situ until Mason landed. The medical team could clean him up after Mason had completed his initial inspection.

Until Mason arrived, the evidence needed to remain intact and undisturbed. As though respecting the situation, McGregor closed the door softly and locked it. They returned to Willis's room to write their second report on Connor, this time on his death.

***

Mason landed half an hour ahead of schedule. Because Antarctica didn't have crowded airspace, arrival times could be flexible. The logging of flight plans was almost unnecessary on the continent. But given all the international agreements in place and the various safety concerns about pretty much everything on Antarctica, it was just the opposite. Every flight had to be scrupulously tracked.

They installed Mason in Connor's office and filled him in on the bad news. Mason looked nonplussed. 'Since it needs special training to organise a suicide watch, neither of you need carry any guilt. We have not taught you two gentlemen the necessary skills.'

'Doesn't common sense count?' barked Willis.

'Not if you're already stressed by the situation. There'd been a vicious murder. I bet both of you were reacting negatively to what happened. It's a very natural reaction. Try to forget it.'

Willis thought his attitude was very blasé, but he let it pass. Although he was sure Mason had a point, he couldn't find it through his guilt.

Mason arrived at Connor's bedroom with his forensic officer – or at least, someone acting the role, as McMurdo would have no reason to have one. Photographs of the scene were taken, then the body was cleaned, made presentable, and loaded onto the plane. 'We'd better have some lunch before we go,' Mason said.

After they had sat down to eat, Mason said, 'This stuff's no better than at McMurdo. If anything, it's a little worse.'

'Even MacTown is civilised compared to here.' McGregor was baiting him, but Mason refused to rise to it.

'This place is a lot cleaner – apart from the pile of empty cable drums I passed getting here.'

McGregor didn't rise to the bait either. Interrupting the verbal duel, Willis leaned over and waved a hand. 'Is there anyone we need to inform about Connor's death?'

'As far as we are aware, he had no family. John and Maria had no children. But no doubt the NSF will know if they have to contact anybody. It's out of our hands now.'

'I saw a photograph of two kids in Connor's office,' Willis said. 'Surely someone will contact them? Who's looking after them?'

'They were his kids, but they were killed in a car accident six months ago. Their grandfather was driving.' As though erasing the words from his mind, Mason closed his eyes and held them shut.

'Shit. No wonder the poor guy lost the plot.' Immediately, Willis's thoughts filled with memories of Carole's death. 'How could Connor have coped with this double tragedy?'

139

'It looks as though he didn't.' As if bracing himself for an argument, Mason paused. He leaned back in his chair, staring at McGregor. 'Mr McGregor, I don't want you to take this the wrong way, as you are doing an outstanding job here, but I have asked the NSF to put Brad Willis temporarily in charge until we can find a replacement Station Leader.' Mason looked at McGregor, waiting for his approval.

The support came instantly. 'Willis has much more experience than I do. He will make an excellent Station Leader.'

'And what about you, Dr Willis? Are you happy to take on the task until we get a suitable candidate?'

Willis hesitated. Either Mason was unaware of his and McGregor's secondary roles, or he had forgotten. Willis had told him about his mission the day he met him at McMurdo. Now Willis realised he was protecting his cover, but Mason was unaware of McGregor's undercover role. That struck him as odd.

'I'd hoped to get off The Ice soon.' Willis twisted a pen in his fingers impatiently. 'I have another job that I need to do at home in England.' This was only part of the story. Sophie was the other part, she was the second reason he was here. And she was pulling him in the opposite direction. To stay.

'The NSF called me. They asked for you.'

'Game, set and match, then.'

***

Mason left as soon as he'd eaten lunch. His plane was out of sight within minutes, leaving only a cloud of fine ice particles in its wake.

Because he didn't even know what a Station Leader did, Willis remained a little shell-shocked by his new post.

He should have asked Mason for a copy of the job description, but it was too late now.

Willis sat in what used to be Connor's office, and read as much of the paperwork as he could understand. He also found Johnny's stylus, his notebook and a hunting knife he assumed that Connor had used to slit Johnny's throat. So Mason and McGregor hadn't done a very thorough job either.

Why the knowledge made him feel marginally better, he couldn't fathom. Willis put all three items in a plastic bag, then sealed it in case they were needed at a subsequent inquest.

McGregor came in and plonked himself down on the chair facing Willis. 'Do I need to call you "sir"?' He ignored the 'Bollocks' that Willis mouthed. 'I guess there's not a lot to do. The murder is solved. The saboteur is dead. The source of the electric surges is no more.'

'But who tried to poison me? That remains an unanswered question. When Connor said he didn't do it, I believed him. Will whoever it was, try again?'

***

When he arrived for dinner, Linda, Gabi and Sophie all curtsied to him. Willis mouthed something a little stronger than he had suggested earlier to McGregor. Since he'd discovered that passing out messages addressed to the base's scientists was part of his job, he handed a printed email to Linda. 'Great, I have a personal secretary now.' She stuck out her tongue, then waved the paper in front of Willis's face.

Linda had done her hair: she'd set it in spikes and dyed the ends green. She reminded Willis of Sonic the Hedgehog. She had put in her piercings, too. She had two diamond studs in one ear. Another in her upper lip. Clearly

Linda didn't intend to go out again today. The cold would freeze the bare metal in minutes.

Sophie and Gabi also looked rather dapper. Maybe they were trying to make themselves feel better by putting on some make-up? After all, they'd experienced a pretty rough couple of days.

Willis kept glancing at Sophie. She looked beautiful. Since he'd arrived, this was the first time he'd seen her wearing make-up. She caught Willis staring at her and whispered, 'Later.' Suddenly Willis wished the evening would end, and that 'later' could be 'now'.

For the first time in ages, dinner was enjoyable. They had bought three bottles of sparkling wine from the station's store, which was unusual as they normally drank a mixture of red and white.

'The galley is very busy this evening,' Willis remarked. 'They must have a hiatus in their work schedules.' Sophie poured five glasses of fizzy wine and distributed them, then stood. She held up a glass towards Willis's. 'Congratulations.'

He lifted his glass and clinked it against hers. Then all hell broke loose. The loudspeakers in the galley strained to the sound of Cliff Richard singing 'Congratulations'. Everybody in the galley got to their feet and started singing. Willis flushed the colour of beetroot. Sophie grabbed his arm in case he passed out. She looked into his eyes and gave him the most beautiful smile he'd ever seen. Then she dragged Willis from the table, gripped his waist with both hands, and manoeuvred him onto the floor, forcing him to do the conga. Linda, Gabi and McGregor joined the line behind Sophie. Soon everyone in the galley had followed her lead. The snake was at least forty people long. It made three circuits of the galley before depositing Willis back at his original seat. He dropped into his chair, embarrassed and exhausted.

Within seconds, shouts of 'Speech, speech!' filled the room. Willis could have killed Sophie. She dragged him to his feet again and put another glass of sparkling wine in his hand. She had trapped him into speaking in front of the crew.

Willis spoke nervously at first. 'I wondered why the galley was so busy for dinner tonight. I asked myself why the ladies were wearing make-up and had done their hair. Since it's not the sort of thing one expects at the Amundsen–Scott South Pole Station, it should have dawned on me sooner. This is a very sad time having lost John Connor and of course Johnny, but I want to thank you from the bottom of my heart, but all that has happened in the last few days has been a team effort. Doctors Foreman, Costa, Fenwick and McGregor, not to mention all of you who co-operated by supplying your fingerprints, made everything come together. We are truly a great team, so here's to your future.' He lifted his glass in a toast. Everyone followed suit.

Two guitar players appeared from nowhere and began to play. Everyone moved tables to make room for a makeshift dance floor.

'May I?' Sophie held out her hand for Willis to escort her onto the floor. He bowed politely, then led her in their first dance in Antarctica.

'I could kill you.'

'Why would you want to do such a daft thing? Kiss me instead.'

Willis leaned forward and planted a big kiss on her mouth. The room erupted in applause as their lips touched. Gabi and Linda were dancing alongside him. Linda guided Gabi until they were directly in front of them, forcing the dancers to collide clumsily.

'Now your secret's out.'

'And so is yours.'

'I've already told you, we don't care.'

At that moment McGregor glided past with a lovely lady in his arms. 'This is Sheila, she's a meteorologist.'

'We're very pleased to meet you, Sheila.' All four stopped, introduced themselves and shook her hand then they continued in a very poor impersonation of formation dancing.

After Willis recovered from the shock, he thanked Sophie for organising the evening. It wasn't she who organised the party; it just happened earlier today. She got a 'clandestine' whispered invitation like everyone else. Willis complained that no one had sent him one. But Sophie asked if he really expected to get one. He smiled and kissed her again.

'You promised me, "after".'

'I did, but now everyone is watching us, so it will need to be after – that is, after the night is over. It has only just begun.'

'Isn't that a song by the Carpenters?' Willis asked.

Sophie walked away, leaving him standing alone in the middle of the floor. By the time she returned, the guitarists were playing the tune.

'Let's make that our song.'

He kissed her again. 'Yes, let's.'

It was a night they would never forget. They danced until their feet hurt. So many of their colleagues came up and introduced themselves. There were so many, it seemed impossible to learn all the names.

But the night wasn't to be over any time soon. After the first shift had gone to bed, the second one turned up. Willis looked at Sophie in dismay. 'Tomorrow?'

'Tomorrow,' she replied. 'I promise.'

CHAPTER 18

Willis woke very early the next morning. He was lying with his arms around Sophie. Memories of the previous night flooded back. He smiled, cuddling up close to her soft body. The celebration had been a wonderful experience. The company, the entertainment and comradeship filled him with warm fuzzy thoughts. Willis didn't even remember coming to bed. Had he and Sophie...? No, he was sure they hadn't. But he recalled being on a promise for tonight. His smile broadened further.

Why had he woken so early? Something was throbbing in his skull. He couldn't expect anything else when he reminded himself of the amount of alcohol he consumed. But it wasn't a hangover. The noise continued to throb in his brain. Willis turned his head to listen more closely. The racket was a fire alarm. He could hear only the bass sounds from the klaxon through the door. How long had it been ringing for? He jumped out of bed and shook Sophie awake. 'Get up now.' They dressed and headed out in less than three minutes.

Loud, jumbled voices were coming from downstairs. Willis's nose stung from the smell of putrid smoke rising from the stairwell. He ran down the stairs. About a dozen men were blocking the corridor, jostling around a doorway about thirty feet away. Extinguishers hissed as they sprayed foam into the bedroom. One man was pulling out a chair and carrying a laptop. The computer was a similar make to his. There was a sticker on its lid… Then he realised. It was his room. They were tackling a blaze in *his* room. He pushed forward, but the officer in charge of the emergency crew blocked his passage.

'Get the statistics book from the shelf!' Willis shouted.

'What?' the large man wearing a full-face mask said, the word barely audible.

'My statistics book — get my statistics manual. It's critically important.'

The masked man stepped back into the dense cloud of toxic smoke and disappeared. Within seconds, he reappeared.

'Is this it?' The man held up the charred remnant of the codebook that Willis needed to decipher Reilly's messages, and threw it over the heads of the men holding the extinguishers. Willis caught it. The book crumpled in his hand. Flakes of burnt pages puffed into the air; the smoke had blackened the remaining leaves beyond recognition.

It was twenty minutes before he could get into the room. 'It's something else for you to investigate Dr Willis,' said the fireman after removing his mask. 'This fire's been set deliberately. Have a look at the floor.'

146

After expressing their condolences, the men dispersed. Following the previous night's frivolity, everybody recognised him. In the wardrobe, his clothes had escaped the flames. But they reeked of soot and dust. They needed to be washed. His parka was lying on the floor, close to the entrance. The Big Red was destroyed. Willis knelt and looked at the floor in front of the door. A quick assessment confirmed that someone had poured an accelerant under the door and set it alight. If he had been in his room, instead of Sophie's, he would have died of smoke inhalation. Willis shuddered. This was the second attempt on his life. It proved that Connor had told the truth. It wasn't Connor who had tried to kill him.

McGregor was soon at his side, wearing his PJs. 'Christ, what's happened here? You are in serious danger.' He put his hand on Willis's shoulder. 'Serious jeopardy, my friend.' He spoke straight into Willis's ear. 'I'll check the room for any forensic clues.'

McGregor went to dress, then returned and spent an hour looking for any clues the arsonist might have left behind. The search was fruitless. McGregor put his hand on Willis's arm in a futile attempt to console him. 'The accelerant was the same thick machine oil that someone used to start the fire that lured Linda and Gabi away from the telescope, but I've discovered nothing else.'

'If we were somewhere civilised, I would put up a surveillance camera to track who was coming and going during the night, but I can hardly nip out to Tandy's anymore to buy one.'

'I found a camera in the equipment store. I'm not sure if it's in working order, but it's in its original box so there's a good chance that it is.' McGregor clicked his fingers.

'Go fetch it. We will find out if it works.'

147

***

Everyone on the base held at least two jobs. This became very clear when the man who'd fought his way into Willis's room wearing the smoke mask returned as a member of the team responsible for cleaning and painting the room.

Willis moved into another room. As the replacement was closer to Sophie's, it pleased him immensely. He was lucky that the full quota of personnel was no longer at the base, as this meant there were rooms available that he could use.

The camera that McGregor brought was ancient. Even its blue case was part metal instead of modern plastic. It was large and heavy.

McGregor spilled the box's contents on the bed in Willis's replacement room and sorted the components into the order they fitted together. 'Its resolution is less than ideal. It only records in black and white, but it's better than nothing. The unit needs to hook up to a computer for it to work. There is an old-style floppy disk in the box, which is a bad sign – it means it's ancient and its program might not operate on a modern laptop.'

Willis's computer didn't even have a floppy disk drive, but McGregor saved the day by locating a unit that they could connect externally. Once they'd loaded the program, they would disconnect the external drive. Everything worked. After they'd done a couple of tests and satisfied themselves that the camera was operational, they set about finding a suitably discreet place to hide it. Outside Willis's replacement room was a fire extinguisher. It sat on the end wall at right angles to the passageway, supported by a thick brown steel frame. The camera would fit inside its mounting, out of sight, giving it an uninterrupted view of the passage. They only needed a short cable to reach Willis's laptop. They installed it around midday, when activity in the corridor was minimal: most people would be at lunch, and anyone who spotted them would assume that they were replacing the extinguisher after the fire. After they connected the cable, they switched on the camera. Then they left for lunch.

***

As they ate lunch, several men put their hands on Willis's shoulder as they passed him, to console him. He tapped their fingers in appreciation. Willis's gaze followed the group while they walked away. 'They're glad that I'm the bloody target, not them. I don't blame them one little bit – I'd think the same thing in their shoes.'

Willis had almost finished his meal when Dr Franck came and sat next to him. 'I know you're busy. I don't suppose you've traced my jacket?'

'The very man – I have. Come to my office after lunch and I'll return it to you. But bring the one you're wearing. I will swap it with you.'

Dr Franck thanked him. Willis told him he'd see him in thirty minutes.

'That's a neat solution,' Willis said. 'Franz gets his coat back. I get a replacement that might fit. That's a bit of luck. I would consider buying a lottery ticket if I could.' He was putting a brave face on things. When he finished his lunch, he and McGregor walked to his office.

When they arrived, Sophie was already there. She handed him a mug of coffee and, because she knew it was his favourite, some lemon drizzle cake. 'Sorry, Callum. I only brought one.'

McGregor shrugged and smiled. He made his excuses and left them alone.

'You're going to have to be careful.' Sophie hugged his arm tightly as she brushed a tear from her eye.

As his teeth cut into the sponge, Willis rolled his eyes in ecstasy.

'But seriously, what if someone tries again?'

'McGregor and I have installed a security camera outside my room. It will record anyone suspicious who loiters in the passage.'

'That's a relief. At least it will give you some sense of security. But I want you to do more to ensure your safety. You should move in with me.'

'That would be a dumb thing to do – it would put us both in danger. What makes you think he wouldn't kill both of us?'

'There would be two of us paying attention, so there would be less chance of his sneaking something past us.'

Willis let out a coarse laugh. 'Just like you did this morning? When all hell was breaking loose, you were fast asleep. That helped a lot.'

'Last night was an exception. We were both knackered and had danced for hours.'

Willis kept silent; he was deep in thought. His gaze darted left and right. 'Of course! Whoever set my room on fire wasn't at the celebrations last night. If he had been, he would have suspected that we'd be together during the night. He wouldn't have torched an empty room. As you pointed out, we danced together for most of the evening – it was clear we were a couple. The culprit would have noticed that if he had been there.' He stopped and shook his head. 'But how can we find out who wasn't there? That's impossible.' Willis fell into his chair, disheartened.

At that moment, there was a timid knock on the open door. It was Dr Franck. 'Here is my jacket. Can you swap it for me?'

Willis got up and reached for the hanger behind his door. He handed the coat to Franz, who thanked him, put it on and left. Willis tried the jacket on. He noticed the tear on its shoulder, but ignored it. He stretched his arms out. 'Dah-dah! It fits perfectly.' Willis was about the same size as Connor. 'Sadly, it's Connor's but I'm just glad to have a parka that fits.' Willis took it off and placed it on the hook. He looked forward to going outside again.

'There are five of us. We could make a list of everyone we saw at the party.' Sophie had returned to their previous conversation. 'If we do it while our memories are fresh, we might remember a lot.'

'But we would need to know everybody at the dance and on site if we are to identify the culprit.'

She disagreed. 'The aim is not to find him. We want to eliminate people, so we find out who it *wasn't*.'

Willis saw the logic of her argument, but as a counter-argument, he said, 'I don't know the names of ninety per cent of the characters here.'

'But Linda and Gabi will, because they were on The Ice for two seasons, and I've been here for months,' she said. 'Some people will have returned.'

Willis agreed that it was worth a try. They would meet in the galley, where they would see familiar faces that might trigger memories, and they would work as a team.

***

An hour later, they sat in the galley, sipping wine again, trying to be inconspicuous. The list was growing. One of them would look up and remark that this guy or that guy had been there. Willis said that if there was someone they recognised but didn't know his name, they should write a brief description to help them recognise him. Gabi devised a simple method that abbreviated the information. For example, *b-h* stood for 'brown hair'. While *6+* was code for 'over six feet tall'. The system was crude but proved effective.

Time flew past. Eventually the process slowed. Fewer people were visiting the galley. It was late in the evening. They decided to give up for the day, but they would continue when they were next in the galley. Sophie suggested that they should arrange a night shift to cover people who worked nights, but none of the team fancied that.

When they finished, it was after midnight. Willis's face was flushed. 'I need some fresh air.' He went to pick up his parka. Sophie did likewise and followed him.

Even well wrapped up and protected, the air stung their skin as they ventured outside. Fine flurries of ice particles floated lazily in the weak breeze. Willis still couldn't get used to the concept of the sun shining at midnight. It was getting lower in the sky. Soon it would set. The shadows it cast exaggerated every bump in the landscape. They made the surface look rougher than it was. If the sun reached the horizon, it would leave Willis stranded over the winter. The idea of it wasn't as alien as it had been previously – the thought of staying with Sophie was attractive, but the pull of his work in Cambridge was also strong.

Sophie interrupted his thinking. 'Let's go back inside. I'm getting uncomfortable.' They retired to the galley for early morning cocoa. It was 1 a.m. and a warm drink would be most welcome. Willis removed his mittens and placed his parka on the bench beside him, then picked up an energy bar for later. He put it in his pocket. When he withdrew his hand, he was holding a folded piece of paper.

'Well, I'll be damned.' Willis threw the paper on the table. 'I've no idea what it says. It's in Chinese.'

CHAPTER 19

The next morning, Willis was impatient to see the results from the security camera. He washed and lathered his hair, turning the shower off while he did so, then used the shower to wash the suds away as he cleaned the rest of his body. At last, he had mastered the two-minute shower. He had also been given a tip: use wet wipes between showers to keep himself fresh. Willis checked his watch. One minute, fifty-eight seconds – it was good enough, he reckoned. He returned to his room and finished dressing.

When he got to his laptop, he opened the file that held the camera recording. The computer played it back automatically. The video folder was over a gigabyte in size. That was too big. It puzzled him – the camera should only record when it detected motion. Then he realised why. At night, the corridor was a hive of activity. With the perpetual daylight, even with blackout blinds at their windows, many people found it difficult to sleep. Others imagined they were getting 'toasted', but it more commonly occurred in the winter. During the summer there was so much going on that people rarely lost it. It was, however, something that concerned many of the people who worked there.

The passageway was a hub of activity for most of the night; people tended to wander aimlessly along the corridors until they were exhausted and sleep became a necessity. He assumed the lower corridor was also busy. On the tape, Willis saw men slowly walking in their pyjamas, glazed expressions on their faces, as though they had lost something and were searching for it. People walked pointlessly, looking in windows, trying to find out what was going on elsewhere. He wondered if he'd eventually act like that too. Willis was lucky because he had reasons to go out, to move around, but a lot of the crew didn't. They spent long periods indoors, supporting the station's activities and recording data from external instruments only going outside for essential maintenance. No wonder they went stir crazy.

He estimated there must be four or five hours of video on the hard drive. The camera was sensitive. Even someone moving twenty feet away triggered it into action. He pressed fast-forward, making the figures dance around, like people in early black and white movies. Another press of the Play button and the action sped up further. People appeared and disappeared as the program skipped frames. This would do. Willis leaned back in his chair. He let the night's activities numb his brain. He was looking for something out of the ordinary, but everything seemed normal. Before 4 a.m., there was a gap when the corridors got quieter. When he saw the time stamp in the corner jump minutes at a go, he felt relieved. This was too much work. In the future, he would keep each recording for two days. If no incidents attracted his attention, he would delete the file.

He took out the piece of paper he had found in Connor's jacket and read it. The top row comprised three double-digit numbers; under them was a line of Chinese characters and below these, a four-digit number. The first line could be map co-ordinates, he thought, but the bottom row looked too short to be another. The Chinese writing could be a cipher. Sophie supervised a Chinese postgrad student on IceCube. Willis decided to ask him to translate it. After re-folding the note, he replaced it in his pocket.

***

When he walked into the galley, Sophie, Linda, Gabi and McGregor were already there. While they ate, they continued to write down descriptions of members of the crew they remembered from the party two nights ago. Once Willis had filled them in on the long recording from the previous night, they looked disappointed but had no useful comments.

Willis had just cleared his plate and moved it away when he heard a timid voice over his right shoulder.

'Dr Willis? Dr Brad Willis?'

Willis looked over his shoulder and nodded.

'May I introduce myself? My name is Justin Rowe. I have read much of your work. Can I say it's an honour to meet you, sir?'

Willis stood, pushed his chair back and shook the young man's hand.

Justin said, 'I was about to do my PhD in observational cosmology, but I decided to take a gap year and spend the winter down here working on the base. It's the first time I've shaken the hand of a Nobel Laureate.'

'You still haven't. I was a member of the team who made the discovery, but my boss and the leader who was

156

running the parallel research received the prize.' Willis smiled. 'Don't worry, it's a common mistake.'

'I stand corrected. Until now, I've never shaken the hand of someone who nearly became a Nobel Laureate.' Justin grinned.

Willis invited him to join them at the table. He estimated the young man to be in his early twenties. Justin was about six feet tall with bushy red hair and a sparse beard. He displayed a slight, nervous twitch on the right side of his mouth that Willis found endearing. Linda, Gabi and McGregor left them to it. They returned to their respective experiments. The next hour flew past while the two men discussed Willis's team's discovery of dark energy and the acceleration of the Universe's expansion rate.

'Before they disappeared, I should have introduced you to Dr Linda Foreman and Dr Sophie Fenwick,' Willis said, chiding himself for not doing so. 'Linda is doing observations of the cosmic microwave background radiation, the remnant noise from the Big Bang, and Sophie is studying neutrinos from distant supernovae. Their work might interest you.'

'I would love an introduction, because what they're doing will be relevant for my thesis, but I'd also welcome spending some time with you to discuss the discovery of dark energy.'

The young man's enthusiasm impressed him. Willis invited him to join them at dinner later. Once again, they shook hands and parted company.

***

Willis took a casual stroll along both corridors. He copied the nightwalkers' habit of looking through every window he passed. Behind most windows, teams worked away at their allotted tasks, some in white overalls, others in boiler suits.

157

Some wore shorts, others Hawaiian patterned shirts. If the temperature was as comfortable as that, he might give shorts a try. If only he'd brought a pair. After passing several departments, he reached the medical unit where Dr Franck practised. Willis shuddered, recalling the time he spent there after he was poisoned. Above the door someone had added 'Club Med' to its official title.

Willis stepped inside to see Franck. 'Now you've got your parka back, how are you getting on with it?' He looked around the facility, which was well equipped. There were three hospital beds, a dentist's chair, a pharmacy, and an office for Franck's PA. An eye chart hung outside Franck's office.

'Unless there's a reason to do so, I seldom go outside. Most of my work comes to me.'

'Aren't you afraid of being toasted?'

'Ah, the dreaded Antarctic stare? We doctors call the condition polar T3 syndrome, or polar triiodothyronine. It's brought on by a decrease in the thyroid hormone T3, hence its name. If I ever enter a fugue state here, they will lock me up. I check my chemical levels once a month, so there will be no winter-over syndrome for me, I hope.'

'How common is it for folk to suffer from these symptoms?'

'We can count the incidents on one hand, but it is worrying to witness. When we diagnose it, we can treat it, in most cases with injections. If you experience any of its effects, come to see me as soon as possible. But it rarely happens in the summer. It's a winter ailment, if it appears at all.'

'Thank you, Doctor. I will.' When Willis made a move towards the door, Franck called after him. 'If you feel unwell in other ways, I'm also a psychiatrist. I can help sort you out.'

Willis stopped at the door. 'Thank you. I will remember that.'

Franck waved his arm in his direction.

Willis planned to find out as much as possible about the day-to-day activities of the members of the team. There weren't so many people on the base that he couldn't hope to learn to recognise them, at least by sight. Since they recognised him, every third or fourth person he passed acknowledged him with a friendly 'Brad' or 'Dr Willis'. Some even stopped and chatted. As the Station Leader, they would expect him to be familiar with most of the crew.

But that wasn't the reason for his walkabout; someone on site had tried to kill him. Someone had malevolent intentions that were not good for him – or the base.

He was on the lookout for any unusual behaviour that might give him a clue to who that might be. However, he finished his walk without incident. Nothing stood out as worthy of any special attention.

He wanted to go to SPT, as he hadn't been there for some time. He wanted to tell Linda and Gabi that he'd invited Justin to join them at dinner, and that he'd promised to introduce him to Linda. The walk to the telescope was invigorating. The harsh coldness of the air sharpened his brain and cleared his thought process. Should he arrange an ambush for his assailant, or let matters take their course? Although setting a trap would flush out any malevolence sooner, the latter would be safer. He decided, as Hamlet had done, to procrastinate. Willis wondered how William Shakespeare would set the plot in this case. He dismissed the idea. If he took Shakespeare's advice, they would all finish up dead at the end. No, he would leave things to unfold.

When Willis barged into the SPT enclosure, he soon found out that he wasn't welcome. The telescope was in the middle of its longest uninterrupted run for some time, thanks to the sinking of the Chinese ship. While they supervised their planned observations, Linda and Gabi were a hundred per cent engrossed. Although Willis considered asking them for a precis of what they were doing, he decided against it. Whatever process was under way demanded their full attention. He would ask them at dinner. 'See you both later,' he said, waving and turning to leave. After what seemed like forever, the delayed reply came: 'Okay, later.'

Willis decided to visit Sophie instead. The walk to IceCube Observatory was equally invigorating. He found Sophie in a much more welcoming mood. She planted a moist kiss on his cheek then offered a coffee. Willis accepted. They sat talking for half an hour about how she used the atomic clock.

Sophie told him how they set up the telescope. 'My observations are partly passive. Once I switch on the detectors and they're running, it's just a matter of waiting. Neutrinos often arrive at the sensors but the cosmic ray muon background coming from the southern sky swamps most of them,' she explained. 'We're interested in particles that arrive from the northern hemisphere. This means that, before they reach us, they have passed right through the Earth, unhindered. Since the detectors can tell from which direction the neutrinos approached, they ignore those that don't fit. Are you listening?' She was looking at Willis, who was staring into the distance.

'Yes, of course I am. Sorry. I was distracted. But I just remembered that I intended to ask you about translating the note I found in Connor's jacket. Is your Chinese assistant around?'

'He's got some study time allotted today. If you want to see him, he'll be here tomorrow.'

'Okay, I'll leave the note with you. Will you ask him to translate it? Then let me have a copy?'

'Of course. Leave it with me. Put it in my notebook.'

Then an alarm sounded.

Willis jumped to his feet.

'Don't panic. The detector has sensed something. You'll need to go.' Sophie started to take readings from recording equipment on the wall. Willis wasn't having much luck. Nobody wanted to speak to him today, but he realised that work needed to come before socialising.

He headed off to the base. So far, it hadn't been a very productive day. First, the video from last night had produced nothing, and now his walk around the installation had been equally unproductive. Also, he'd failed to get Connor's note translated.

Once at the base, he proceeded to his office, took off his jacket and checked his email. He found no new messages. That was unusual, so he walked along the corridor to the communications room. Mick was the new comms operator – Johnny's replacement. He was a fresh-faced young man with thick black hair. His upper lip sported a heavy moustache. Willis stared at him. He thought he could have left school yesterday. Perhaps he grew a moustache to make himself look older?

'I have received no messages today, Mick, which is unusual. Are things that quiet?'

'No, Dr Willis. I don't have a copy of Johnny's password to open the email window.'

Willis had seen Johnny enter his password several times. He told Mick the password. Soon emails were being printed out. Willis sorted them into piles for redistribution.

These were business emails rather than the private ones that the crew could receive on their personal laptops. One caught his attention, as it was addressed to Connor. The source address was the Vostok Station. That was unusual. Vostok was a fair distance from Pole. It was Russian run and was located at the geomagnetic pole just over 800 miles from the geographic south pole. In the message, a general, with a surname that was very familiar to Willis, was asking permission to visit the base. He'd sent it at 9 a.m. Willis glanced at his watch. It read 4.15 p.m.

'Please send an answer, Mick. Apologise for the late response, say it's because of comms problems. Ask when he intends to be here.'

Mick typed the reply and hit Send. Within a minute, a reply came.

Have arranged for transport to arrive by 11 a.m. General K.

Willis lifted the rest of his mail and returned to his office. 'Tomorrow has got to be more eventful than today,' he said to himself. 'What a coincidence that the general has the same family name as Boris.' Willis thought back to his assignment in Kazakhstan. His friend and ally, Boris Korolev, had been killed during the assignment; he had been shot in the stomach and had died a painful death. Willis pushed the unpleasant memory from his mind and swung the door to his office open. He paused. He was sure he'd locked the door.

Inside, he froze in shock. The floor was strewn with papers from his desk. All the drawers had been pulled out and their contents spilled onto the ground. His coat lay on the floor, covered with loose pieces of paper. Someone had been

162

hunting for something. And Willis knew what it was. They had pulled out the lining of his jacket pockets, then emptied them. Somebody had been searching for Connor's note.

Thank God he'd left it with Sophie.

CHAPTER 20

Willis was busy tidying his office when Sophie joined him to lend a hand. When she arrived, he kissed her. 'I can't remember where Connor kept things. I don't have time to work out a system for myself, so for now I will bundle papers together then thrust them into whatever drawer will take them. Once I've done that, it will be tidy. If I can't find anything, then as sure as hell any intruders won't either. Luckily my parka escaped damage. When the bastard didn't find what he was searching for, he threw it on the floor.'

Sophie tried to convince him to work out a filing system, but he resisted.

'When you need to find something, you'll regret stuffing everything away.'

Willis sat for a moment, deciding what to do. 'No one was around to hear you ask me to put it in your notebook, so the note will be safe there, at least for the time being. But whoever is looking for it won't give up that easily. The next logical step would be to try my room. So, just in case, I will go there now and set up the camera.'

When Willis got to his room, he switched on the recording device, then chose the motion-sensor setting. He only wanted it to trigger if someone came close to his door, so he turned down the motion-sensor's sensitivity, then turned off the screen so it wasn't obvious that the machine was running. Once satisfied, he closed the door, without locking it. There was no point in risking the door getting damaged if someone tried to force it. Having to change room once was enough.

After setting everything up to his satisfaction, he checked it thoroughly, then walked to the galley, where he expected to find the rest of the team at dinner.

***

Justin was at the table before Willis. He'd forgotten to tell them to expect Justin, but it didn't seem to matter. The young man was busy ingratiating himself into their company. Because he was such a personable fellow, thought Willis, he would make friends anywhere. After they had chatted about the food and the accommodation, they asked Justin how he was faring with the restricted nature of the base. 'There is a lot of work for me to do here – I'm already preparing to restart my PhD once my gap year is over.' He turned and looked at Willis. 'And being lucky enough to meet Dr Willis is a bonus. I'm planning to get as much information from Dr Willis as I can. If he doesn't mind, that is.'

'Less of Dr Willis – please call me Brad.'

'But I must leave to do my chores. I apologise for having to leave so soon.' With that, he vanished into the kitchen.

What a lovely young guy, everybody agreed. He was so pleasant and easy to chat to. Willis nodded. 'When the opportunity arises, I will have to ask him more about his background. I didn't even ask him which university he studied at. Still, that will wait. There are other matters I need to talk to you about.'

Willis told them about finding his room trashed. 'They haven't taken anything, but whoever carried it out must have been looking for Connor's Chinese message. Whoever did it carefully searched my parka, then discarded it on the floor. But thankfully, I gave the note to Sophie earlier. She has it with her in a simple hiding place where no one will look.'

Willis turned to Sophie. 'Have you had time to ask your Chinese assistant to translate it for us?'

'Not yet. I'm not sure that Tao will be able to read it – he's a third-generation American. His English is better than mine, there's a good chance that he doesn't speak any of the Chinese dialects at all.'

'Well, it's worth a try. Can we find him now? Even if he's working, it will only take him a few seconds to explain it to us.'

'He doubles as a cook in the galley,' Sophie told them. 'Cooking is his second love.'

They asked a chef to fetch Tao, who appeared within minutes. He said no, he knew a few common words in Mandarin but he couldn't read its message. They thanked him, and he hurried back to finish his job in the kitchen.

'Now we'll need to find someone else.' Willis slid the paper in Sophie's direction, smiled at her, and asked her to replace it in her notebook. 'And it's got to be somebody we can trust. Because anyone who can understand any form of

166

Chinese is a potential suspect. We will need to be extra careful. Anyway, let's sit down – I have more news.'

Willis explained that a Russian general had asked to visit the base tomorrow morning. But he was a little worried that he'd given his permission too hastily. Allowing military people on the base, especially Russian, would almost certainly be frowned upon. But it was done now, so he would have to live with his decision.

'His name's General Korolev.' He looked at Sophie.

'Now there's a name that brings back sad memories.' Sophie turned to Linda and Gabi. 'We met Boris Korolev while Brad and I were working in Kazakhstan at the end of last year. Unfortunately, he was shot in the stomach and died a very painful death.'

Willis and Sophie's eyes met. They could read each other's minds. 'It was the saddest part of our trip.' Sophie's gaze dropped, and the overhead light reflected off a tear forming in her eye. 'He was a very good friend indeed. I still think about him.'

Willis wished that he could have prevented Korolev's death. 'While we were raiding a gang's stronghold, a lone gunman appeared from a side door. We couldn't have prevented the shooting, because no one on our team knew that door existed. Boris died in hospital, but not until after we'd completed our mission. It was successful, partly thanks to Boris, who organised a fleet of armed helicopters to attack the gang. Boris saved not only their lives but the lives of their Russian friends who were taking part.'

'Wow! That was tough. What a sad story,' Linda said. 'Sometimes it's better not to dwell too much on the past.'

Willis disagreed. 'It's always a good thing to reminisce a little – it ensures that people who deserve to be remembered, are. Anyway, you'll meet his namesake tomorrow.' Willis perked up and forgot about his negative thoughts. 'He's arriving by plane at eleven in the morning.'

'You might see him, Dr Willis. But Gabi and I will be working. We're at a critical part of the current experiment. If we finish in time, maybe we'll find him at lunch or dinner.'

'I doubt he'll be staying for dinner,' Willis said. 'I'll probably want to get him off the base as soon as possible, but you might meet him at lunch if you're lucky.'

'They've organised an unusual surprise for tonight,' Gabi cut in. 'The comms team has stolen some spare capacity from the satellite and downloaded a movie.'

'I hope it won't be displayed on the three monitors.' Willis hated those screens.

'No, they'll show it in the gym.'

'Which movie have they downloaded?' Sophie asked.

'I've heard it's the latest Bond. If it is, I want to see it.' Gabi rubbed her palms together.

'Blimey. That was only released just before I left England.' Willis couldn't believe his ears.

'We don't ask too many questions,' Gabi tapped her nose. 'It's likely to be a pirated version. The film will still be in cinemas as a new release. If the site supervisor finds out, we'll get done for bootlegging a movie – but only if he finds out.' She gave a wide grin.

'There's a cinema room on the base, but the projector got damaged during one of the surges,' Willis said. 'That's why they'll be showing it in the gym. When will the film begin?'

Gabi said, 'It's usually around eight, but if anyone misses it, they repeat it several times until everyone is sick to death of it.'

Willis looked at his watch. It was only ten to seven. He glanced at McGregor. 'Let's check my laptop in case it's recorded anything. We'll be back before the movie begins. Please could you bring chairs for us and keep our places, in case it gets busy?' Willis said.

'Don't worry,' said Gabi. 'The gym is large enough to hold everyone.'

***

When they reached Willis's room, he checked that a moistened hair that he'd stuck across the door jamb was still intact. 'It's a tip I picked up from Sean Connery in one of the old Bond films. What a coincidence!' he said to McGregor. He swung the door open. But everything looked tidy and as he had left it. Satisfied, he switched on the laptop and played the new recording. It revealed nothing spectacular. There were only about a dozen triggers. Each ten-second burst of action showed someone passing Willis's door, heading for the stairs. Faces had been recorded clearly. That gave Willis confidence that the camera would work when needed. A negative result was what he'd expected. If it was common knowledge that they would show a movie that evening, the culprit would wait until it was in full swing before making his move.

'After the film, we'll come back and re-check.' He nodded to McGregor. Willis switched the laptop's screen off, replaced his strategically placed hair on the door jamb, and headed to the gym. It was mobbed. A few people stood against the walls, too idle to bring a seat. Some were wrapped in blankets. The women had had to protect the men's places. They almost lost them on several occasions. Once they had settled down, Willis leaned over and whispered to his four colleagues, 'Watch out for anyone who leaves while the film is running – it could be our man.'

The movie started with the familiar John Barry theme music. Willis studied the room. The lights had been dimmed.

At first, he couldn't identify a thing, but his eyes quickly adjusted. Because he was an astronomer, he was used to seeing in the dark. Light coming from the screen and the poorly fitting blackout blinds provided ample illumination.

The film continued, with Bond carrying out some heroic act that might, or might not, have a bearing on the story later. The sound was loud, much louder than it needed to be. Willis fought the temptation to look at the screen. He wouldn't hear anyone leave, so he would need to watch out for movement. His peripheral vision allowed him to detect anything moving from everywhere except behind him. That was fine. Because there was no door near the screen, he would keep his attention on the two doors at the rear. A glance to his side revealed Sophie, Linda, Gabi and McGregor engrossed in the action. He shrugged. He would expect no help from them. Two hours passed. Nobody left or entered the gym. The music was building to a crescendo. Something exciting must be happening. While no one left the gym, Willis glimpsed a shadow cast on the wall outside the far exit. The effect was momentary, then it vanished. The shadow had looked too short to be a person, anyway. Willis had likely imagined it.

The movie came to its usual ending, with chauvinistic Bond getting the woman.

'Wow! Did you catch the bit where—'

'Stop!' Willis interrupted. 'I want to see it first.'

His friends looked sheepish as they realised they had failed in their task of observing the exits.

After the film finished, Willis waited until the room had almost emptied, until only a few stragglers remained, having a nightcap or a hot drink they'd brought before going to their rooms.

'Shall we check?' Willis got to his feet. McGregor followed.

***

The hair on Willis's door jamb was missing. He looked at McGregor. Someone had been in the room. Willis swung the door open. When he did, he was greeted by the same kind of a mess as when he'd opened his office door that morning. Once again, papers were strewn everywhere. Drawers had been emptied onto the floor. The laptop had moved; it sat at an awkward angle, not as Willis left it. At least it didn't look damaged. Thank God for that, he thought. Willis was about to power up the laptop's screen when McGregor put his hand on his arm to stop him. 'Let's do fingerprints first.' He left the room to fetch his kit, and returned after a few minutes. He started to dust the surfaces, beginning with the laptop. Thirty minutes later, he had finished. He stuck the prints he had lifted onto cards, then placed them in the satchel containing his gear. 'We have a full set of prints for everyone on the base. Now it will be easy to trace whoever did it – if he wasn't wearing gloves, that is.'

Willis powered up the laptop's screen and hit Play. There was the usual collection of miscellaneous figures passing by until eight o'clock. Then a gap followed. This was when the film had been in full swing. The program activated itself again at five past ten – during the climax of the movie. A short figure hunched in front of Willis's door. Shit, he thought. Only his forehead and the top of his hair were visible. The bent silhouette was playing with what Willis imagined were lock-picks, trying to open his bedroom door. Willis couldn't see his features. After apparently realising that the door was unlocked, he disappeared inside. The video stopped. No one else was moving along the corridor. The Bond film was still running. Then the laptop screen burst into life. The small shape appeared again. Double drat! He was facing away from the camera. Willis heard the door to his room close. The man stepped away. After that, a noise came from the stairs. A couple of men approached, shouting and discussing the movie. The figure swung around, so that he faced the camera.

Willis gulped. It was Franz Franck – the duty medical practitioner for the base.

'Let's nab him,' McGregor said.

'Why? Where's he going to go? He can hardly leave the base. And he doesn't know that we're on to him. Let's compare the prints, then grab him in the morning. It'll be better if we challenge him with as much evidence as we can. Lock those prints away in a safe place, then let's go for a drink. We deserve it.'

CHAPTER 21

McGregor and Willis rose at seven sharp and prepared for their visit to Dr Franz Franck. They recruited two bigger men to accompany them – not because they would need to overcome the diminutive Dr Franck, but because they might need witnesses. When he opened his door to Willis's knock, Franck's jaw dropped. His look of surprise changed to one of guilt when McGregor told him he was arresting him on suspicion of attempted murder. The heavies led him away and ensconced him in a room that just contained a bunk, a chair and a basin. Willis intended to make it impossible for Franck to attempt suicide. There was no way Willis wanted a repeat of what had happened to Connor. They removed his shoes then stripped him down to the bare essentials. Willis sat opposite him on the bed. 'Is there anything you want to tell us?'

Franck gave an almost imperceptible shake of his head.

'Is that a no?'

This time Franck nodded, but again, it was barely visible.

'Why did you need the note? What does it mean to you?'

His left eye twitched. He looked down at the floor, trying to avoid their gaze.

'We will send you back to the States – to a state that still has the death penalty.'

Still nothing. Willis shook his head and moved towards the door.

'I want a solicitor.' The words were hardly audible. Willis made him repeat them. 'I want a solicitor.'

'No solicitor for you – traitors don't get solicitors. They don't get trials. They get lethal injections.'

McGregor gave Willis a frown that could kill. His face turned crimson and he clenched his teeth, frantically shaking his head. Willis pretended to go to the door for a second time.

'It's a map. It's a location. And it was mine, not Connor's. I am not saying another word until I get a deal.'

'This isn't civilisation; there'll be no deal for you. You poisoned me! I don't care what happens to you, Mr Franck. You will rot here until I decide how to dispose of you, so the best deal you'll get is if I let you live.' Willis walked out and slammed the door.

'What the fuck was that all about? You broke every rule in the book,' McGregor stuttered, near apoplectic. 'That crap about traitors not getting solicitors is exactly that – crap. We haven't even read him his rights. Fuck you, Willis.'

It was Willis's turn to throw him a murderous look. 'There's been one person killed so far, and one attempted murder. We don't even know yet if Franck is acting alone – he could have half a dozen accomplices, for all we know. I don't have time to faff around with rule books.' He strode off and didn't look back.

***

It was almost 11 a.m., and General Korolev was due to land. When his plane landed, Willis had to be there – because he would get into enough trouble inviting Russians onto the base without leaving them unsupervised. At precisely eleven o'clock Korolev's plane touched down on the skiway. Willis waited. It seemed to take forever before the door opened and the general finally stepped out.

He didn't look like a general. There was no sign of an entourage or any military regalia. He was quite short, and a thick Russian Arctic jacket and a pair of padded trousers bulked him out. There's no way he'll get cold, thought Willis. This man clearly didn't worry about status or rank. As he walked towards Willis, he was alone, with no guards or other personnel accompanying him. When he got to about eight feet from Willis, the general paused. What's he doing? Willis wondered. The general stopped to inspect Willis, then he took a step forward and stopped again. He raised his hand and slowly removed his goggles.

Willis's jaw dropped, and he staggered backwards in alarm. 'You're a ghost.' Even as he heard his words, he didn't believe them.

'Brad Willis?' the short general said. He allowed the final 's' to disappear into the wind.

'Boris? Boris Korolev? But you're dead. I saw your coffin being taken off the plane. What the—'

'Two bags of sand, my good friend – just enough to make box seem heavy. Dear friend, I am sorry for deceiving you. Get me a warm drink and let me tell you what happened.'

They walked to the base in silence. Willis shook his head and ground his teeth. Korolev had a lot of explaining to do.

They sat in the galley drinking coffee, and Korolev began. 'You remember that I am member of the GRU?'

Willis knew he was a member of the Main Intelligence Directorate, part of the Russian Federation's secret service. After the Soviet Union broke up, the Russian authorities changed its name to the GU, but old habits die hard and most people still referred to it as the GRU.

'Because it is important that I stay as anonymous as possible, as soon as I finish my work in Kazakhstan, I needed to vanish. Faking my death was quickest way to disappear. I was needed in the Balkans, so it had to be done quickly.'

'But I shot Klaus Fauler in the stomach. Because I wanted him to die in the same horrible manner that you did – but now you turn up alive and healthy.'

Klaus Fauler had been the leader of a rogue element of the Russian Mafia called the Golden Triangle, and Willis and his team had been sent to bring them down.

'That was unfortunate, or maybe not so unfortunate. Fauler was evil man and deserved to die. And I *did* suffer pain. I almost didn't survive.'

'Even so, I killed him for the wrong reasons.' Willis shook his head and frowned. He gazed over the table top, focusing everywhere except on Korolev.

The general seemed to see Willis's irritation and changed the subject. 'Since there is less chance of people raising the eyebrows, I thought it better not to appear military.' Korolev spoke English with the occasional endearing turn of phrase, but Willis was in no mood to forgive, not yet at least.

Despite his short height and stature, he had demonstrated his bravery on more than one occasion. He had saved Willis's life in Kazakhstan. Willis owed him for that.

'I'm here on your base because I suspect there's a common thread running through our objectives.'

Willis watched the general's dark brown eyes staring, observing everything.

'What a coincidence. "Of all the gin joints…" I forget the rest. *Casablanca* is my favourite movie.' Korolev had deceived Willis. The way he was wringing his hands gave away his discomfort.

'And why are we both here? And stop being frivolous.' Willis spat the words out.

'I need you to trust me again, but I don't blame you for being cautious. I am here because of blackouts we've experienced. My department informs me that your navy sank a Chinese vessel in the Ross Sea for transmitting a pulse of interference. But that's not the end of it. There are more.'

'More what?' Willis asked. 'More ships?'

'No, my good friend. More pulses; you have only detected the more powerful ones. At Vostok Station, we have recorded many weaker ones. And before you ask, no, we haven't traced their location yet. They are bouncing off the upper atmosphere, the ionosphere, which scatters the signal, making it impossible for us to track them.'

Willis frowned. His eyes narrowed. He'd hoped the pulses were gone forever, so this was serious. 'The Chinese must have found a way of generating pulses that are strong enough to be weaponised.'

'I don't think it's the Chinese.' Boris was adamant. 'The Chinese have reassured us that it is not their doing.'

Willis told Boris of the coded note he had acquired. 'I think it's written in some kind of cipher, in Chinese.'

Boris's focus dropped to his clasped hands. Then he became pensive. 'If you will allow me to see it, perhaps I can shine some light on it. All Russian generals need to study a little Chinese. I am no exception.'

'Because someone tried to steal it from me, I have put it in a safe place, but I will let you read it. When do you need to fly back to Vostok?'

'The plane will wait for me until tomorrow evening. If we agree to co-operate, we can decide what plans we need to put into action.'

'Good. That will give you the chance to meet Sophie Fenwick again before you leave.'

Boris's mouth fell open. Then he chuckled. 'The whole of England must be here. Are you two still playing the cat and the mouse?'

'What do you mean?' Willis looked away.

Boris smiled, then put his thumb and forefinger to his mouth and made a horizontal motion, pretending to zip his lips closed.

Willis needed to do some housekeeping. For starters, he had to find a room for Boris. He showed the general the layout of the building and suggested that he come to fetch him from his room in thirty minutes for lunch. He messaged Sophie to ask her to bring the note with her to the galley when she came for lunch. He also promised her a pleasant surprise.

***

Sophie nearly passed out when she saw Boris at lunch. When she saw him, she asked if he was her friend Boris's twin. But

178

Boris assured her he was Boris Korolev. He explained what had happened, and why. Sophie reacted as Willis had, with disbelief and disappointment.

'But you *did* get shot?' Boris immediately opened his tunic and showed her his battle scars. His stomach was a maze of healed wounds. He seemed very proud of his collection. Sophie found it incredible that he could have survived so many serious injuries. 'I wish I hadn't asked now. It wasn't intended as a challenge.' She held out her hand to block the view. With her right hand, she signalled that she wanted him to cover up. If nothing else, it was proof that she was speaking to the real Boris Korolev.

'This food is same as we get at Vostok. I hoped that I would have pleasant change, but it's not to be.'

Sophie remembered he loved his hamburgers, and offered him a hamburger tomorrow. His eyes lit up.

'That's a deal,' Sophie said, amused.

'Let Boris see the note,' Willis said. Sophie reached for the notebook that sat on the table beside her. She produced the small folded piece of paper and handed it to Boris.

Boris unfolded the paper, read it, then grunted. He shook his head. 'I have no idea what the numbers represent. But the writing is old Chinese proverb. It's in Mandarin and reads *Masters open the door. You enter by yourself.*'

'What the hell does *that* mean?' Willis asked.

'Your guess eez as good as mine.' Korolev handed the note back to Willis.

No one discussed it further. When they finished their meal, the conversation returned to when they had last met. Sophie told Boris about Willis getting treatment in St Petersburg for his PTSD. So far, it appeared to be working, she said. She tapped her head, smiled and said, 'Knock on

179

wood.' Boris burst into hysterics. He'd clearly never seen that done before.

Linda and Gabi arrived and sat down.

'Why did you tell me you wouldn't make it to lunch today? What's changed?' Willis asked.

'I guess we're just nosey. We were curious about what a Russian general looks like.'

Willis introduced them to Boris.

'I bet you didn't imagine me to be as handsome as I am,' Boris said arrogantly, then stood and offered his hand.

'Bloody men, they're the same all over the world.' Linda took his hand reluctantly.

Gabi asked the inevitable question. 'Are you related to Sergey Korolev?'

Willis and Sophie answered together. 'He's his great-uncle.'

Everyone had heard of Sergey Korolev, except Linda. They explained that he was the father of the Russian space programme. He had designed the original rockets. He'd helped construct Sputnik, the first satellite. Linda was impressed. She leaned over and shook his hand a second time.

Then Linda and Gabi gave their apologies. They had to leave. They were running an observation at the telescope that required their attention.

Willis updated Sophie and Boris on the morning's adventure with Dr Franz Franck. Sophie remarked that she hadn't seen Franck at the party, so it could have been him who had started the latest fire. Willis told them that Franck was admitting to nothing, but that he was almost certain it was Franck who had poisoned him. After all, he had access to a pharmacy and he could easily have put something in his food while Willis was standing in the line or when he was distracted at the meal table. The only thing Franck had revealed was that the numbers on the note were co-ordinates. Try as they might, Willis and McGregor couldn't work out what the co-ordinates were for. There weren't enough digits to represent latitude and longitude. Latitude might be possible with the top group of figures, but the lower set only comprised four numbers – not enough.

They chatted for some time, reminiscing. It was a nostalgic trip. Willis thought of the warm memories he cherished with Sophie and Boris.

'Talking of McGregor, where has he gone?' Willis asked after a while.

'I think he went back to his room or to see Franck. Perhaps he is looking after the prisoner,' Sophie said.

Willis jumped to his feet. He raced to the room where Dr Franck had been held that morning. It was empty. As he thought, McGregor had moved Franck to prevent Willis from breaking any more regulations. Since there were still a few rules he wanted to break, he needed to find where McGregor was holding Franz Franck.

CHAPTER 22

McGregor's door burst open with such force that it bashed against the wall.

'What the hell are you playing at?' Willis wasn't hiding how he felt. 'Where is Franz Franck? What have you done with him?'

'He's safely locked up where no harm can come to him. I've read him his rights. I have also signalled McMurdo to ask Glen Mason to assign a team to take him into custody.'

'You did what? I'm the Station Leader. I'm in command of this base. I'll say when he goes to McMurdo.'

'I'm sorry, Brad, but I've been put in charge of security, so I'll decide when and where we send him.'

'You're not the security officer, you're an undercover CIA agent. You have no legitimate authority in the station.'

'CIA or not, I did the interview. I got the job. You overstepped the mark on this, Brad. You know it.'

Willis slumped onto the bed; he knew he had taken things a little too far. 'Look, I need to get as much information out of him as I can before Mason takes him off-site. We'll only have one go at this.'

'Okay, you can have twenty minutes with him, but I insist on being there. Remember, twenty minutes only, and no threats. Play it by the book, Brad. Or I'll close it down.'

Willis nodded. McGregor was right. There was no other way. 'There's something else I need to confess to.' He started to tell him about Korolev, but McGregor interrupted.

'What the fu— Are you mad? You can't invite Russian military personnel onto this base without clearance. They'll lock you up.'

Willis told him about Boris: about them working together in Kazakhstan, and that Joshua Baker in the CIA knew of Korolev and would act as a referee if asked.

'Jesus H. Christ, Brad, you'll get us all shot.'

Willis held up his hand. 'Boris has translated the Chinese writing on the note. I would appreciate the chance to face Franck with the information, to see how he reacts. I would also like Korolev to be there in case we need his Chinese knowledge.'

'Hey Ho, line up the firing squad, here we go.'

Willis, Korolev and McGregor entered Franck's temporary prison cell.

After McGregor's intervention, he'd become more confident.

Somehow, Willis would have to break his confidence. Willis introduced General Korolev, then told Franck that he'd come from Vostok Station to take him to Russia.

'Shit,' McGregor said under his breath. He kicked Willis's ankle. Willis looked over and threw a wink in his direction. McGregor shook his head.

Some of Franck's new confidence vanished. His face drained of colour as he bit his lower lip. He swallowed hard.

'Now, we know about the door.' After Willis made the statement, he made a play of taking the note out of his pocket and unfolding it. When he finished, he rotated it in his hand, laid it on the table, pretending to smooth it out, lengthening the awkward silence. '*Masters open the door. You enter by yourself.*' Willis paused again for effect. 'You'll be in deep crap, my man, when the powers-that-be see this…'

'Moscow will be very interested.' Boris had twigged what Willis was trying to do, so put in his tuppence-worth. 'That you acted against the Federation won't amuse them.'

'Can I have a d-d-drink of water, p-please?'

McGregor went to the sink, filled one of the plastic beakers that sat on the shelf, then handed it to the doctor.

Franck gulped the liquid. 'It's on The Ice. I don't know exactly where it is, but it's somewhere near the sea. The co-ordinates give its precise location.'

'The co-ordinates are incomplete,' barked Willis. 'There are not enough numbers.'

'I know nothing about that. I'm just a middle-man. I was paid for my efforts. It was slipped under my door with instructions. All I had to do was post it on a company noticeboard. It had a Chinese IP address.' Willis looked at Franck and raised his eyebrows. Franck took the hint. He recited the eight digits of the address slowly, so Willis could write them down.

'Shouldn't there be twelve digits in an IP address?' Willis asked. 'This only has eight.'

McGregor looked over his shoulder and told him that they'd left out the leading zeroes in each set of three digits.

Willis refolded the paper. He placed it back into his pocket. 'We will check this out. But God help you if you're sending us on a wild-goose chase.' As it was clear that Franck was shit scared, Willis didn't think for a minute that he was lying.

'One last question – where is your boss based?' He wasn't expecting an answer.

But Franck seemed eager to help. 'In Beijing. The Chinese government is also trying to locate the source.'

***

Once they were back in his office, Willis grinned. 'There, that didn't hurt.' He looked at McGregor, who was still smarting from Willis threatening to send Franck to Russia.

'The co-ordinates make no sense,' Willis kept repeating. 'And if Franck is telling the truth that someone slipped the instructions to him on the base, then there's someone else involved.'

On the wall was a star chart. Either Connor or his predecessor must have been interested in the sky. Willis kept staring at it. Something about it nagged at him. The answer wouldn't come, but it felt as though it was trying to tell him something. The map covered the southern constellations. As Willis looked at the South Pole on the star atlas, he could see the Southern Cross. He pictured two imaginary lines drawn on it to indicate the position of the South Pole. The map was telling him something. But what?

'Let's go for something to eat.'

***

'When is your flight out?' McGregor asked Boris.

Because, as usual, Korolev was speaking with his mouth full, the reply was muffled. 'Seven p.m.'

It always amused Willis that Boris never hesitated to speak when his mouth was full. Willis had concluded long ago that it was a cultural thing. He chose to ignore it. But not so with McGregor. He was looking at the general in disbelief. The general said, 'I didn't think I could risk staying for longer.' As he spoke, grease sprayed from his lips. It landed in front of McGregor, who stood and took a step away from Boris.

McGregor spoke directly to Boris. 'Mason is due at 4 p.m., so, it might be a good idea if you kept out of sight. The less Glen Mason knows about all this, the better, at least until we are clear what the next step is. And it would be a good idea if you moved your plane to the furthest end of the skiway, so that he won't spot it.'

Willis nodded. It surprised him that McGregor was being clandestine. Because he'd been part of Willis's risky strategy in the end, Willis guessed McGregor felt there was no option but to agree to his wishes until Franck was off the base.

***

While Mason was present, they hid Boris away in the room Willis had assigned him. Willis hoped Mason didn't recognise the Russian plane sitting at the far end of the runway, partly concealed by a mound of snow that remained after the skiway had been groomed. To prepare for take-off, the plane from McMurdo would taxi and turn around. Its position would further conceal the other plane. So there was no reason Mason should look back and spot it. But Willis still worried about it. Willis met Mason as he alighted from the plane and tried to distract him by directing his attention to the observation platform.

McGregor finished typing up a report on their interviews with Franck, leaving out the shady bits. He kept to the facts that Franck had revealed. Until the next available connecting flight to the USA, Franck would be securely held at McMurdo. Two burly giants had manhandled Franck onto the plane. The process went smoothly. By 4.30 p.m., Mason's plane was only a spot on the horizon. Once they had satisfied themselves Mason was far enough away, Willis and McGregor brought Boris out of hiding. Because Boris needed to be gone by seven, Willis suggested they have an early dinner.

Boris was unenthusiastic about accompanying them to the galley, and it wasn't until Willis gently reminded him that he had been promised American hamburgers that he capitulated and followed them.

Gabi produced several quarter-pound burgers, so they could all enjoy Boris's luxury meal as a team. 'I thought coin would never fall,' Korolev said.

They were used to Boris's translated idioms, so Willis and Sophie chanted, 'the penny has finally dropped'.

Once again, Willis was quiet. He was still trying to work out why he kept returning to the star chart. He was missing something. As he resurfaced from his thoughts, he heard someone make an unkind remark about Mason's rotund shape.

'He is at least fifty pounds overweight,' Gabi said. That was ten more than Willis estimated. Then she added, 'His stomach is almost spherical.'

Willis jumped to his feet, excited. 'I've got it! I know what was bugging me about the star chart. Spherical – it uses spherical geometry.'

'What the hell is spherical geometry?' McGregor asked.

'It's used a lot in astronomy – Linda, Sophie and Gabi will understand.' Willis took a bowl from the table and turned it over. 'Let's imagine this is the Earth.'

McGregor rolled his eyes, but Willis ignored him. He took a felt-tip marker from his pocket and drew lines of latitude and longitude on the bowl. 'One degree represents seventy miles on the Earth's surface. That's true of degrees of latitude everywhere on Earth. It's also valid for degrees of longitude, but *only* at the equator. Look.' He pointed to the lines of longitude. 'The circles become smaller the closer they get to Pole. A degree at the equator might represent seventy miles, but as they get nearer to Pole, they become shorter. By the time they reach Pole they are infinitely small.' Willis produced the note from his pocket. 'If the top number is the latitude and we put a minus in front, it's about seventy degrees south. That's at the edge of Antarctica. If we take the bottom number and assume a decimal point between the second and third numbers, then it represents about seventy-six and a half degrees of longitude. At that latitude, a tenth of a degree would be equivalent to just over two miles – and that gives the location, accurate to a fifth of a mile.'

'Is it east or west?' McGregor asked.

'Without a plus or minus sign, we can't know for certain. We'll need to check the map and work it out.' Willis checked that Boris had finished his burgers, then stood up and headed to his office. Boris followed, chewing as he walked.

Willis pulled a map from the bottom drawer of his desk. 'If we travel westwards, it's towards the Antarctic Peninsula *but* if we go eastwards, it's to the north of Zhongshan Station, which belongs to China, and to Progress II Station which is Russian. So my money is on it being eastwards.'

'If I can use your email system, I will order high-resolution satellite image of the area.' Korolev waved his hands in the air. Drops of fat sprayed from his mouth. 'I will also order a scan using ground-penetrating radar. The probe can penetrate a couple of hundred metres in ice. Less if we go for the highest resolution. I will request that they take images at both resolutions.'

Willis left him alone to send his email, then looked at McGregor and took a deep breath. 'Things are about to get interesting. We'd better prepare for a trip.'

Boris returned, and confirmed that he'd placed an order for both. Since it was a polar-orbiting satellite, it would require less than two hours to fly over that part of Antarctica, but longer to download the images. By sheer luck, the satellite would pass almost directly over the right spot where the GPR would take the image. He said he would email Willis when he received the results. It would be sometime tomorrow morning.

***

At seven, Willis saw Boris off. The departure was emotional. How do you say farewell to a friend who you'd believed was dead? thought Willis. They hugged. Boris tried to kiss him on both cheeks. He failed, because their ECW was too bulky between them. Boris turned around and walked to the plane without looking back. That's how it's done, thought Willis. Embarrassingly badly.

***

Their group was in the galley when Willis returned. He was getting bored with the place. And this was after a short while. What would it be like if he 'wintered-over' here? He wasn't even sure if 'wintered-over' was a proper word. Despite the challenges that lay ahead, he relaxed, because this was the first time – other than the day he had landed – that his life wasn't in danger.

Because the other three were sitting with drinks, Willis poured another to be sociable. 'The place is uncommonly busy again this evening,' he said. Gabi informed him that the Bond movie was being repeated tonight.

'I'm not watching it again.' Linda threw back her drink and stood to leave.

'Or me.' Gabi rose like a trained poodle and followed her.

Willis looked at McGregor, who shook his head, got to his feet and pursued the other two.

'It looks like it's just us, Brad,' Sophie said. 'We can sit at the back and snog?'

'No. I want to see this bloody film. Perhaps later.' He kissed her on the cheek then walked to the coffee machine.

Sophie put her hands over her mouth to simulate a cone and called after him. 'I'll miss you when you've gone home.'

CHAPTER 23

'Quickly – go and use the shower near your own room.' Sophie threw Willis's clothes at him the next morning. 'I'm late for work. I should have been at the observatory fifteen minutes ago.'

Willis pulled on his pants and T-shirt. He was acting like he'd been caught in a lady's chamber by her husband, who had come home unexpectedly, and had to scarper. He hopped on one foot while trying to put on his trousers, then lost his balance and fell backwards on the bed. Sophie leapt on top of him then landed a soft kiss on his lips. 'I shouldn't have been so physical last night. It makes us sleep in every time. Now get showered. If I wrap up in time, I'll try to see you at lunch.'

'I love it when you get physical that way. I enjoy all the pleasure without having to make the effort.' He struggled to finish pulling on his pants.

'Sod off, you lazy monkey.'

Sophie was in the women's shower room long before he had dressed. She switched on the shower, then she rushed out of the shower room and into the corridor. 'Hold on,' she waved at Willis. 'The shower's not working.' Water was dribbling from the shower head.

He threw the light switch to have a better look. Nothing happened. Or at least, nothing appeared to happen. The bulb came on, but with only a dull orange glow. He pulled the short cord above the basin. The same thing.

'We're having a brownout. The voltage has dropped. Leave it, it'll recover in a minute.'

Willis was right. The lights flickered then, flashed on at full power. The shower gave a gulp and a splutter, sending a powerful jet of water drumming off the plastic base of the cubicle.

'There you are, all fixed. Hurry, your two minutes have started. I'd better disappear before someone catches me in the ladies' showers.' Willis threw her a kiss before disappearing into the corridor.

***

When he reached his office, an irate Linda was already there. 'This is getting repetitive. After the voltage dropped at the telescope over half an hour ago, all the circuitry reset. Now it'll be another four hours, at least, before we can do any useful work.'

Willis had assumed that the brownout at Sophie's only affected the local supply. It didn't. He grabbed his jacket. 'Go back to SPT. Try to find out an accurate time for the voltage drop. I'm going to IceCube to see if I can determine which direction this pulse – if it was a pulse – came from.'

At the entrance to the observatory, Willis met Tao, Sophie's assistant. Tao told Willis that Sophie wasn't there yet. Willis, of course, knew the reason, but just smiled.

'The sensors on our equipment have reset. I am panicking because I don't know how to restart them. I have to switch them on manually to get everything running again, but I don't have a clue how to go about it. Neither have our other two assistants.' They stood sheepishly behind him. Willis looked at the control panel. He had an idea for how to start it, but he told Tao that it was too risky. He'd prefer to wait for Sophie.

At that moment, Sophie came through the door. She looked at the lack of lights on the board. 'What's happened?'

Willis pointed to the control panel. 'The voltage drop occurred here, as well as at the base. It also affected Linda's telescope, but it reset itself.'

Sophie pressed a dozen buttons in quick succession, like a demented xylophone player. The panel burst into life, and Tao looked relieved. Sophie switched on one of the desk computers, pressed six or seven keys then hit Enter. 'It's up again, but I don't know whether we've lost any observations.'

'Can we check the sensors?' Willis asked. 'Is there a chance that they might have detected a surge?'

Sophie switched on a workstation, then she scrolled through several pages of information that flashed on the screen. 'No, it recorded nothing. If there was a pulse, it must have been weak, not strong enough for the detectors to pick up.'

'How about a time? Is there any way you can detect the time it happened?'

'Is a two-nanosecond accuracy any good to you?' She smiled smugly.

'That might be sufficiently accurate,' Willis said, more than a touch of sarcasm in his voice.

'I can give you the accurate start times of the outage.' Sophie pressed a key. A laser printer burst into life. She handed the printout to Willis.

'The power that these people are generating must be huge. If I thought it didn't sound so pathetic, I'd call it astronomical.'

'How is the time useful to you?'

'It isn't – not on its own. But if I can get a similar time from Linda, I might work magic with both of them. If I can tell the time delay between the start of the brownout at the SPT and the IceCube I can work out the direction of the pulse. It works like this. Sit down and concentrate. It's really quite simple once you get your brain around it.' Willis took a deep breath, 'The interference travels at the speed of light. When I divide the speed of light by the time difference between its arrival at each observatory, it will give me the difference in distance the source is from each observatory. Remember, speed multiplied by time equals distance. If the distance I calculate is the same as the actual distance between the observatories, then the direction is on the straight line joining both. If the distance is zero, then the direction is at right angles to the line joining the observatories. So there are two solutions to the calculation, one at each side of the line. If it is somewhere in between, and I expect it to be, then there are only two directions that it can have come from. If you draw it out on paper it will be clearer. I know it sounds complicated but just trust me, it works.'

'You mean it works like parallax? Why didn't you just say that in the first case?'

'Exactly. The source will appear to come from a different direction at each observatory. I need to visit SPT and ask Linda if she can give me the time the interference arrived at the SPT.'

Sophie turned to Tao. 'This is running now. I'll be with Dr Willis at the IceCube Observatory if you need to find me.'

Tao's hand went to his mouth, and he nibbled a fingernail. Her three assistants would sweat until Sophie returned.

***

'What are you pair wanting? Nothing's happening here. Before I can get any bloody thing out of the instrument, it'll be several hours.' Linda threw a folder on the bench with enough force to make Willis jump.

'Can you find out for me the time of the outage, using the system clock? I know you're occupied, but it would be very helpful.' His reluctance to ask was clear in Willis's voice.

'That's the bloody trouble – the reason we're not busy is there's nothing we can do. The equipment needs time to reach equilibrium.' She was almost screaming. Linda clasped and unclasped her hands until her knuckles cracked. Willis was sorry he'd asked. Linda pounded on the keyboard of a computer, then smashed the Enter key with a flourish. The printer came to life, sucked in a piece of A4 paper, and spat it out the top. Linda picked up the sheet and sent it sailing across the bench to Willis. He caught it in mid-air.

'There are your bloody times. I'd kill for some caffeine.'

'I need a calculator.' He sat down at the workbench. Gabi brought him one. Linda slapped a cup of black coffee in front of him. 'I hope it's Brazilian.' He was trying to wind her up.

'Fuck off.' She clearly wasn't in the mood for frivolity.

Willis ignored her. First he measured the distance between the South Pole Telescope and IceCube on a map of the base, then he took the difference in time between the outage at both instruments. While he was doing this, he explained to Gabi that if he knew the delay between the disruption at SPT and IceCube, and how far it was between them, it would tell him from which direction the pulse originated. Unfortunately, with only two positions and times he wouldn't able to work out exactly where it came from. The arithmetic would give two solutions: each offset by the same angle to the line joining the observatories. He would only know the direction, not the location.

Gabi frowned and rolled her eyes. 'It's beyond me, but I'll take your word for it.'

'Don't worry, we do it regularly to measure the source of gamma ray bursts. If it interferes with three or more space probes, then we can get an accurate location in the sky by measuring the time the signal reaches each probe. However, in this case we only have two timings instead of three.'

'Before it gets cold, drink your damn coffee.' Linda was in a talkative mood again. 'I have a chart in the cupboard. I'll fetch it.' She smoothed the map out over the bench. Because it was too big for the surface, it flopped over its edges. Willis drew two sets of lines in pencil. Each pair of lines differed in length by the time difference between when the signal had reached each observatory. One set pointed to a barren area of no-man's land, but the other was more interesting. The lines pointed to a location toward the Amery Ice Shelf and crossed the point indicated by the co-ordinates

Willis deduced from the Chinese note. This was the confirmation he needed. He had discovered the source of the pulses. He would tell Korolev when he contacted him later. He made a mental note to tell Reilly of his discovery too.

'When you find whoever is doing this, give them a kick up the arse from me.' Linda grinned from ear to ear. Willis folded the map.

'It's the physics of this that puzzles me,' Willis said. 'I can't even begin to imagine how they manage it. To affect us from as far away as the Amery Ice Shelf is mind-boggling – the power they're consuming has to be enormous. The ice must be melting around them.'

'Right, you guys need to go. My equipment is nearly stable. I'm going to risk running everything again. And you can take that map with you, Brad. I won't need it.'

While Linda and Gabi set about their work, Sophie walked back to IceCube. 'I hope Tao didn't panic too much in my absence.' As she strolled away, she threw Willis a kiss.

Willis stuffed the map in his pocket. At last, he was making some progress. He lowered his gaze and followed the vehicle tracks back to the central complex. Willis's return route took him to the rear of the main building. He walked around to where the four sections of the base jutted out from its backbone, then stopped. He climbed to the summit of the zigzag stairs leading to the top floor of the second section, he looked across into the windows of the adjoining block, but all the room windows were blacked out. Willis didn't have a clue what he was looking for. These stairs were meant to be used for emergencies only, so he sat on the top step, his chin in his hands, and tried to figure out how the physics of the surges might work, but nothing came to him. Finally, he gave in and stood up. He shuffled down the steps and headed for the galley. 'I'm talking to myself. That's the first sign of madness. But there must be a way to work out the science of this.'

***

Willis sat in the galley, drinking yet another cappuccino. He was conflicted as to what to do. Willis missed Cambridge and his work but he had thought about joining Sophie over the winter. He was still indecisive. Sophie had her day job. She would be busy most of the time. Unless he could find something to keep him occupied, he would go crazy. Thank goodness this current challenge kept his mind active. When he was with Sophie, he wanted to stay with her forever, but staying out here on The Ice with her made little sense. To make it last as long as possible, and to help him concentrate, he sipped his coffee slowly.

'Where have you been? I didn't see you at breakfast.' McGregor sat down beside him.

Willis hadn't realised he'd missed breakfast. Maybe his low sugar level accounted for at least part of his melancholy. 'I didn't go for breakfast.' He played with some froth floating on his coffee. 'But I ought to have something now.'

'Did you suffer from the fall in voltage earlier?' McGregor asked. 'The drop seems to have affected everyone.'

Willis filled McGregor in on his visit to Linda's and Sophie's observatories. 'I found out the dropout timings and, by using the distance between the two locations, I've estimated a position for the source of the interference. It was another pulse, but it was a lot longer than the previous ones. It also came from the location we worked out from the co-ordinates on the piece of paper.'

'I'm going to fetch you something to eat.' McGregor disappeared, and soon returned with two plates piled high

198

with roast lamb. McGregor doesn't seem interested in my discovery, thought Willis.

'That's a bit heavy for breakfast.'

'Since it's nearly midday, you can treat it as brunch.' McGregor sat down with his plate. 'If you can't finish it, I volunteer to come to the rescue.' He wasn't joking. Willis knew how much food McGregor could consume. 'So, what's the game plan? How do we stop these bastards from screwing with our electricity supply?'

'I will contact Boris Korolev later. We should find out the results of the GPR images. Once I finish eating, I also need to email Reilly, to ask him to get a satellite photograph of the area to support whatever Boris sends me. I'll request an infrared image. That will show up the immense heat that is produced to create the surges if it's still visible.'

Before Willis had finished talking, McGregor's plate was empty. Willis cut a slice off his lamb chop. He put it into his mouth, then pushed his plate onto McGregor's tray to finish. 'Welcome to your first heart attack.'

CHAPTER 24

McGregor barged into Willis's office, breathless from the run along the corridor, carrying a sheet of paper.

'I said you'd have a heart attack. Sit down. Get your breath back.' Willis pointed to a chair that was facing his desk.

McGregor dropped into the seat, panting. 'There's a plane down – it crashed into the sea heading into McMurdo. It looks like everyone on board has perished. They're out searching, but no one could survive in that water.'

'What time did it happen? Did they say?'

McGregor picked up the printout of the email. 'The base lost contact with the plane around 7 a.m. There was no mayday message; communications just cut off.'

Willis shook his head in disbelief. 'The brownout happened at 7:06. The same happened when I was flying into

McMurdo – the pilot lost control and the plane went into a dive, but the pulse was shorter so the pilot could regain control in time. If the brownout affected this plane, there wouldn't have been time for the pilot to recover from the dive because the brownout lasted for seven minutes. That's much longer than the previous pulses. Poor buggers, they didn't stand a chance. A plane left here at 8 a.m. to return some crew who didn't contract to winter-over – it was lucky they weren't in the air then as well.' Willis put out his hand to take the email. 'Have any messages come in from Korolev?'

'I didn't see any, but not all the emails have been downloaded yet. I'll go back and check.'

'I'll join you. Reilly needs to know about this.'

When Willis reached the comms centre, two emails were waiting. One was from Reilly. It read:

I have ordered the infrared image of your target. Will deliver it as soon as the satellite passes over Pole. I estimate I will forward it to you in three hours.

The send time on the mail was two hours ago. With luck, he would receive a photograph in an hour. The second email was from Korolev, and it was more informative. He had attached a ground-penetrating radar image of the area near Zhongshan Station. The picture revealed a discontinuity in the ice about eighty miles inland, north of the Chinese and Russian bases. He included an explanation of the radar image and an artist's impression of the anomaly's position and orientation. Willis selected the shot that illustrated both the object's direction and its location relative to the two bases, then sent the image to the printer. While he was waiting, he rattled off an email to Korolev, telling him about the downed aircraft and the approximate time it had disappeared, adding that it happened at the same time as the brownout. After he hit Send, he plucked the artist's sketch from the printer. The drawing showed a narrow object about five hundred feet long and fifty feet below the ice. Willis folded the printout and stuck it into his pocket. 'I'll put this on the map of Antarctica and see what it tells us.'

***

Carefully Willis spread the map out on his desk, then copied the artist's impression onto it, exaggerating the object's size to show its orientation. Its position was crossed by the line that he'd drawn earlier with his timing calculations. Finally, things were coming together. He had a hunch. He drew a line through the long axis of the object, then extended it until it covered the Antarctic continent. It passed halfway between Pole and the McMurdo Station, then the line cut across the Ross Sea where both his flight and the missing plane had flown.

It would still take a lot of energy to produce sufficient power to achieve this range, but if it had been focused in some way, that would substantially reduce the amount of energy needed. But why would anyone want to focus energy in this direction? That's what he didn't know.

After he'd seen Reilly's infrared image, he would contact Boris Korolev again to work out a strategy. Whatever that plan might be, it would involve a trip to the other side of the continent.

'I'm getting hungry.' He turned to McGregor. 'If you want a double helping, get it yourself because. This time, I'm eating my own dinner.' They were in the galley earlier than usual. Only a few people were eating, but a bunch of guys worked in the far corner. Many of the tables were gone. Staff were replacing them with smaller, more intimate dining tables. At the far end, another group of staff were wheeling in couches. Soft, luxurious couches. Willis wondered what it was all about, so he stopped one of the men, who was carrying a long table folded under his arm.

'What's going on here?'

The man, who introduced himself as Jim, said, 'The flight that left earlier was full. Many of the crew were heading home after finishing their stint on The Ice. Didn't you hear we polies cheering from the observation deck as the plane took off?'

'I didn't. When it lifted off, I was with Dr Linda Foreman at SPT.'

Jim continued, 'It's normal for those left to cheer as folks leave The Ice, because they would have been looking forward to leaving for weeks.'

Willis understood the feeling.

'Once all the crew who've stayed for the summer months have gone, the number on the base will tumble from over a thousand to fifty. That means we don't need as many seats in the galley, so we can spread out in relative luxury. We don't normally do this until the winter starts, but the numbers are dropping fast this season.' Jim marched away with the table.

'Dr Willis?' It was Justin Rowe.

Although he liked the lad, Willis would rather not spend too much time with him, not while there were so many other demands on his time. 'May I join you for dinner?' Before Willis could reply, Justin had plonked himself down on the seat next to him. 'I have several things I want to ask about your research. For example, when you were researching supernovae—'

'Let's get some food first, then I will answer your queries.' Willis decided it would do little harm to provide answers during dinner.

Instead of returning to their original long table, they collected their meals and sat at a smaller round table.

'This is a lot more friendly.' McGregor smiled.

The questions Justin asked were mainly about Willis's dark energy cosmology project, but he was equally interested in the neutrino work Sophie did and the background radiation research that Linda was involved with. After about half an hour, Justin's questions had dried up. Willis offered to send him some articles to read. This pleased Justin. He said he hadn't decided on the topic of his PhD thesis. Before the winter is over, he'd better decide, thought Willis.

'I'm going for a beer – fancy a glass?' Willis got up. Justin had returned to the kitchen to continue his chores.

McGregor nodded. 'And let's be the first to sit on the comfortable chairs.'

Willis disappeared and returned with two beers.

'You weren't fast enough.' It was Sophie. She'd grabbed one of the couches before McGregor could get there. 'Never mind, there's plenty of room.' She patted the couch. Willis sat beside her. He offered to fetch her a drink, but she declined.

'I've got some news.' She sounded excited. 'I detected my first burst of very high-energy neutrinos.' Sophie emphasised the 'very high' then looked expectantly at Willis.

'That's bloody marvellous. Were you able to work out which direction they came from?'

'Of course I was. But I know why you're asking. And no, it's not a false reading because of today's brownout. I checked. There was a simultaneous detection at a neutrino detector in Japan. They confirmed it. A lot of people, including amateurs, are searching to see if they can image the supernova that caused it.'

'Well done – that calls for a beer.'

At that point, Linda and Gabi turned up for dinner. Sophie told them what she had discovered.

'Since we're in a celebratory mood, I might as well get you two ladies a drink too. What will you have?' Willis listened while they gave him their order.

Willis returned with a tray of drinks for the women and another couple of beers for McGregor and himself. Sophie was busy explaining to McGregor that a supernova is the death of a star: it's an enormous explosion that is always accompanied by a burst of neutrinos.

'I'm a little wiser, but not a lot.' McGregor picked up his beer, clinked it against the other glasses, and took a slug from the can. 'Cheers, many congratulations.'

'We should really play Cliff again, but there hasn't been time to arrange it.' Willis grinned, leaned over and gave Sophie a congratulatory kiss.

When Willis told them about the missing plane from New Zealand, the mood of the evening lowered. There had been four people on board. The plane was carrying much-needed spares for the generators that had been damaged during the surges.

'Winter's coming. I don't mean in a *Games of Thrones* way. The weather's going to get bloody cold. If more surges happen and we don't have replacement parts, we'll be well and truly scuppered.'

'Cheers, everybody.' McGregor was trying to change the subject and cheer everyone up.

'That's marvellous news – congratulations, Sophie.' Justin had arrived at their couch.

Because Justin hadn't been around when Sophie made her announcement, McGregor asked, 'How did you find out?'

'This is a tiny village. Everybody knows everyone else's business.' Justin grinned. 'Besides, it's showing on the galley monitors. Everybody knows.'

In true tradition, they used it as an excuse for a party. Once a crowd had gathered around their couch, they decided to move back to one of the long tables.

Willis nursed his second beer for most of the evening, trying to make it last. He needed a clear head the next morning to devise an action plan with the general. At about 10 p.m., he made his excuses and left. It was Sophie's celebration, and it didn't look like she wanted to leave early. She was enjoying herself too much. Willis kissed her on the cheek and said goodnight.

'I'm going to check the email system for replies from Reilly and Korolev,' Willis said to McGregor.

McGregor stood and followed him. 'I've had enough. I'll come and join you.'

The lights were off in the comms centre when they arrived. A green light flashed on the console, showing that messages were waiting. Willis opened the program, entered his password, then scanned down the list of emails. One email showed 'Mike' as the sender. Willis double-clicked on it. It was from Reilly. It contained two images taken several minutes apart. The first revealed nothing at the target location; the other showed a bright halo of infrared from a position that corresponded to the southern tip of the structure on Boris's image.

'That's odd. It isn't emitting infrared all the time. It must do it in bursts.' Willis envisaged an extractor system that switched on when the heat exceeded a certain threshold, but where was it extracting from? He printed the photograph and passed it to McGregor.

An email had also arrived from Boris Korolev. It read:

Brownout also experienced at Vostok Station. Duration seven minutes but only marginally detected. Sorry to hear about NZ plane. We need to act. If you agree, I will fly in tomorrow 11 a.m. and then on to Progress Station. We will pick up a team there and proceed to the target location. Reply ASAP. BK.

'Bloody hell, things are heating up. Sounds like Boris will go on his own if we don't agree.' Willis looked at McGregor, his brow furrowed. 'We're about to break the Antarctic Treaty.' He pressed Reply, then typed, *Agreed. See you at 11 a.m.*

Willis hit Send and the screen turned blue. He'd done it now.

CHAPTER 25

It was a typical morning on The Ice. The sun was only a few degrees above the horizon. It cast long shadows that made everything look exaggerated and unreal. It was difficult to avoid its stare. The sharp rays penetrated Willis's thoughts, making him squint.

Willis could see for miles with his snow goggles. Without them, he'd be almost blind. He came out of the communications centre on the upper level and turned right onto the observation deck. The platform stood on top of a metal structure, which had stairs leading down to the main entrance. Members of the safety crews had designated the door below the observation platform Destination Alpha, but the other way in, Destination Zulu, was an insignificant set of stairs on the first floor at the other end of the building between wings A1 and A4. The numbering system puzzled Willis.

Before coming out, Willis asked the comms team whether they were expecting a flight at 11 a.m. They were. Willis planned to have breakfast, then return closer to the time. When Boris flew in, Willis would be ready to leave. He'd packed his kit bag.

As Willis walked through the door from the observation deck then along the corridor, he passed the admin offices, the science labs, the computer suite and the medical department before arriving at the dining area. Sophie was already there when he arrived. Willis collected his fry-up and joined her. He hadn't yet told her he would soon leave with Korolev for the other side of the continent. He wasn't looking forward to telling Sophie as he knew she wouldn't be happy. Once he sat down, he said, 'I need to go and investigate where the electrical interference is coming from. I'll probably be away for a few days.'

'I suppose you're going with Korolev. When you're with him, you always get into trouble. You were almost killed the last time.'

'This trip shouldn't be dangerous,' he lied. 'It's only to check out the source of the surges. I promise we'll ask for backup before we do anything stupid.'

Sophie rolled her eyes. 'I don't believe you. I've heard your promises before, but since there's no way that I can stop you from going, I might as well agree. But I want you to promise that you won't take any unnecessary risks.'

'Of course I won't. I promise.'

'I knew you would say that, but can I believe you? When is he coming for you?'

Willis decided not to argue. 'He will land at 11 a.m. After we've had lunch, I suspect we'll take off at about 1

209

p.m. Boris will have missed breakfast to make it here by eleven. When did you eventually go to bed last night?'

'Gone midnight. I promised my mother I'd be in bed before dark.' She grinned at her own joke.

'Hilarious. I suppose you have a delicate head today too?'

'Not at all. It's only you big powerful men who drink too much who get headaches.'

Willis shook his head, then tucked into his bacon. He reckoned he'd got off without too much hassle. After he finished his breakfast, he said, 'I have to see McGregor. I want to leave him some instructions. He'll stay here to run the base while I'm away.'

Willis met up with McGregor, expecting a confrontation. 'Someone needs to stay to manage the base. To make sure it's secure. You're the best man for the job.'

'But I assumed I would go with you. I'm disappointed that you want me to stay here. There are things I could help you with.'

'I would rather you came too, but somebody has to keep the complex up and running.'

McGregor agreed, but he looked far from pleased.

***

At five to eleven, Willis strolled back out on the observation deck. Although he didn't like to admit it, even to himself, he was nervous about flying. What if there was another pulse? Willis planned to see Boris land, but there was nothing he could do if something went wrong. He lifted his binoculars every few seconds and scanned the horizon. Eleven o'clock passed. No sign of Boris. This was unlike him, as he was always prompt to a fault. Willis scoured the ice again. He saw a tiny dark spot, followed by a mass of disturbed snow. Surely he isn't driving? thought Willis. No wonder he's late.

210

The dot got closer and bigger. It didn't look like a vehicle. It was broader and higher. The snow cloud covered its rear, making it difficult to see its shape. The outline got clearer. It was a plane, but travelling very low, hugging the surface of the ice. Crafty. Willis smiled. Boris was skimming the surface of the snow in case radio interference caused the pilot to lose control. Flying this low meant that Boris's plane would land safely on the ice, but flying this low took skill and focus, as the ice was anything but level and smooth. Over time, the wind blows the ice into ridges. Willis was pleased that, as it was early in the season, the wind wasn't strong enough to form the larger ice ridges, called sastrugi. These develop perpendicular to the wind direction, their peaks resembling anvils.

The aircraft was flying slowly – another reason it was later than expected. The plane bounced once, then landed. Korolev and three others alighted. By the time they had reached the ground, Willis was waiting at the entrance of the facility to greet them. They bumped their gloves together in place of a handshake.

'Let's go for some food. I imagine you guys are starving, as you had an early start to get here.' As Willis had expected, none of the plane's crew had eaten breakfast, but they'd stowed some snacks before leaving.

'I've arranged some burgers for you as a special treat.'

Boris's grin was as wide as the Cheshire Cat's.

'You must have used a lot of fuel flying so low and so slowly.'

'We did. We don't have enough to get to Progress Station. Will we be able to refuel here?'

Willis nodded. 'I'll arrange it.' After he ordered the refuelling, McGregor came to join them at their table in the galley. Willis told Boris about the images Reilly had sent. 'They suggest that the heat from the equipment is being vented at intervals rather than in a continuous stream. While one image shows the area cold, another shows a hot spot where one end of the object on your picture is located.' Willis produced the two images and passed them to Boris.

'I agree. Look at this.' He handed a photograph to Willis. 'This is another image our satellite captured. It records the same feature as before, but this time there is a black spot on the opposite side from where Reilly's photo detected heat. This is also an infrared image.'

'That tells us it's cold. It's probably something that's made of metal on the outside, exposed to the low temperatures. It might be a door, a way in.' Willis thought for a moment. 'Might this be what the Chinese proverb was talking about? "Masters open the door but you go through", or words to that effect?'

'That's a distinct possibility, but let's wait until we can inspect it up close.'

'Your burgers are ready.' Justin walked up and placed a tray of food on the table. 'I made these especially for you.'

Boris thanked him. Justin loitered, looking as if he planned to hang around. Willis took him aside. 'Justin, I'm sorry, but we need a little privacy for the next few minutes. Can you leave us for a while until we finish our discussions?'

'No problem, Dr Willis, I understand.' He left them and walked off.

Willis felt guilty for treating him like this, but decided he'd make up for it on another occasion. McGregor caught Willis's eye. 'There's no reason to feel guilty. I'll talk to Justin at dinner, he'll be okay.'

'You've got quite close to Justin.' Willis looked at him and waited for an answer.

'He's easy to get on with.'

'We need to go as soon as possible,' Boris said. 'It's not a short journey at the best of times, but it will take a lot longer…' – he paused to swallow, as he was talking with his mouth full again – '… since we have to travel at snail's pace.'

McGregor changed seats after whispering to Willis that he didn't want to sit beside Boris, where there was always a chance of being sprayed with burger grease.

'As soon as we've eaten, we will leave.' Willis looked at Boris's two companions. They smiled. Perhaps neither spoke English?

Boris seemed to be getting more comfortable on the base. He went to the serving hatch, made himself a black coffee and returned. 'Right. If everybody's ready, let's go.' He made his way towards the double doors, sipping the hot liquid from the cardboard cup.

In a rush, Willis said, 'Goodbye, Callum. Look after the place until I get back. Oh, and will you say goodbye to the ladies for me?'

McGregor grunted, and shuffled off.

***

The pilot took off in the same direction from which he had landed. He swung the aircraft around through one hundred and eighty degrees. Since this necessitated lifting it higher in the air than Willis was comfortable with, his knuckles turned white as he gripped the seat in front of him. But all was well: the manoeuvre was completed without mishap. As he flew towards Progress Station, the pilot continued to hug the ice. The sound inside the plane was deafening. The engine noise was worse than usual, because their whine reflected off the ice and back into the cabin. Willis was developing a headache. There were hours to go before they reached their destination. Part of Willis wished that Boris would take the risk and climb higher, but he knew that would be foolhardy. The small plane skimmed the surface of the ice, rising and lowering with the undulations of the endless whiteness. The pilot struggled continuously with the joystick only feet away from where Willis sat. The door of the cockpit was jammed open and Willis watched as the nose of the plane rose and obscured the horizon with every pull on the joystick.

Boris handed him a large brandy. 'Drink this – the alcohol will help you sleep. It'll make the journey seem shorter. It will also help drown out this damned noise. We will fly this low for the entire trip.'

'I'll take anything that might ease the racket.' He swallowed the fiery liquid in a single gulp. 'I think it's helping already. How much of this stuff do you have with you?' After the second glass, Willis fell asleep.

He woke with a start when the plane's skis bounced off the ice, throwing him from side to side. If he hadn't fastened his seat belt, the force of the impact would have tossed him across the cabin. Boris held on to the arms of his seat, frozen with fear. His knuckles were as white as his face. Without realising it, Willis had been clinging to the seat in front of him. The plane came to a sudden halt, its nose buried deep in the snow.

'That was surge, General.' The veins stood out on the pilot's face, he had been gripping the joystick with such force. 'The controls stopped responding. I couldn't raise or lower elevators.'

Willis was so numb with shock; it took several seconds before he realised the guy could speak English.

'You did a good job, Leo. You saved the plane.' Korolev patted his pilot on the back.

'How far are we from Progress Station?' Willis asked.

Boris shook his head. 'Too far to get helicopter. What is it you say in English? We're the pigs in the middle now and just over halfway there. Leo, can you radio the base? Let them know what's happened. We'd better start shovelling snow.'

There were half a dozen shovels, two more than needed. Willis, Korolov, Leo the pilot, and the co-pilot, fastened their parkas and slid down the emergency chute onto the ice. It looked useless. The plane's props were buried under a deep, icy blanket of snow. At least ten feet of snow had accumulated covering the propellors and part of the plane's nose.

Willis picked up some particles of snow and let them fall between the fingers of his gloves. 'Because we're far from the centre of the Antarctic Plateau, the flakes are fresher and not so compacted, so we should be able to move the snow without too much effort. If we can shift enough snow to clear the rotors, we could try to start the engine. If it starts, it might be possible to use the propellers to blow away some of the rest of the snow.'

'Da! Good idea, Brad,' Boris said. 'Let's concentrate on clearing props. Even if Brad's idea doesn't work, we'll still need to switch on the engines soon to stop the fuel pipes freezing.'

To describe it as cold outside was an understatement, but within ten minutes they had warmed up enough to work. Their goggles kept steaming up as they worked, so they had to keep raising them to demist them. They tried to move the snow near the bottom of the props first. As they removed each shovelful, another fell from above to replace it. It seemed a thankless task, but there was no other solution, so they had to keep going. The air temperature was only a few tens of degrees below zero, but the added wind chill made it almost unbearable.

'The wind is blowing strongly from behind us,' Willis said, looking at the wind carrying the white powder back again. 'But it's taking some snow back to where we just shovelled it from. Is my imagination playing tricks on me, or does the top of the snow look as though it's getting lower?' After another hour, he stopped and looked up. 'It's at least four feet lower than it was an hour ago. We've moved a lot of crap, so that's encouraging.' But after three hours of toiling, the men had slowed down. All four seemed to be struggling, but they knew that if they stopped, that would be the end. They needed to sleep. They were feeling warm now, and the sensation of being cosy was wonderful. Surely a ten-minute rest wouldn't hurt?

Willis looked around. 'You're slowing down. If you go any slower, you'll stop. I know you need to rest, but your breaks are coming more often. They are getting longer each time.'

Boris was leaning on his shovel, staring into the whiteness. Leo was doing something similar, but his eyes were closed. Boris's other comrade was leaning, motionless, against the fuselage of the plane.

Then there was a roar and a rumble. They jumped to attention. Their eyes were wide in disbelief.

The wall of white was no more.

Willis shouted, 'The wind has eroded the wall of snow on the far side! It's travelled over the top of the ridge. It's blown it away, crystal by crystal. Let's get back inside.'

The slow but steady katabatic wind, gravity-fed from somewhere behind them on the plateau blew snow particles into their backs. The breeze was strong for this time of year, but who was complaining? It was saving their lives.

They climbed back into the plane, but the ordeal wasn't over yet. The plane's front was pointing down. They couldn't rotate the props until they had raised the nose.

'Let's bring the tail down,' Willis suggested. 'Push these crates back – shove them up to the rear.'

The four men started to manhandle the first crate. After fifteen minutes, they'd moved all six containers. The plane still wasn't level.

'Leo, go and sit in the pilot's seat while the rest of us stand in the back. Now jump. Not like that.'

They were jumping out of synch.

'All together, on a count of three, one, two, three…'

They jumped. The plane lurched. Its tail dropped, and the nose rose ten feet. They stopped and held their breath, waiting for it to tip back into its original position. But it didn't. They remained where they stood to keep the props pointing upward.

'Switch on the engine and rev it up.' Willis closed his eyes and crossed his fingers. The engines burst into life. Leo adjusted the feathering of the propellers for forward thrust, but set it on minimum. The plane lurched forward, driving the skis up a ramp in the ice. It held fast. Leo revved even harder and increased the feathering. Clouds of loose frozen pellets raced by the cabin windows. After five minutes, the barrier of snow that remained covering the nose of the plane had all but disappeared.

'It's gone!' Leo shouted. 'It worked.'

They moved to the cockpit window. A gap had opened up in front of them, but it was still impassable.

'The remaining bank of snow is lower than the wings. Rev the right engine and idle the left.' Willis was chancing his arm now. He was glad of the flying training that Reilly had given him for use in emergencies. If they could force the plane to turn using the engines, they might get clear from this mess. Leo did as he instructed. The skis creaked noisily as the nose tried to turn to port. Then they ploughed through the snow. The plane swung around until it faced in the opposite direction. Leo cut the starboard engine. The plane stopped. Its skis were sitting in the tracks they had gouged when it dropped from the sky.

'Strap in.' Leo's command came over the tannoy. He revved the engines and the plane juddered forward. The ski struggled to stay in the original ruts. As the skis released themselves from the mound of ice they had created while turning, the fuselage jolted, its steel supports creaking and threatening to break. Finally, the joystick shook and vibrated. Their speed increased. The vibrations got stronger, reached a crescendo. Then they stopped. They were airborne. A cheer filled the cabin. The four men congratulated Leo on his piloting skills. Leo steered the aircraft around, navigating towards their intended destination.

Boris turned to Willis. 'It was you who got us out – thank you,' he whispered, taking Willis's gloved hand in both of his and shaking it.

CHAPTER 26

Although it would only take three more hours to reach Progress, there was no way that Willis could relax during the second part of the flight. The chassis continued to vibrate. Leo was taking no chances; he was still hugging the snow. Willis adjusted a little to the perpetual shaking, but his body ached for peace and he longed for bed – any bed would do, as long as it was quiet and motionless. It was an old plane. Its cabin was spartan. There was no lining on the walls, which showed the bare struts that gave the fuselage its strength. A lot of heat would disappear through the exposed surface, but it didn't matter; the cabin filled with warmth. The heaters were blasting out hot air.

Although Willis's eyes closed, sleep eluded him. He lay with his head leaning on his shoulder. Doing this reduced the rattling. He thought again about who was causing the surges and their apparent naivety. They must know that they would be under scrutiny. That someone would come to investigate. Why hadn't Progress Station investigated them already? Or the Australian base? Davis Station wasn't that far away. But this was all speculation. He would find out soon enough.

Willis let his thoughts run loose. He fantasised about a future with Sophie, about how they would live together, how they would reconcile their career conflicts. But no solution appeared. He struggled with the dream, but reality kept intervening.

And intervene it did. Leo announced via the tannoy, 'We're about to swing around, ready to touch down.' The radio crackled. Then he spoke in fast Russian. Willis picked up only the odd word.

'Prepare to land' was his last announcement.

Landing on wheels on a proper runway is the epitome of smoothness compared with landing on ice on skis in an old plane. Making contact with the ice jarred every bone in a person's body because these old skis had little suspension, if any. Willis readied himself for the inevitable jolt. The cockpit radio barked something in Russian. The message sounded urgent.

It was.

Leo pulled hard on the joystick, aborting the touch-down. Willis heard him let out a long slow release of breath. 'We have problem. We have damaged one of skis. I am to perform a fly-by while ground crew make inspection.' Leo raised the nose of the plane, swung around and made a low pass over the station. The plane shook as Leo lowered his altitude to about thirty feet. Willis wished he could see what was happening as well as listen to it, but the cabin had no windows. Leo lifted the nose preparing for another fly-by.

Once completed, he travelled in a wide loop, circling the site. They waited. Finally, the radio crackled into life. A babble of Russian followed. '*Da, da, okay, da.*'

Willis could only hear Leo's reply. '*Spaseeba, okay, Spaseeba, tovarishch.*'

Leo opened the throttle and flew to the other side of the base. 'One of our skis eez broken. It's almost torn off, so we can't touch down. I have been instructed to land along a line of bulldozed snow and to attempt to lower faulty ski on the mound. If I can hold plane straight, I should be able to bring it to a halt before we run out of snow, so make sure you're strapped in.'

The plane circled and reduced its speed. Leo brought it down gradually. Willis felt the ski hit the line of ice. The plane rebounded then came down again, harder this time. The plane was travelling too fast. It bounced a second time. Leo let it ride into the air. He would try again, but this time coming from the opposite direction.

The plane shuddered. Leo reduced its airspeed much lower than Willis considered safe. There was a grinding sound and a tearing of metal. Willis assumed it was the faulty ski ripping off. They could feel ice scraping against the belly of the craft. Suddenly, the aircraft swung through ninety degrees and they skidded sideways. The slide seemed to last forever. The plane skidded broadways, its left wingtip buried deep in the snow, before coming to a halt.

Leo deserved their thanks, yet again, for saving their lives. They sat in silence for several minutes. It was true silence. The engines had stopped. The persistent vibration was gone. Then they flung the door open and piled out onto the welcoming snow. Being back on solid ground was a relief. They grouped around Leo and patted him on the back.

Within minutes a train of skidoo-style vehicles drove up, each pulling a trailer. The men climbed on and they sped towards the base. Once inside, they stripped off their damp clothing. Warm cocoa and generous glasses of vodka followed. Korolev introduced Willis to a tall, heavy man with long black shaggy hair. 'This is Dr Nabokov. The good doctor is the boss of Progress Station and is in charge of everything that happens on the base. Anton, this is Dr Brad Willis – he is astronomer and a very good friend.' Korolev told Anton about their near-death experiences: first, the forced landing; second, landing with only one ski. Anton seemed incredulous. He offered his hand to Willis. 'You look exhausted, Dr Willis. You must be ready for bed?'

'I am, but please call me Brad. We have lots of questions to ask before we go, if we may?'

'Go ahead. I will answer as many as I can.'

Willis was keen to know about the times of the pulses at Progress, but Anton surprised him by saying, 'What pulses? We have observed no pulses or radio interference whatsoever.'

Willis's eyes widened, and he stared at Anton. 'The base is so close to the suspected source – you must have noticed some interference.'

'If there was any disruption like you describe, we would have detected it, but there hasn't been, I can assure you of that.'

Words eluded Willis for several seconds. 'This throws everything we suspect on its head. We might need to think again. Maybe my arithmetic is wrong? Maybe the source is somewhere else? No, I double-checked my maths. I'm certain that my calculations are correct.'

'You look puzzled, Brad.' Anton glanced at Willis, a disbelieving look in his eyes, while waving his hands in the direction of the bedrooms. 'You also look tired. Sleep. Everything will make more sense after you have slept.'

'You are right. I would love to fall into bed.' The vodka was affecting his thinking process. 'I will go to my room and crash out. Tomorrow is another day.'

They directed Willis and Boris to their rooms. The bed was very inviting, but Willis couldn't drop off. If you get too tired, this can happen, he told himself. On the ceiling, there was a circular lamp. Beside it, a small fleck of paint was peeling off, which absorbed Willis's attention as he struggled with the problem. Why had no interference been detected at Progress Station? The question repeated itself over and over in his mind, and he kept staring at the tiny mark in the paintwork until his eyes closed and he fell into a deep, comatose sleep.

***

Willis awoke the next morning to someone knocking on his door. He staggered out of bed, half asleep, and opened it.

'It's noon. I left you as long as I could.' Korolev stood there, grinning. 'I'm sorry, but Nabokov has arranged a trip out to the suspect site in an hour, so you will need to eat and get ready fast.'

Willis nodded, his eyes still closed, and shut the door. He took a quick shower under one of the few spray heads – the Russian base was much more spartan than the Amundsen–Scott Station, then he headed for the dining area. At first, he took several wrong turns. His head still hurt, making him wish he'd paid more regard to the direction he'd taken last night, but the sounds of cutlery and plates rattling helped to guide him to the canteen. Korolev stood up and waved to attract Willis's attention. 'Sit here.' He pointed to the seat opposite him. 'I will fetch you something to eat.'

Willis looked around; it was almost a replica of the galley at Amundsen–Scott. The tables and chairs were identical. Even the couches at the far end were the same colour. He wondered whether a common contractor fitted out all the stations on The Ice. Boris returned and placed a plate of meat in front of him. It was as though he could read his mind. 'The requirements at all bases are similar, so they all look alike.'

Willis was so ravenous that he gulped his food down. It was all gone before Boris had time to ask how it compared to the food at the South Pole Station.

'I ate it too fast, so I have no idea. If I eat here again, I'll let you know.' He wiped his face.

'Anton has supplied some fresh outer clothes for you, so there's no need to run back for your own.' Boris indicated a coat rack behind him. 'They will fit. I gave him your approximate size. But we'd better go – he will be waiting.'

'I feel much better now I've eaten. I feel fit and ready to tackle the day.' If Willis had known what he was about to face, he might have thought differently.

Willis didn't recognise the truck that waited for them, but it looked like a Tucker Sno-Cat. If he wasn't on a Russian base, it could have been. A track sat at each corner of the monster vehicle, with five drive wheels powering each mighty track. The cab was bright orange, and twice Willis's height. A second Sno-Cat appeared and lined up behind the first.

Willis put a foot on one track and lifted himself so that his other boot could reach the short step that would bring him within distance of the cabin door. Once inside, he offered Boris a hand. When the door closed, the warmth was reassuring. Because they were wearing outdoor clothes, he wondered if he would get too warm. No sooner had the thought occurred to him than the answer came.

'It's almost a hundred-kilometre trip, so I'd take off your outer clothes if I were you. Before we climb out again, we will have plenty of time to dress, so you might as well be comfortable for the ride. It will take about six hours,' Anton said. He led the way by stripping off his parka. He continued, 'The plan is to stop two or three kilometres away from our destination, then continue on foot. That will prevent anyone from hearing our approach. There will be an hour's hike, in soft snow, to reach our goal. We aren't carrying arms, and I don't expect anyone we meet to have any weapons either.'

The Antarctic Treaty states that no arms are allowed on the continent.

'We have, however, brought some "tools" that we might need.' He threw a tarpaulin back to reveal several large adjustable spanners and torque wrenches. 'Just in case we need them.'

The trip was smooth for a vehicle of this size, thanks to its tracks, which extended further in front and behind its length. The surface wasn't as flat here as at Pole. It was also windier – Willis assumed, because they were nearer the coast. Despite the speed of the wind, the visibility was excellent. In the warm cab, he leaned against a window. Once they were on foot, things would be very different. He imagined the cold air biting into his face and shuddered. Although all directions leading away from the Pole were north, Willis always thought of this area as being the north of Antarctica. Maps always showed McMurdo Station at the bottom, which reinforced this erroneous idea. He was seeing more of the continent than he'd planned to when he left England; then again, he'd also been on The Ice longer than he'd expected. The days came and went: how many had passed since he'd been here? He didn't have a clue. When he returned to base, he would check the calendar.

The view was beautiful here. He could make out subtle shades of blues, purples, lilacs and mauves. The snow was a vivid white, but the sun's rays refracted through its transparent surfaces and, like crystals in a chandelier, they scattered the light into a multitude of hues. The low sun sparkled off individual snow and ice particles on the ground, creating a field of fairy lights flashing on and off as the Sno-Cat moved forward. Each Sno-Cat stirred up a cloud of ice and snow particles in its wake and the sunlight illuminated it, producing a rainbow of colour that formed an arch ranging from violet through to red. Parts of the rainbow faded and then reappeared as the swirling powder caught, then missed the sun's rays.

Anton's voice dragged him from his daydream. 'There are crevasses in this area – they can be invisible. They get covered by moving ice and drifting snow, so we need to drive slower than the vehicle is capable of going. Even with these large tracks, it can come, how do you say, a cropper if it dips into one.' At that moment, the Sno-Cat lurched, throwing them in the air. They landed with a crash.

'Just like that.'

Until the tracks found their grip, the engine roared, then the Sno-Cat reversed. 'That was a narrow one. The bigger crevasses are the dangerous ones.'

Two hours later, they shut down the engines. 'It's on foot from here,' Anton said, taking a deep breath and furrowing his brow. 'There are some long backpacks under the seat. Please take a pack each and put one of our "tools" in it. We might need them.' Willis put on his outdoor clothes, then placed a large adjustable wrench in a backpack and dropped it onto the snow.

The snow was as flaky as Anton had promised. Willis's feet sank into the drifts and walking became slow and laboured. Anton walked ahead, prodding a long pole into the snow, searching for crevasses.

After a while, the going became even more difficult. The snow was deeper; it reached halfway up Willis's calves. Despite his thick scarf, the bitter air was biting. In front of them, the land was barren. Behind, their footprints disappeared as soon as they had formed. Even with darkened goggles, the harsh light irritated Willis's eyes. They watered, and the cold threatened to freeze his tears against his cheeks. This was the first long trip he'd undertaken outside the South Pole base. He wasn't finding it easy. Willis considered himself fit, but this took more energy than he wanted to spend. Boris was also struggling, but the man leading the way was coping well, as were the other members of his team.

The figures following Anton started to straggle, staggering off the straight line made by his footprints. Anton stopped and shouted for them to get back into position. Willis copied the guy in front, but he drifted off the correct path once more and Willis tracked behind him. To return to the track left by Anton, the man ahead of him swerved to his left, so Willis followed him. The frozen powder crackled beneath his feet, then he skidded on a patch of yellow bird guano in the snow.

Instantly, darkness engulfed him. A feeling of weightlessness pervaded his body. He was falling.

An intense pain inside his chest brought immediate unconsciousness.

CHAPTER 27

Feeling returned slowly to Willis, as did consciousness. As did the pain in his chest. Only the shallowest of breathing was possible or the agony intensified, threatening to return him once more to unconsciousness. Even though he was conscious, he was having difficulty seeing. All around him was semi-darkness. White ice glowed above his head, turning to deep indigo the deeper it reached. He turned his head and his face brushed against the chilly dampness of melting snow. Then the realisation penetrated his stunned senses. He'd fallen into a snow-covered crevasse. He strained to see upwards. The narrow slit of light that seemed miles above him confirmed his worst fears. His heart was thumping in his ears so hard that he could hear nothing else. Taking shallow breaths demanded all the concentration he could muster.

For what felt like an eternity, Willis remained motionless, hoping the pain in his chest might lessen. It was easing, but only slightly. Perhaps, he thought, I'm thinking more logically, but how am I qualified to decide what is, or is not, logical in a nightmare world like this? Warmth replaced the cold. Willis dreamed of warmth and sleep, but he shook his head – he knew he had to avoid falling asleep at all costs. Sleep would mean the end for him. The outcome would be inevitable anyhow; it was just a matter of time. Why not close my eyes now? he thought. Get it over with. Yes, that's what to do – sleep, a warm, gentle sleep…

Then something hit Willis on the back of the skull. Something moving, he thought, something alive, something furry? I'm under attack. But the sensation stopped. Then he felt it again, this time on the other side of his head. Then again. He reached out and struck it with his hand. He caught it. Once more, he strained to look up. Willis made out Anton's silhouette across the slit of visible sky above his head, then he saw the long, meandering outline of a rope. Willis pulled the lifeline towards him, threaded it under his armpits and secured it across his chest. Then he became aware of a hissing noise. It was becoming louder. A crackling, the sound of ice rubbing together. A stark realisation flooded into his brain. The damned ice was shifting. The crevasse was closing… Slowly, but still closing…

Gently at first, the rope was being pulled from above, then more strongly. It was soon taut, tightening around his rib cage, restricting his breathing, making his breathing more difficult. His discomfort worsened as Anton heaved on the tightening lifeline. Willis was stuck fast. None of Anton's efforts was effective. Willis was trapped between the sides of the crevasse. The walls that were preventing him from falling deeper into the abyss were now preventing his release. His foot snagged on something, but he couldn't see what. The padding in his boot stopped him from feeling where the restriction was. He tugged. Nothing happened. His foot wouldn't move. The ice continued to hiss, reminding him that it was still moving. What had begun as a gentle crackling developed into a cacophony of sighs and screams from a choir of out-of-tune sopranos.

Then the wall pressing against his stomach and chest moved. It shifted inches, perhaps two. And in the wrong direction; it was tighter. This forced more air from his already compressed lungs. The restricted supply of oxygen was draining Willis's strength. Pins and needles began in his fingers and toes, then spread up his arms and down his legs.

Suddenly, the crushing pressure on his chest vanished. The ice disappeared. And the slit of light from the sky flashed before his eyes. Once more, he was weightless and falling. The walls of ice that had been his saviour separated by several inches, releasing their hold on him, letting him fall into the black void below. As he plummeted, Willis's head smashed against the rock-hard ice. He dropped for over six feet. After that, tension returned to the rope, which stretched and contracted like a rubber band, bouncing Willis's aching body upwards. As the line slackened a second time, he plunged again. When the rope finally took his weight, the pain in his ribs became excruciating as his crudely tied knot tightened around his rib cage, squeezing more air from his starving lungs. He lapsed into a state of semi-consciousness. But he could see himself moving towards the light. So, this was how it felt. He'd read that death started with travelling towards a bright light. The glare approached ever faster. His body crashed against the ice, making him spin on the end of his thin lifeline. The blue glow of the crevasse gave way to the blinding whiteness of the ice, and dazzling sunshine.

Anton and Korolev pulled him over the last few feet of the chasm and let him lie on the ice. Anton removed the rope around Willis's chest. Then the thunderous roar of crashing ice made the men turn towards the crevasse. Willis's heart sank as he watched the ice close, spraying a cloud of fine snow particles into the sky.

That was the last thing Willis remembered. Pain returned to his chest with increased intensity, forcing him to slip once more into unconsciousness.

***

Periods of lethargy punctuated by brief intervals of total awareness accompany the exit from any comatose state, while images of silhouetted figures move across backgrounds illuminated by soft, unfocused lights. The outlines approach and recede with hypnotic regularity. Sounds are exaggerated and loud. These quick observations last only minutes before the effort becomes too great and the person slips into a relief-giving sleep.

Willis experienced all these sensations during the hour he was unconscious. When his eyes opened, he explored the heavy bandages around his ribs. Even the slightest pressure on his chest was painful. He tried to sit up. He was back in the Sno-Cat. Anton helped to lift him into a sitting position. 'Take it easy. We thought we'd lost you.'

'Thank you for saving my life. As you pulled me up to safety, I could see your face. How long have I been out for?'

'Over an hour. Now that you're awake, we can risk the shaking of the transporter as we drive back to the base.'

'No way. Before they kill any more people, we have to discover the source of these surges. We carry on.' He swung his legs off the bench seat in the Sno-Cat and stood up. Pain stabbed his chest. 'I suspect I have bruised a couple of ribs,' he said with a grimace. 'But I want the investigation to go ahead.' The pain in his ribs was intense, almost overwhelming, but he struggled to overcome the agony, he said, 'There's no point returning to Progress just to come back another day, so let's stick with it, finish the job we've started.'

It took little to convince Boris and Anton that they should proceed. 'Right, people, let's get moving. We've still a long way to travel.'

Anton clapped his hands. The Sno-Cats' engines stopped and everyone jumped to attention. They'd left the engines running to keep the cabins warm. Willis tried to fit the rucksack that Anton gave him onto his back. Anton lent him a hand to draw the straps over his shoulders. As he let it go, its weight sent a racking pain through his chest. He closed his eyes until it subsided.

Willis climbed down out of the transporter. The snow that once was soft now felt hard and unyielding, making every step he took vibrate through his body, jarring his damaged ribs. He trailed after Anton and Boris so that neither could see him grimace in agony. Willis remembered Anton saying that it would be an hour on foot from here to the site. He hoped he would make it.

Willis kept falling behind, and needed to speed up every so often to catch up. The more he walked, the less he felt the discomfort. His body must be producing its own home-made analgesics, he thought. After about forty-five minutes, Boris announced they should be almost there and confirmed that the source was in this general area, so they spread themselves out to cover more ground. Except for Willis, that is. He stayed close to Boris. He didn't want to risk dropping into another crevasse. Twenty minutes passed; nothing was visible. An additional fifteen flashed past. Everyone was beginning to think that the location was wrong, so they stretched out further. After a few hundred yards, one of Anton's men waved his arms, gesticulating. The group closed around his position. Fifty yards ahead, the ice sloped downwards. Anton beckoned to two guys, and they went to investigate. Willis joined him. He wanted to see for himself. As they drew nearer, it was clear that the snow sloped upwards at first. Ruts scarred its surface, caused by tracks similar to those left by the Sno-Cat. They were old but, despite fresh snow accumulating and obscuring their outlines, still partially visible. They followed the trails over the rise in the snow and down the other side. Anton halted at the top of the slope and raised his arm. The men following him stopped. Before him, stood a large, smooth, shiny vertical door made of metal and set into the ice. Willis estimated it was over thirty feet high, and about the same wide. They approached it, expecting it to open or an alarm to sound as they got closer. Nothing happened.

Willis placed his hand against the door. He hit it. It clanged and shuddered. But no one appeared to be inside. It was painted a stark white, blending in with the dazzling snow. Now, Anton was signalling to the rest of his group. They stood and stared in awe. Anton pointed to a member of his patrol and waved his arm. The man gave him his backpack. Anton took out an infrared viewer. Before passing it to Willis and Boris, he glanced through it. Willis then put the instrument to his eye and saw the door: jet black in infrared. This told him it was colder than the snow that surrounded it – much colder. A roar emanated from somewhere close by. Willis swung around to catch it in the viewer. A plume of white steam ejected from the ice several hundred yards ahead. This gas was hot – it was white in the infrared viewer. Willis signalled to Anton to come with him, and led the way to where the gas had originated.

Meanwhile, Anton instructed two of his men to follow the ruts the opposite way, away from the door, hoping they might lead them to their source. Then he caught up with Willis and followed him. As they got closer, they could see a dark circle in the snow. The snow surrounding it was melting. After another fifty paces, the cause became apparent. Twin exhausts, eight feet in diameter, sat a few inches below the snow. As they approached, they burst into life, spraying hot air upwards, disturbing the ice and snow and blowing a white plume of steam over sixty feet into the sky.

Willis moved closer to study them better. As he leaned over the edge and looked in, the enormous blades of the fan slowed to a standstill. Through the blades he could see a massive horizontal cylindrical chamber about thirty yards in diameter. He assumed it reached back towards the door, and it probably stretched a similar distance in the opposite direction. 'It's huge.' He turned to Anton. 'We need to find a way to gain entry.'

'Unless we can get them to open that door, or we blow it up, I can't find a way in.' At that moment, a figure wearing a white coat appeared in the chamber below. They watched him check a control panel and write something on a sheet of paper he carried attached to a clipboard. Anton asked, 'Is he Chinese?'

'I don't know. He's too far away to tell. Can you make out what he's doing?'

Anton strained his eyes, but he couldn't see enough to be sure. 'It looks like he's setting something up. He's entering information from his chart into a keyboard on a control panel. Now he's moving away, out of sight. He's moved towards the far end of the tunnel.'

Anton put his hands to his face to shout at the figure but Will put his hand on his arm and said, 'Let's not alert them to our presence. Not yet. Let's go back and find out if we know where the tracks originated.'

They were about twenty feet from the exhaust when the air began to vibrate. Their faces started to tingle. Walking became tricky. They lost their balance and fell to the snow. Lights flashed before their eyes. Their ears buzzed. They tasted imaginary flavours in their mouths. When it stopped, they staggered.

'Feel this.' Willis held the metal tag on his zip against Anton's cheek. 'It's hot. We've just experienced our first up-close surge.'

'Bloody hell, we're lucky we're not dead. Such a powerful burst of radio frequency might have melted our brains as though we had been in a microwave oven.'

Willis nodded, 'Now we know that the interference we felt elsewhere was due to an intense surge of radio frequency.'

They made their way back to the rest of the team. One man said, 'The tracks ran out about two hundred yards further on.'

Another man said, 'The snow covered them about a couple of hundred yards on. We have no way to find out where they came from, but they appeared to be going in the general direction of the Russian and Chinese bases.'

Willis walked up to Boris. 'We'll need to try something else. Have you recovered after our little adventure?'

'What little adventure?' Boris screwed up his brow. He gave him a quizzical look.

'What we just felt – the tingling, the buzzing, the flashing lights.'

Boris looked even more confused. 'What are you talking about, my good friend? I have seen no lights or felt any tingling.'

CHAPTER 28

It was unbelievable. The surge had disorientated Anton and Willis: they had lost their balance yet here, only five hundred yards away, the men had felt nothing. 'There must be protection preventing the interference from coming in this direction,' Willis said. 'It would need to be huge and very efficient.' He was talking to Anton. 'We saw the man who entered the settings into the control panel head out of view. The shield has to be somewhere to the right of where we were standing, and much closer to the door.'

'We have to get inside. What if we do the obvious thing? Bang on the door again?' Anton took a big spanner out of his rucksack, approached the large sheet of alloy that covered the entrance, and waved to several of his team to follow. He banged on the door. He waited a few seconds, then repeated the procedure. No response. Anton tried again.

Still, nothing. All three men hammered on the metal at the same time, and continued to do so for several minutes. Dents appeared on the smooth surface and paint flaked off. The coating had become brittle in the sub-zero temperature. Then they stopped and listened. In the vain hope of feeling some vibration, Anton put his gloved hand against the metal. Zilch. 'We need to return to base. We'll bring some cutting equipment.'

Willis was getting impatient. 'It's getting late – you lost time rescuing me. Then it took an hour to hike here. It'll take another hour to walk to the vehicles. If we leave, heaven knows what will happen here. The men inside could disappear, or they might even destroy the site. I have a plan. How much rope do you have?'

'Lots. What do you have in mind?'

'It should be possible to abseil down through the extractor fans.'

Anton grimaced. 'We have no belays. We must have connectors to make abseiling safe.'

'You have carabiners for climbing on ice and glaciers. We will use them instead.'

Anton shook his head and frowned. 'What if the blades start turning while we are dropping? It's too dangerous.'

'I reckon the fans kick in every fifteen minutes. But let's time it to make sure. I'm also certain that we can predict the surges. As soon as we spot someone approaching the control panel to set it up, we will abort.'

Willis had dismissed Anton's principal objections but he was not one hundred percent certain that the pain in his chest wouldn't prevent him from taking part.

'Okay, let's do it,' Anton said. 'We need to get the rope and the carabiners from the vehicles, and that will still take a couple of hours.'

'If you drive the trucks right up to the entrance, you'll save time. If they've already heard us, they'll know we're here.'

Anton selected two of his younger, fitter men and sent them to fetch the equipment. Willis headed towards the extractors to time their outbursts. Because Boris wanted to see the inside of this facility for himself, he accompanied him.

***

According to Willis's estimations, the fans switched on every fifteen minutes. He'd timed them five times before the Sno-Cats returned.

The ropes were thicker than those used for abseiling: two strands barely fitted inside the carabiners and they rubbed together, but that would slow down their descent a little, making it safer. Willis hoped that a swift drop wouldn't become necessary. To make sure the pain was still there, he pushed on his chest. It was.

So far, he had spotted no weapons, but he had seen only one man, and he was a researcher. But there might be armed guards further along the tunnel. As he had other problems to concentrate on, Willis put these thoughts out of his mind. While he lowered himself, he would have to lean back and let the rope tighten around his chest and back. That would hurt.

Willis said, 'We need to drop down the rope one at a time. I volunteer to go first – not out of any false sense of bravery, but because I want to get to the control panel to disable it. While men are dangling in the air, we daren't risk a surge happening.'

They attached a rope to the outside frame of each extractor: this allowed two abseils to take place, one through each fan. They waited for the next outburst of activity to happen, then threw the ropes into the extractor.

Willis drew a deep breath. It might be his last until he hit the floor. He stepped down inside the cylinder that housed the extractor and slipped between its stationary blades. Gravity took charge and pulled him downwards. The rope squeezed his lungs, forcing the air out, and his throat made a sick gurgling sound. The sooner he reached the ground, the sooner the agony would go away. Willis released his grip on the nylon as much as he dared, letting his fall speed up to the maximum the carabiner would allow. He stopped inhaling for seconds at a time, as this reduced the pain that was invading his rib cage and back. At one point, he breathed out. The rope tightened around his chest, restricting his respiration even further. Breathing in again would cause excessive discomfort. He stopped inhaling for the rest of the fall.

His feet hit the floor harder than he expected. His ribs complained. Willis disentangled himself from the rope, leaving it free for the next abseiler. He took a deep breath and walked towards the control panel. As he gulped in oxygen, his lungs felt as if they were on fire. Every breath burnt its way in. At first, he thought his damaged chest was causing the burning sensation when he breathed, but soon he realised that the air was hot – searingly hot. The need for the two extractor fans was obvious. The equipment was creating a tremendous amount of wasted energy. Willis was certain that he would meet nobody else in this room. Unless it was absolutely necessary, they would avoid entering this part of the cavern.

He went around to the back of the controller, where a row of circuit-breakers lined the rear wall of its cabinet. To be on the safe side, Willis ran his finger along them and tripped every single switch.

Three other men were now on the ground. The fourth and fifth were on their way. He made out the familiar shapes of Anton and Boris as they came over to join him. Willis looked at the cavern. It was hundreds of yards long and had been hewn out of the ice. The stark whiteness seemed to stretch for miles. What Willis assumed was a huge Tesla coil dominated the centre of the tunnel. This was a device for transmitting electricity. Connected to its front was something that looked like a maser. This is like a laser, but works at radio instead of light frequencies. Was this how they had achieved such an immense power output? Although Willis didn't understand the physics, he imagined the Tesla coil and the maser working synergistically to achieve enormous bursts of energy.

He walked down the length of the long, thin coil. At the furthest end of the chamber was an enormous piece of shiny steel. 'This is a parabolic reflector; it will reflect the radiation forward and into the heart of the continent.'

Since the steel sheet didn't reach the wall on either side, he moved around its edge. Behind it, a mesh of steel covered the width of the chamber.

'And this is a Faraday cage. That's what it is – a giant Faraday cage,' Willis said. 'That's why your men and Boris didn't feel the surge. The cage absorbs radio waves, to prevent them from passing through.' He saw a huge earth connector attached to it. Its end disappeared deep into the ice. 'Marvellous – this is a marvellous work of engineering. It must have taken millions of dollars to finance.'

Straight ahead, a sliding door led through the mesh. Willis signalled for Boris and Anton to follow. In front of him were a well-equipped laboratory and a heavy engineering workshop. The facility was behind a triple-glazed glass barrier intended to help the air conditioning to cope. Willis made out eight men, each in a white coat, all busy with tasks of various sorts. They seemed oblivious to their presence. They looked Eastern, maybe Chinese, and they weren't armed. What was more surprising was that Willis saw no soldiers. This had all the hallmarks of a military installation, but no guards.

While they decided what to do, Willis, Anton and Boris formed a huddle. This laboratory seemed too well equipped to be a civilian undertaking, and Anton and Boris fidgeted uncomfortably, voicing their concerns about the apparent lack of any armed protection. They saw the underside of the steel door they'd hammered on earlier. There was nowhere a guard or armed man might hide.

'We've come all this way,' Boris said. 'It's too late to withdraw now.' Like everyone else's, Boris's face was dripping with sweat.

'I, for one, don't fancy climbing back up that rope.' Willis rubbed his chest.

They slid open the door in the triple-glazed wall, then crept in, under cover of twelve six-foot-tall computer cabinets that stood in a row, thick communication cables snaking behind them and connecting them. Cool air-conditioned air hit their faces. Their sweat chilled their skin. A loud drone emanating from the powerful air-con filled the workshop. The idea was to get as far into the room as possible before the men in white coats saw them. If there were any armed guards, they would have a better chance of spotting them first.

'Why isn't this place protected?' Anton kept repeating the question every few minutes. 'It doesn't make any sense.'

Now concealed behind the rack of computer cabinets, Anton's group awaited his instructions. 'I don't like this. I don't like this one bit.' Anton signalled his guys to follow him as he stepped out into full view of the white-coated men. Anton held his rucksack containing the wrench out horizontally in front of him. The white coats froze and raised their arms.

'Don't shoot,' pleaded a lanky Chinese man.

'Who are you? What are you doing here?' Anton asked.

'We research facility,' the tall Chinese man spoke again in broken English. 'We work for Hōng Corporation in Shenzhen. Here, we do experiments so we not interfere with anyone near us. We produce much electrical noise, so must avoid other people equipment. Who are you? What you do in our facility?'

Willis nudged Anton in the ribs and pointed to the rack of computers. Above the central computer sat a prominent LED display that was counting down in real time. It read 10:33. 'It's a timer. That can only mean one thing. This place is about to blow up.'

'Open the door. Now.' Anton aimed his rucksack at the tall man, then waved it towards the exit.

'But … the cold…'

'Open the exit,' Anton shouted.

The Chinese man walked to the side of the massive steel panel and pressed a button. Like an oversized garage door, it swung up. Damn. Behind it was yet another door – that was why no one had heard their banging on the outside. That, and the hum from the air conditioning. Then Willis spotted four security cameras, positioned at each corner of the room. Perhaps that's how they knew we were here; perhaps that's how they knew to trigger the timer. He passed

243

a workbench on which lay an open loose-leaf folder. He picked it up and tucked it under his arm.

Anton ushered everyone inside the gap. He signalled for the next door to open. 'Get it opened, now.' The Chinese man pressed another button. The first door began to close, but at a snail's pace. Willis hoped they'd have enough time to escape before the place exploded. Despite its colossal size, the massive panel closed softly.

Anton signalled for the man to open the outer airlock. He hesitated.

'Now the other.' Anton poked his rucksack hard in his ribs.

The man pressed another button, but the outer exit took even longer to rise than the inner had to close. Before it was fully open, Anton's men had rolled beneath it. They headed for the Sno-Cats. The researchers were forced to run out into the freezing temperature, with insufficient clothing, and guided towards the waiting vehicles. When they bundled the numb, cold Chinese men into the cabins, the engines were running and the cabins were already heating up.

'Christ, this is like a sixties event where students would see how many people could fit into a public phone box,' Willis said. The scientists made muffled sounds of complaint. Their engines roaring, the Sno-Cats made a swift turn and raced away.

No one was wearing a wristwatch – at least, not one they could read under their bulky clothing.

'Does anyone know how long it's been since we left the chamber?' Willis asked. The scientists glared at him, their faces blank. While the Chinese men watched on, confused and bewildered, Willis, Anton and Boris turned around and stared into the whiteness.

Willis caught the attention of the tall man, and signalled for him to look around.

'See what you've only just missed.'

At that moment, the ground shook and a huge plume of black smoke rose high into the sky. The Sno-Cat shuddered as the shock reached it. A wall of snow raced towards them. When the snow enveloped the vehicles, it went dim inside and all visibility vanished. In case they tumbled into a crevasse, the drivers rammed on their brakes and waited for the snow cloud to disperse.

Once it had, a red glow flooded the cabin. As the snow on the windows melted, the light brightened, revealing a crimson sky interspersed with pockets of deep black. Willis imagined he saw flashes of lightning high in the sky above the explosion. Another blast followed. This one was bigger. The light from it was almost pure white. Small sparks of silver flashed from the hole left in the ice by the detonation. Then there was silence. Nothing remained but a wisp of black smoke rising into the cold Antarctic air.

The tall Chinese man leaned forward and insisted on shaking hands with Anton, Boris and Willis. 'You save our lives. Thank you. We didn't know that would happen.'

The engines of the Sno-Cats burst into life. They drove, with care, back to Progress Station.

CHAPTER 29

The journey was slow until they were well clear of the explosion site and the crevasse that almost cost Willis his life. From then, the Sno-Cats' earlier tracks became visible, allowing them to increase their speed. But it was the early hours of the morning before they reached the base.

When Progress appeared, it was a most welcome sight. Anton's men and the eight researchers bundled into the dining area for hot drinks and food. They allocated rooms to the newcomers, then told them they would meet them at nine in the morning to discuss what to do next.

Willis, Anton and Boris spent the following hour emailing their respective bosses on the day's events. Willis sent a message to Reilly, asking for as much information as possible on the Hōng Corporation in Shenzhen. He needed to find out who owned it – and where its financial support came from. The Hōng Corporation was a new name to Willis; if it was a big company, he was sure he would have heard of it. Willis suspected he knew already what Reilly's reply would be. The Hōng Corporation didn't exist. He also fired off a quick note to McGregor to tell him all was well and that he would contact him again later that day. Then they all retired to their rooms. Willis placed the folder he'd taken from the laboratory onto the desk, climbed into his beckoning bed, and fell fast asleep.

***

Willis was up early and showered. Unsure whether protocol allowed showers longer than two minutes, he conscientiously kept to the rules. There was no reason to suppose that the Russians were more proficient at managing their resources than the Americans. A short time in the shower suited him. His ribs hurt like hell. The effort of washing shot pains around his chest. Willis had expected the pain to be worse on the second day. After an injury, it always was.

When they finished breakfast, they gathered in a large room with Anton and a few of the rescued researchers. The questions began. Most of the men spoke reasonable English, but it was the tall man who volunteered most of the answers.

The company had recruited them from various companies in China and had interviewed them in Beijing at the New World Hotel in Dongcheng.

'That on Qinian Street,' somebody added. The scientists had all been invited to interview; none of them had applied. The interviewer, Mr Chang, explained they had been selected and headhunted, based on the specialist areas they were currently researching. Willis asked what these were. They listed almost every area of electronic and electrical engineering he could imagine.

Yes, they knew that their research would emit interference, that's why their employer insisted they work for a year in Antarctica. They had assured them that the magnetic noise would be directed into the heart of the continent, and it wouldn't interfere with anyone else. The object of their experiments was to devise ways to transmit electrical power without using cables. The plan was to provide usable energy to underdeveloped parts of central Africa. Willis thought it was a reasonable cover story. But how could they have been so naïve?

They continued to explain that a team had already cut the facility out of the ice by the time they had been recruited. Most of the heavy equipment was also in situ. Willis intervened again. 'How did they know what apparatus you would need if this was blue-sky research?'

The Chinese man said, 'The Corporation previously researched principles, so our task was to increase efficiency of project and to drive it above sixty per cent.' He held his head high. 'The team exceeded seventy-five per cent on last trial. We worked mainly on our own, making our own decisions, but there were visits from Hōng Corporation every month to deliver supplies and to receive updates on our progress. Latest visit was four days ago. Communication was via satellite link that was in polar orbit. We have schedule detailing its trajectory so we know when it pass over.'

Willis produced the folder he had taken from the laboratory. 'Is this it?' He opened it and pushed it across the desk.

'Yes, that is set of tables.'

'We will need this redrawn and translated into English. Can you do this for us?'

They were more than eager to assist.

'Would you also make a rough list of all the trials that you carried out? I realise that some of the times might only be approximate—'

The tall Chinese man interrupted. 'I have full details here.' He produced a small notepad from his pocket and slid it across the table. 'The language is English, so no problem.'

Willis knew that researchers often kept private notebooks, so they could access important reference information. He opened it on the first page. There was a name on the inside leaf. 'Is this your name?'

'Yes, I am Shan.'

'I'm very pleased to meet you. I am Brad.'

There was a flurry of activity around the table as everyone introduced themselves. Willis knew he wouldn't remember all the unfamiliar Chinese names, so he suggested that Anton produce lapel badges for everyone.

'Now for the bad news.' Willis looked seriously at the group. 'Your experiments have created chaos all over Antarctica.' He hesitated. 'Only the bases behind you escaped the disturbances. Although your Faraday cage did its work by protecting them, your experiments affected people in every other direction. The American base at South Pole was without electricity because of electrical interference, and the electrical surges caused a considerable amount of damage. That's not the worst part. A New Zealand plane crashed because of your radio surges. All four members of its crew perished.'

The scientists looked horrified.

'The bursts affected many other aircraft, including two that I flew in. And other planes nearly came down or were damaged.'

'We have no idea that happening.' Shan dropped his head. 'The surges shouldn't have been that strong – not from calculations we make.'

'Might your bosses have swapped some components, perhaps changing them to a stronger power level without your knowledge?'

'The only items we didn't specify were Tesla coil and maser. They were both in place when we got here, but I suppose they might fit higher-graded ones than those specified and failed to tell us what they do. The model numbers on the identification plates are correct for the power we need. The plates might be wrong, of course.'

Willis said, 'We will have to keep you all in custody until we can verify what you've told us. There will need to be an enquiry into the plane crash too. That will take some time.'

Shan was contrite. 'We not expecting to get home for twelve months, so anything we can do to help…'

'Thank you.' Anton's face lit up when it became obvious just how willing to help they were. 'We will make you as comfortable as possible here. We realise that you were nearly killed too.'

'Will we be able to contact our families?' a younger member of the group asked.

Willis had forgotten his name already. 'Not right away, I'm afraid. We must check your identities first. After that, we will see what we can do.'

'You lock us in our accommodation?'

'I don't think that will be necessary, Shan,' Anton said. 'You can hardly run away, but you will keep to your rooms and the dining area. Unless one of us accompanies you, don't enter the working areas or the laboratory.'

Shan nodded. Anton arranged for pens and sheets of paper to be handed out to them all. 'I'd like you to write down anything that might help us discover who's behind this. Remember, you eight gentlemen are in the firing line. If we can't find anyone else, you will carry the blame on your own.'

When Willis and the others left, the scientists were babbling in some dialect of Chinese.

***

'What will we do with them?' Anton looked uncomfortable about the situation.

'We will need to hold them until someone comes to collect them,' Boris said.

'I recommend we don't send them to China until we are certain we can eliminate that country as the source of the problem,' Willis said. 'Until we're sure, I propose we contact our respective countries to suggest that a United Nations peacekeeping force holds them.'

They exchanged glances; all three nodded in agreement.

Willis asked, 'Has anyone checked the email system this morning?' The three of them shook their heads, so they headed off to the comms room. Two replies awaited Willis: one from McGregor confirming receipt of Willis's email from the night before, and the second from Reilly. The email from Reilly reported that the Hōng Corporation was a shell company owned by a long chain of similar companies. In other words, it didn't exist. Willis swivelled the screen so that Boris and Anton could read it.

'That's no more than I expected.' Anton shook his head. 'If it was anything else, it would have surprised me. I should have asked our new friends for their IDs. I will do it later. It might also be useful to obtain their bank details.

What about their salaries? Maybe we can trace the origin of payments?'

Willis was about to speak when Anton interrupted. 'I know – the Hōng Corporation paid them. But they must have a bank account to do that. And someone had to transfer the money in.'

'I will ask Reilly to get our financial forensic experts on the job to see what they can dig up. Will you also follow up with your guys?' Willis asked Anton. 'We can check one against the other in the event they miss something. Can you do something similar, Boris? I'm sure your people have excellent ways of finding things out.' Willis grinned.

Boris smiled back, sat down and started to compose a long email. They moved away to give him some privacy.

'In case anything has survived, it might be worthwhile returning to the site of the explosion to see,' Willis said. 'Even pieces of paper can survive explosions if they're in the right place at the right time.'

Anton agreed, and promised to organise a team to visit the site tomorrow morning.

After Boris finished his email, Willis sent one to Reilly to ask if he had discovered anything more about the ship the Royal Navy sank in the Ross Sea. He suggested that although it was flying a Chinese flag, it might not have been Chinese. It may have belonged to another nation. Willis pressed Send and stood up, allowing Anton to take his place.

***

When Shan approached him, Willis was sitting in the Russian galley sipping cocoa.

'I redraw tables for satellite.' He handed Willis the translation.

Willis scanned the list. 'This only covers the next six days. What happens after that?'

'We get additional information. We go back and start over again.'

The left-hand column indicated the times that the satellite was due over Antarctica, and the column on the right gave the frequency that applied to that transit.

'That's odd.' Willis was perplexed. 'Why would they change the frequency on each pass?'

'They tell us it was for security reasons, so no unauthorised persons listen in.'

'Why didn't they just encrypt the message? Surely that would be easier?'

'I not know. We had no way of decrypting messages in lab.'

'Thank you very much,' Willis said. 'This will be most useful.' He tucked the translated notes into the original ring folder.

After Shan left, Willis returned to the email computer and composed another email to Reilly. He put Shan's translation in the scanner, then he attached the image to his message. Then he did the same thing with the original Chinese sheets. He emailed Reilly: *Can you find a specialist in orbital mechanics to study the list? Is it possible to extend the times that the satellite would pass over into the foreseeable future? If so, how far into the future? Can someone examine the frequencies to see if they can recognise a regular pattern? How often does the same frequency appear? Is it feasible to work out what frequencies they might use in the future? Last, who bought the bandwidth on each of the days identified?*

That wasn't too much to ask of Reilly, he thought. He's not got a lot else to do, anyway. But he decided that those were enough questions for one email. He grinned and walked to his room.

253

Willis was thinking over the timings. They weren't logical. They didn't make sense. Something was amiss with the timings. That's it – Shan had said that their contact communicated with them every month. He'd also said that he had updated them four days ago. Surely they would deliver at least a month's data at once? But only six days of data remained on the list. Willis opened the ring folder and turned to the back sheet. He found a sliver of paper snagged around the bottom ring. He then checked the original sheets. They were all intact. As he had suspected, pages were missing.

Willis went to Anton's and Boris's rooms to convene an urgent meeting. According to Boris, most Russian generals must learn a smattering of Chinese as part of their training, so he handed him the list written in Chinese and asked him to translate the first column. The values were nothing like those in the column Shan had produced. Willis leaned back in his chair, took a deep breath and explained to Boris and Anton his suspicions. He pointed out to them the discrepancy between the amount of satellite info present on the sheets and the frequency at which Shan previously had told them they updated it.

Anton slapped his hand on the table. 'You and Boris make an excuse of some kind to call another meeting with them this evening. While you keep them busy, I will search Shan's room and look for the missing papers and anything else I can find.'

Willis looked satisfied. 'If this works out, we'll have found the first link to whoever set up this charade.'

CHAPTER 30

After the scientists had all gathered in the meeting room again, Willis said, 'We need to do some checks, so we need your full names and addresses. Since the explosion destroyed your passports and papers, Jack here will also take your photographs. That will help us to confirm your ID. Have you filled out the paperwork I asked you to do earlier?' There were a series of nods and a few shaking heads. Willis collected the papers and put them in a pile to one side. One of Anton's men set up a camera and took individual headshots of all the men.

'If there is anything else that might help with your IDs, let me know. That will speed things up.'

While the cameraman took photographs, Willis browsed the forms the men had supplied. Unfortunately, they contained nothing useful that he could see. That some people could work for a company yet learn so little about it amazed him. At the end of the exercise, there was a full list of their names, addresses and bank details. Because he needed to keep them occupied for longer, Willis whispered to Jack, the photographer, to slow down.

Stealthily, Anton slipped into a seat to join them. 'Are you satisfied?' he asked Willis. That was the signal they had agreed to show that Anton had finished searching Shan's bedroom.

'Yes, we're almost all done here. Jack only needs to take a few more pictures then we'll be finished.'

Anton waited until the cameraman had finished and the group had dispersed. 'It's as you thought, Willis. Here are the missing pages. There are six sheets in all. How Shan imagined that this would go unnoticed, I don't know. These are photocopies. I left the originals in his room.'

Although he didn't understand Chinese, Willis looked at the number of lines in the copies. He could see that hundreds of passes by the satellite were due in the next month.

'I wish we could fit a keystroke logger to the email system.'

Anton asked what that did. Willis told him it recorded every key the operator pressed then stored it in a secure location in the computer's memory so even if the user deleted his work afterwards, a record remained of what he typed.

Boris smiled and tapped the side of his forehead. 'Although I don't have keylogger here, I can have one sent from Vostok Station within the hour.'

'You're a lifesaver. Why would you need a keylogger at Vostok? No, I won't ask.'

'Da. You could ask, but if I told you, I'd have to kill you.' Boris gave the mischievous giggle that Willis remembered from before. Boris was a fan of old American films, and he loved to quote from them.

'Let's do it. Send for it. While we're waiting for it to arrive, we might as well have some lunch.'

***

Less than ten minutes later, Boris returned to the dining room. 'How's that for Russian efficiency? The logger is here and installed. I waited while it downloaded. We're all set.'

Willis shook his head, then ate another mouthful. 'You never cease to amaze me, General. Well done. After lunch, we can let them loose on the email system. There had better be someone present to oversee them, or Shan could get suspicious. Whoever it is should not supervise them too strictly. He will need to leave the room on occasions, or somebody might come in to chat and distract him.' Willis gave a wide grin.

Shan appeared, and thanked them for treating him and his men so well. While he was there, he also asked again if they could contact their families.

How serendipitous, thought Willis.

'We can give you access to our email system, but we will need to supervise you for security reasons,' Anton said. 'We will need to limit you to using it to once a day. Is that acceptable?'

'Yes, yes,' Shan answered. 'You so kind. It means much to contact our loved ones and let them know we are well.'

'After we've eaten, we'll set it up. Tell your friends what we've decided. We can show you where the email system is and leave you instructions for how to log on.'

'Thank you.' Shan's eyes lit up. He was clearly delighted by the decision. 'I want to tell them splendid news.' He marched off; his head held high.

Boris caught Willis shaking his head in disbelief. 'Things couldn't have been easier … and it all happened so naturally.'

Willis stood up stiffly to stretch his legs. 'Well, that should make Shan feel confident and make him believe that we arranged it on the spur of the moment. He won't think that we could set up anything devious in such a short time.'

'Nevertheless,' Anton said, 'he's keeping his eye on us. He hasn't raced off to tell his friends, like he said he would. He's sitting watching us.'

'Let's make it easy for him, then. We'll stay here for as long as practical.'

***

Anton briefed Leo, Boris's pilot, on what he wanted. Anton needed surveillance, but he wanted it done 'incompetently'. Leo joked that he was good at being incompetent. Anton patted him on the back and laughed. All the while, they stood out of earshot of Shan, who continued to watch them. Anton ushered Leo over to Shan and introduced him. 'While you and your friends use the system, Leo needs to supervise.' Leo and Shan shook hands and chatted. That's a good sign, thought Willis. If they feel relaxed together, it will be more natural for Leo to act the same way.

Willis watched Leo pick up a novel to read. Brilliant, he thought. The man was a natural.

Shan called the team of researchers together, and they followed Anton into the comms room. Anton showed them the relevant screens and wrote the password down on a piece of paper. Once they had finished emailing, he told Shan, they would change the password. Shan understood, and thanked him again for his kindness. Anton winked at Leo and left Shan to repeat the instructions to the other members. Then he left to arrange some 'interruptions and distractions' for Leo.

'The system's all set up,' Anton told Willis. 'All we need to do now is wait and hope that he communicates with his contact.'

Anton frequently walked past the door of the comms department. Shan let his associates use the system first. Letting them go first wasn't just good manners; Shan observed them closely. Anton watched him looking over their shoulders and he assumed that Shan was checking that nothing out of the ordinary was evident before he used the email. On his last pass, Anton called Leo out of the room. He apologised to Shan for the interruption, then pretended to talk to Leo in the corridor before nodding for him to return to his post. Anton kept Leo chatting for ten minutes. As Leo left, he called after him, 'When I get back to my office, I'll look that out for you.'

Anton went back to his office, where Boris and Willis waited. 'Fingers crossed. There's nothing we can do now but wait. Time will tell.'

***

Two and a half hours passed. After the last man had finished his emails and left, Leo locked up and headed to Anton's office.

'Let's not rush to check,' Boris said. 'We might need to allow them on the system again, so we mustn't let them see us rush back to the comms room. The information is safe; it's not going anywhere.'

It was too early for dinner, so they decided to have a drink. They thought it would be good if the Chinese team watched them relaxing. Because they had to act as casual as possible, Boris went to the hatch and asked for his favourite

259

cognac. Willis recalled, from their time together in Kazakhstan, that Boris preferred brandy to vodka, unless he was celebrating.

'It's a little soon to celebrate.' Willis grinned. 'General Korolev always likes a quality drink to follow an achievement.'

'I'm not celebrating, not yet. I just fancied a refreshment, that's why I chose brandy. If you don't want to, you don't need to join me, Dr Willis.' Korolev replied with the same level of formality as Willis.

'I would love to join you,' Willis said, pushing an empty glass towards Boris. He poured the alcohol generously. 'Don't overfill it – we need to savour the aroma first.' Willis took the glass and swirled it around in his hand, allowing his body heat to warm the amber liquid, then raised it to his nose. 'Excellent.'

Anton pushed the other glass forward. 'I might as well join in. Because I want to be sociable, you understand?' He raised his filled glass and clinked it against Boris's.

They sat for several hours chatting, then hung about for the first diners to arrive. Then they waited a little longer until the Chinese contingent had collected their food and were busy eating.

'Let's go,' Korolev said.

In the comms room, Boris plugged a memory stick into the computer and hit a couple of buttons, then waited. In a few seconds, a progress bar had appeared on the screen, showing that the file was being transferred. When it vanished, Boris disconnected the stick from the system and removed it from the USB socket. 'Let's go to your office, Anton, to see what fish we've caught.'

The information looked garbled. The keylogger recorded not only the words that were typed, but also the control characters. The program recorded every input, even the Enter and Shift keys, and every other button they pressed. Boris decided it would be easier to print out the file. There's a lot of data in two and a half hours of emails. Willis was glad that none of the Chinese men appeared to be touch typists, otherwise they'd have far more files to read. Boris took a yellow felt-tip and highlighted the body of each message. When he finished each sheet, he passed it to Willis. He scanned the first five messages. None was in the least incriminating. Unless something surfaced soon, this could all have been a waste of effort. However, the sixth message was different. It read:

Facility destroyed. Being held at Russian Progress Station. They have part copy of satellite schedule. Request extraction.

Boris took a green marker and emphasised the sender's name. *Cai Shan.* He highlighted the destination address, originelectronics.com.

'That's not a Chinese address – it's Western, probably American,' Willis said. 'If it is American, the WHOIS system will list it – that's another task for Reilly. That site registers all domain names: if it's not there, it means they're hiding something. On the database, there's a list giving the details of every domain name with the dot com extension, and many more. Let's check the last two emails.'

It was just as well that Willis suggested this. Both of the remaining emails had gone to the same address, and both repeated more or less the same message. Willis made a note of the names and checked them against the list. Neither showed up on his file. 'We need to assume that these are their actual names, and the ones they gave us are false. Since

I spotted it written in his notebook, Shan admitted his first name, but he's given a false family name.' His suspicion was borne out. Cai wasn't anywhere on their sheets. Shan's name was there, but with a bogus family name. The Cai name was absent.

'We have a problem that we didn't count on.' Boris frowned and his brow furrowed. 'They requested an extraction. If their bosses listen to them, we can expect an attack on the base sometime soon.'

'Shit,' Willis said. 'I'd better get in touch with Reilly. We need support. If there is an attempt to extract them, you can bet it won't be by unarmed men. You would be wise to make a similar request, Boris. Whoever arrives the soonest wins the prize.'

Boris looked at his watch. 'The satellite is due over soon. As it is quicker, we can make voice call. There are four satellites in the constellation, so we have forty-five minutes to speak.' Together they proceeded to the comms room.

'You go first.' Boris sat at the computer keyboard and arranged his seat until it was the correct height for the desk. 'I can speak fast to get my message over, and I'll back it up with an email while you are talking.'

Willis dialled Reilly's number and hoped that he was in the office. 'Mike, Willis here. Because I only have minutes to speak, put on your recording machine. I need to talk fast.' Willis brought Reilly up to date with everything that had happened so far, and identified the three men he had associated with the host company. He gave the email address for the domain he wanted Reilly to investigate. 'Now for the urgent part. You need to get support to us at Progress Station – Cai Shan has asked to be extracted so we're expecting to be invaded by a team soon. We don't know when, but as soon as they can get organised, they'll be here. We have no weapons here to defend ourselves with. The leader of the base has given his permission for you to send United Nations help.'

'Fully understood, Willis. I'll action that right away.'

'Once we hang up, I'll follow this conversation up by email. Now I need to disconnect – Boris Korolev also needs to call his people.'

'Good luck, Brad.'

Willis replaced the receiver and gestured to Boris. 'It's your turn.'

Boris logged on and started talking quickly in Russian.

As promised, Willis composed a message to Reilly, then emailed Sophie and McGregor with an update. Willis then emailed Greg Mason, the US Deputy Marshal at McMurdo, with a rundown. When he'd finished, Willis met Anton and Boris in Anton's office. 'I suggest we continue to let the Chinese scientists use the computer every day. They should get a reply that tells them when the extraction will take place.'

'We'll need to put an unobtrusive guard on them,' Boris said. 'Once they know the extraction team is on their way, they may decide to try sabotage.'

'Agreed,' Anton said. 'I ordered the comms team to show a movie in the dining area tonight, so to ensure that all eight are together and we can monitor them.'

'They're being treated like Tsars.' Boris threw a critical look in Anton's direction. 'I have instructed Leo to organise a team, ready to defend the base with any makeshift weapons that they can put their hands on. With a little luck, Cia still thinks that we have arms, because you never showed him the wrench inside your backpack.'

Anton nodded. 'But I'm not sure how having a wrench in a rucksack will help if a team arrive with automatic rifles.'

'Let's not worry about that tonight.' Boris forced a smile.

'We haven't eaten yet.' Anton rubbed his stomach. 'If we're quick, there might be something left. I want to see this movie.' Anton's last sentence was full of false bravado. 'And in any case, we haven't emptied that bottle of brandy you brought.'

They ate dinner and enjoyed Boris's treat. The film was an old one, *North by Northwest, starring Gary Grant on DVD,* Boris told them. Boris loved old American movies, so Willis spent the evening watching the eight Chinese men.

'They're behaving normally – not that I expected them to do anything different.' Willis kept his eyes on them at all times. 'I know that three of them are associated with the people who organised this set-up, but I have only identified one of them. The other two are a mystery. I want to watch Shan Cia. Maybe he prefers being with some members of the team more than others – if he does, that should be the clue we need.'

While the movie was on, they sat in silence, sipping Boris's brandy.

'There's a problem.' Willis looked at Korolev. 'Keyloggers can only record outgoing messages, so we won't be able to read any replies they get.'

'That might be true of American keyloggers, but in Russia we do things differently.' Korolev tapped his nose with his finger and gave a mischievous smile.

CHAPTER 31

Willis came to breakfast the next morning carrying a sheet of paper. 'Reilly's sent a reply. He says there's a UN ship on its way, but it's only a UN observation vessel. That means it's unarmed, otherwise it wouldn't be allowed to land in Antarctica, as you know. I'm not sure what help it can be to us without weapons; you can be sure the extraction team won't pay any heed to the treaty. It should arrive in two days. As soon as he heard we were coming to Progress Station, Reilly requested the ship, so it should get here before any extraction team. That will give the peacekeeping force time to disembark and for the vessel to hide offshore at Davis Base. The Ozzies have already given their permission. And … Reilly has ordered a remote-control sub to investigate the wreck of the ship that the navy sank in the Ross Sea.'

'If they arrive from that direction, they might spot the craft sitting off Davis.' Anton scowled.

'No, they won't. Don't forget that UN ships are usually white. It will merge with the ice. Stop panicking, Anton.' Boris nodded in Anton's direction.

'I've been thinking,' Willis said.

'I hope it wasn't painful?' Boris laughed.

Willis cast his gaze skyward. 'I think the confusion caused by the extra characters in the keylogger files has damaged our mental abilities. It must have affected our logic. There are eight men. From the names they gave us, three of them we recognise; that leaves five suspects. Two are using email addresses that don't contain any identification so we don't know who sent them. Those two sent what looked like ordinary family greetings. That suggests we have three possible candidates out of five, meaning the two we can't reconcile plus the three whose names we are aware of but didn't delete their messages. We can therefore reduce our list of suspects to any three out of the five.'

'God, that sounds complicated. That's all very well, but we're still stuck with five possibilities. It's not very helpful.' Korolev gave a sarcastic smirk.

'I have been watching Shan, and he doesn't seem to sit with any particular members of the group. That also isn't useful.' Anton held up his hands, spreading his fingers wide.

'So have I. He's devious,' Willis said, 'but I can cut the five down to four. There's a scientist who seems to be a loner: he keeps to himself. He won't make up one of the three we're looking for, and only three wrote to Origin Electronics.'

'This is like a logic test, where you write out a truth table to discover who does what.' Anton leaned back in his chair. 'Mary is married to someone with dark hair. Ann is married to John's brother…'

'Except we don't have enough information to fill in all the spaces. Not yet, anyway.' Willis shook his head. 'Until they trap themselves, we will need to let them send more emails.'

At that point, Shan walked into the dining room. Willis waved him over. 'Our satellite is due over at eleven o'clock. Would any of your men like to send emails to their families?'

'That be great.' Shan smiled. 'They will be so pleased. I tell them right away.' He walked over to their table and joined his colleagues.

'Let's hope that this session is more helpful.' Willis sipped his coffee.

'Da, let's hope that they don't have ship in the vicinity, as we do,' Boris said.

'If they have, at least we'd find out about it.' Willis was chewing on a piece of well-cooked bacon. 'This stuff tastes better the more of it I eat.'

***

At eleven o'clock, Leo was in place. Six of the eight men were in the comms room. Four waited to get on the system. The other two said they would return later. Shan joined the first group. For a while, Willis stood chatting to him, trying to act casual. He asked Shan how his family was getting on. That he hoped they weren't worried about his safety.

'They are all well. Now they know where I am, they are thrilled and relaxed.'

You're lying, thought Willis. But he held his tongue. Before leaving, he asked some other trivial questions, then spoke to Leo.

267

He met Korolev at the end of the corridor. 'Are they on the system?' he asked.

'Some are. Although they didn't all want to send emails, I suspect the important ones did. All we have to do now is wait. And see what we catch on this occasion. Let's leave them to it and go for a coffee.'

After they poured their coffees, Willis asked Boris how his keylogger recorded incoming emails.

'It works like a standard keylogger for outgoing emails, but it scans for all incoming mails and transfers a copy to a secure folder. Even if the user deletes the original message, a version stays on the hard drive.'

'That's clever – devious but clever.' Willis touched an eyelid with his finger. 'I'll need to keep an eye on you. I'm glad you're on our side.'

Boris laughed and winked at Willis. 'You should always watch us Russians.'

Anton joined them. 'I have a team of ten standing by to prevent any attempted extraction, but the most powerful weapon they have is a long-handled shovel. Let's pray that your UN ship arrives before we need them.'

After an hour, Leo came back. He informed them that they'd sent all their emails. Somehow, they'd got through them faster this time.

Boris produced the memory stick from his pocket. He stood up and told them he'd be right back. Within five minutes, he'd returned. 'Let's go to Anton's office. We'll see what we've caught today.'

As before, he printed out the keylogger information then highlighted the messages in yellow. 'Forget this one, and this one, and this one. Ah! This one looks interesting.' Boris had marked the sender in green. 'It's from Shan Cai. He tells them "That is great but please hurry".'

'We'd better look for the email he's replying to.' Boris pressed a few keys. The printer sprang into life again.

Willis picked the sheet from the printer's out tray. 'This is formatted well. Why couldn't you get the program to format the outgoing mail as clearly as the incoming stuff?'

'It looks like we will have ample time.' Boris read over Willis's shoulder. 'A ship's due to arrive in four days but the UN men will be here at least a day before them.'

'Let's go through the other mails,' Willis said.

There were six in all. The one from Shan Cai they'd already read. As before, two men were using names other than their actual ones, but the emails looked harmless. No emails, other than Shan's, went to Origin Electronics.

'He's clever,' Willis said. 'They are all routing formal communications through Shan. There's nothing else to find out here.'

'We've found out enough.' Boris tapped his fingers impatiently. 'I think you should email your friend Reilly to let him know they're scheduled to be here in four days.'

Willis keyed a quick message to Reilly, updating him on the expected arrival time. While he was on, he also asked for the mini-sub report as soon as he received it.

'The couple who didn't send emails today are likely Shan's accomplices. Which two were they? Did anyone spot who they were?' Willis looked around and raised his eyebrows.

'I did.' Anton nodded at Willis. 'I'm sure I can pick them out.'

'Okay, let's check if the two you think match the ones I choose.' For once, the cards fell in their favour. Willis and Anton selected the same men. 'We know who the three likely suspects are. All we need to do is to keep an eye on them as much as possible.'

The following days passed without incident. The night before the arrival of the UN ship, Boris suggested that they should rise early the next day. Anton planned to mount a lookout on the roof with binoculars first thing in the morning. When he spotted the ship, he would alert Anton. They relaxed in the dining room that evening, pretending it was a normal day. All the while, they kept their three prime suspects under surveillance. While the previous night's movie played for a second time, they sat drinking brandy without paying attention.

Willis was bored. Since the next day promised to be interesting, that was surprising; then they would hand off their 'prisoners' to the UN for interrogation. All that would remain for them to do would be to alert the UN of their suspicions and inform them of Shan's duplicitous dealings.

Right now, Willis's thoughts were with Sophie. He was missing her. Despite the excitement at the base, the days since he left her had dragged. Willis dreamed of being with her again. He wished he could visit her. He cursed himself for neglecting her when he returned from Kazakhstan. If he got a second chance with her, he swore he wouldn't make the same mistake again. It was with these thoughts that he returned to his room. When his head hit the pillow, he fell sound asleep.

***

The next morning, he woke much earlier than expected, to a cacophony of noise. He glanced at the clock. 06:30. More sleep would have been welcome. The racket continued. He rose, then walked to Anton's office, but he wasn't there. As he entered the main corridor, a soldier in a white camouflage suit pointed a semi-automatic weapon in his face.

'Into the dining room. Now. Move your ass.' The soldier pushed him through the dining-room door. 'Now sit there still and quiet or a sure as hell I'll give you a bellyful.' He waved his gun at an empty chair. Willis did what the soldier ordered and sat in the chair. The officer spoke with a pronounced American accent. Willis guessed it was Texan. He seemed to have met a lot of Texans in the past few days. Anton and Boris were already there, looking a little sheepish. 'They came a day early.' Anton stated the obvious. 'They must have suspected we were monitoring their emails. They misled us.'

In the far corner of the room stood five men with automatic weapons, while around them gathered three of the Chinese men. Surprisingly, Shan wasn't one of them. The three were the two that Anton and Willis had agreed were absent during the second email session, plus the guy that Willis had called a loner. They were in deep discussion. After a few minutes, the soldier who appeared to be the leader of the armed group made an announcement. 'We're leaving now. If you know what's good for you, you'll stay in your seats until well after we're gone.' He turned with his team and marched out of the room, with the Chinese trio following. Shan and the remaining four Chinese men remained seated at the table.

Only seconds after they disappeared, Willis heard shots being fired, then the clatter of metal hitting the floor. Then silence. Leo staggered through the door. His leg was bleeding and his eyes were tightly shut. He took two steps into the room and collapsed on the floor. Willis ran to support him. A bullet was lodged in his thigh, and he was losing a lot of blood. Willis took off his shirt and ripped the sleeve off to make a makeshift tourniquet. He tied it around Leo's thigh then, with Anton's help, he lifted him onto a table. A doctor arrived within minutes, so Willis left him to it.

271

'That wasn't too clever,' Anton said to Willis. 'He's a brave guy, but impulsive. How could he have hoped to overcome automatic weapons with crude tools?'

Willis walked over to Shan. 'We suspected you were the leader of this group. I owe you an apology. When I saw an email written from a Shan Cia, I assumed you were the head man.'

'But I not Shan Cia. I Shan Cheng. I have no idea who he is.'

'He is the loner, I suspect – the guy who didn't mix much with the others.'

'His name Shan Qi or, so he led us to believe. It probably false. Shan very common Chinese family name, it is also common first name. He very...' – he paused, searching for the right word – 'antisocial. He kept very much to himself.'

'Well, it looks like he's the leader.'

'He in charge of the computer systems at laboratory. He probably set timer going that caused explosion.'

'That makes perfect sense.'

'His Chinese was awful. He was always misusing words. But now I realise, along with his friends, that he is likely another American.'

'Whoever they are, we've lost them. They've gone – and with them any chance of finding out who they are has gone too.'

'I wouldn't be too sure about that.' A massive fair-haired Swede strode in the doorway. 'I am Major Lars Andersen. Somebody sent for me. You must be Brad Willis?'

Willis stepped forward and shook his hand. *Thank you, Mike Reilly,* he thought. 'Do you mean...?'

Lars moved to one side. Their heads drooping and their expressions forlorn, fourteen American mercenaries, including three distraught Chinese scientists, shuffled past him. A dozen or more UN troops herded them into the dining room.

'Welcome back, gentlemen.' Boris aimed his forefinger at each of them individually. 'Now it's our turn to say these words. If you know what's good for you, when we ask you questions, you will co-operate.'

'We made excellent time,' Lars said. 'And it looks as though that was just as well. Another half an hour and these crooks would be well away. When we came across them, they were in a barge trying to get back to their boat. We confiscated their weapons. After we left, I put several men on board their boat. They will pull it apart for any information we can find.'

'Any idea where the ship was registered?' Willis asked.

'Assuming that the registration is genuine, the paperwork says it's the port of Baltimore in the USA.'

'That's as we suspected. The domain of the email addresses they were using suggested they were American. But we still need to find out who they're working for, because they need to account for several murders.'

'We are most grateful that you turned up in time,' Anton said. 'Boris here has a mean brandy that I am sure he'll be happy to share with you later.'

'We will look forward to that.'

'The man you'll want to speak to is the short, dumpy Chinese man. He's the leader. He calls himself Shan Cia.'

'I will leave that pleasure to you, Dr Willis. Since we don't need to leave for at least another forty-eight hours, he's all yours.'

'I know the perfect person to question him but in the meantime, lock him up somewhere, Anton. Then we'll see how Leo is getting on with the doctor. I'm sure that Leo will want to meet Mr Cia.'

Boris and Anton crowded around Lars, declaring their gratitude. The more they chatted together, the more their gratitude became evident. Because he knew how angry Leo would be, Willis kept away from the base's medical unit.

Anton grinned at Lars. 'Haven't you broken the Antarctic Treaty by bringing arms onto the continent?'

'I didn't. We took the arms off their ship, which was guarded by a skeleton crew when we boarded it. The place was a virtual arsenal. We did our duty and confiscated their weapons. Without weapons, we would have been incapable of stopping them.'

An hour later, Leo hobbled into the room where the short Chinese man was being held. Willis chose Leo to do the interrogation. Shan Cia was part responsible for Leo being wounded. Willis knew he would be ruthless. As Leo leaned his crutch against the wall, the blood drained from the man's face.

'Now, Mr Shan Cia, there are a few things I'd like you to discuss with me…'

CHAPTER 32

After a few hours, Leo appeared in the dining room. 'I can't get a word out of that Chinese guy.' He slumped into the chair opposite Willis. 'Cia must have set the explosion, so obviously he was willing to die for whatever cause he supported, but nothing I did would make him talk.'

'Let me try,' Shan said. 'We have methods to convince him to co-operate.'

'What about the Geneva Convention? The humane treatment of prisoners?' Willis asked. As he did so, he grinned.

'This isn't war, it doesn't count. We will bully him a bit. It happens in workplace all time. Since we just his workmates, we like to visit him, please.'

Willis put his empty coffee cup on the table. 'I'm off for a walk.' As he left, he threw a glance at Shan.

Boris stood to join him. 'Haven't you heard of Chinese torture? It can be brutal. There's water torture and lingchi, death by hundred cuts.'

'Death by a *thousand* cuts, Boris. But you're well out of date. Anyway, I don't know what you're talking about. Cia is being visited by some workmates, that's all. We're running out of time. When Lars leaves, he will need to take Cia then. After that, our world will be full of red tape, so we have to get any information out of him before that happens.'

They walked away in silence.

Willis checked for emails from Reilly. There was one. It read:

Received a report from the mini-sub that was investigating the wreck in the Ross Sea. They recovered a box file from the ship. They managed to recover the contents despite its saturated state.

Reilly listed the findings from the file, but they revealed nothing that Willis didn't know already. The corporation that leased the ship was Origin Electronics. They were based in Baltimore. Reilly confirmed the sub had seen several pieces of electronic equipment on the ship's deck, including a smaller version of the Tesla coil like the one Willis had discovered at the Chinese laboratory. There was no chance of recovering anything else, as the wreckage was becoming almost inaccessible and winter was approaching fast. Reilly went on to say there was no information yet on the company or its owners, but that investigations were continuing.

Although he wasn't holding his breath, Willis hoped the interrogation was proceeding okay with Shan Cia.

He left the office and walked to Anton's office, where Boris and Anton sat. Boris said, 'We come up empty with everything we try, but we still don't have a clue who is behind this project or where they are, apart from the fact that they're in the US.'

'Exactly.' Willis sounded irritated. 'And Reilly has just confirmed what we knew already. He hasn't added anything new.'

Wondering what their next steps should be, they sat in silence. Boris suggested they should all get drunk. Willis concurred, but all that would achieve would be three hangovers. It was a good idea but it would wait until after dinner.

'Has the team gone to check the site of the Chinese laboratory for any clues? We agreed that was the plan.' Willis looked in Anton's direction.

'Not yet. With everything that's happened this morning, I forgot. I'll arrange it now. They can do it this afternoon.'

***

After dinner, Shan Cheng came to join them. Leo accompanied him. Willis gave Leo an enquiring glance.

'Well, I thought Shan could do with a hand.' Leo grinned. Boris and Willis looked at him, expecting some news.

Leo spoke first. 'As we know, Cia works for Origin Electronics. He was part of what Americans call a skunk team. That's a group that operates off the books on blue-sky projects, many of which never amount to anything. They carried out some research on the basics of electricity transfer, but the company lost interest as it was costing too much to develop. Then someone came up with the idea of trying to weaponise the product. If they could develop it to a stage

277

where they could show it to the American government, money would pour in, the government would subsidise further research, which would enable them to resurrect the project. Even though the original inventor had failed, they believed they could make it work. They had claimed they found files that showed that Nikola Tesla had got a primitive version of electricity transfer to succeed. There's a conspiracy theory that claims much of Tesla's paperwork went AWOL,' Leo continued. 'If you look, the internet is full of theories about where the files might be. That the US government confiscated many of Tesla's papers after his death seems to be true. Supposedly they removed eighty trunks of notes, but when they returned the notes to his nephew, only sixty trunks remained. Ever since, there has been speculation about what happened to the missing projects.'

Shan put in his pennyworth. 'Whether Tesla experiments are foundation for this group's work is unknown, but Origin Electronics achieved some success by combining Tesla coil with maser. You saw that in laboratory, but what we not know was Origin Electronics upgrade components. They supply higher powers than we specify. They also alter identification plates on units to mislead us. But we not suspect this, so we struggle to find out why trials use so much energy. We try both long and short switch-on times for pulses, but the power source fail to cope. Whoever authorise the upgrade of components don't boost electrical supply at same time. We work in continual danger. The driver unit could explode at any moment. Cia knew all this and say nothing.'

'What about Origin Electronics?' Willis asked. 'Did he mention who owned it? Who was financing the operation?'

'Cia only know what they tell him. Origin Electronics is registered in Baltimore but with many owners. Although he did say they have access to great deal of money, he doesn't know who partners are. As fast as they supply it, project haemorrhage money.' Shan slid his notepad onto the table. 'I think Cia tell us everything he know. Towards end of visit, he ramble. If he know anything else, he would tell us.'

'I fear they will charge Cia not for murder, but manslaughter.' Boris sounded disappointed. 'He's admitted knowing they upgraded the components, so that will make him at least partly liable for the deaths in the New Zealand plane crash.'

'Let's have a word with Lars,' Willis said. 'We must be able to get some information from the mercenaries he captured. They must have known who hired them. Who paid them.'

But Lars wasn't co-operative. He insisted he was responsible for the prisoners, and he didn't want them interrogated until he handed them over. When Willis pushed him about who he would hand them over to, he became cagey. Although Reilly had asked for the intervention, Lars was still working on a UN brief, so he had to find someone in the UN to make that decision. Since the detainees were American, it was likely that they would be handed over to the US. If that happened, there would be no chance for Willis to get any information from them. Willis challenged Lars further. Might they have other accomplices on Antarctica? Lars would be negligent if he left without investigating the situation, but he wouldn't budge. Willis gave up.

'I fear I've lost more time as I haven't sent my team to the laboratory yet. I completely forgot to do it.' Anton said. 'I better send them first thing tomorrow. It's getting too late for them to go today.'

Willis thought that was an odd decision. It was late afternoon, but it wasn't going to get dark. But a few hours won't make much difference, he decided. He wasn't expecting to recover anything from the site after the strength of the explosion, so there was little point in rushing.

***

After dinner, they met to convince Lars to reconsider, but they were wasting their time. His mind was made up, and he wouldn't budge.

Boris produced yet another bottle of superb brandy. He poured copious amounts into their glasses. Willis thought they were larger than their usual goblets, but he didn't complain; he could sup brandy with the best of them. As the evening wore on, Anton and Leo gave their excuses and left. Boris was in a talkative mood, regaling them with tales of his childhood in Russia, his parents, and his adventures as a general during the many Russian wars in which he'd been involved. Willis suspected the tales were, at the very least, embellished. But his conversation was amusing. The anecdotes enthralled Lars to the point where he was pushing Boris for more and more details, which Boris was only too pleased to provide. Every time he started a sentence with 'Da. And there was the day that...', he leaned over and refilled their glasses. Willis was a little more than tipsy. Lars was holding his own, drinking as fast as anyone, pushing his glass forward without waiting for an invitation.

Suddenly Lars staggered to his feet. 'I don't feel so well,' he announced, then fell backwards, landing with a resounding crash, loud enough to attract the attention of his men and to bring two of them to his assistance.

'It's time for bed, Lars,' the taller of the soldiers said. 'He never knows when to stop. In the morning, he will be most apologetic.' He lifted Lars in a fireman's lift and strode off with him to the dormitories.

'That's killed the evening.' Willis stood to leave. 'It's time to go to bed.'

'Nyet! Not yet, my dear doctor. We need to see how Anton and Leo getting on.' Boris stood, swaying at first, but he soon regained his composure and marched off.

'How fucking stupid of me. I ought to know you better by now.' Willis stood and staggered along the corridor after Boris. Boris's duped me again; I should have twigged, he thought. That man is a menace. He always does his own thing.

Boris knocked twice on the door – a coded knock to let Anton and Leo know it was okay to open up. Sitting in the centre of the room was the leader of the mercenaries. His lip was bleeding. His head sagged against his chest. Blood congealed above his right eye. Blood spatter covered the front of his tunic.

'What the shit have you done?' screamed Willis. 'You'll have us all locked up. This could turn into an international incident.'

'It is already an international incident,' Anton said. 'When we tell him what we've discovered, Lars will be grateful, so don't worry. If Lars left Antarctica without doing a proper investigation, they would have reprimanded him. We've saved his Swedish bacon.'

'When you began to talk about your wild adventures, I should have known.' Willis looked at Boris in semi-disgust. 'You conned me. Those extra-large brandy glasses should also have given me a clue. Will I never bloody well learn?'

'You enjoyed the evening, at any rate. And before you ask, all the stories I told were true.'

'Like hell they were,' Willis said. 'You wouldn't recognise the truth if it hit you in the face.'

'Oh, be quiet, Willis. Sit down and listen to what Anton and Leo have to say, then if you're not happy with the outcome, you can blame it on us bloody Russians. We always break the rules, but we get things done. Without even having to ask, I know by the look on Leo's face that it will be worth your while.'

Anton sat in front of Willis, Leo to one side, and they told Willis and Boris what they had found out. As they spoke, Willis stared at the white-painted wall, choosing to ignore the spots of red that adorned its surface. The more they spoke, the wider his mouth opened. Willis added intermittent words like 'hell' and 'shit' to punctuate the details. After Anton finished, Leo added a few facts.

While listening to Anton's report, Willis shook his head.

'Lars will be happy you discovered this,' he croaked. 'He's going to have a very challenging day tomorrow.'

'We all will, by the sound of things,' Boris added.

'I'm off to bed.' Willis was swaying quite badly. 'Can someone point me in the right direction?'

'Follow me,' Boris said.

'I'll never follow you ever again,' Willis said. As he followed Boris, he hiccupped and bounced off the wall of the corridor.

CHAPTER 33

'What the fuck did you think you were doing?' Lars screamed at Willis.

This wasn't the time to deny his involvement. 'What we've found out will please you.'

'I don't give a crap what you've found out. What you've done is illegal – against every international rule that I can think of.'

'Screw your international rules,' Willis said. 'These guys don't play by any rules. There have been dozens of deaths so far: four in a plane crash, a couple on South Pole base, God knows how many on the ship that the navy sank in the Ross Sea, and there would have been eight more if we hadn't got the scientists out of the Chinese laboratory in time. There were several other near crashes in which, by sheer luck, no lives were lost. Don't preach to me about international rules. The only rules I understand are those that save lives, as many as fucking possible, and that's exactly what we're trying to do.'

'Don't rely on my support. I won't have anything to do with it. I will not involve the UN in anything illegal.'

'Nothing we've done is unlawful – don't keep using that word to justify your inaction. There are still lives at risk here. We're dealing with international criminals. They operate in Antarctica; it's no-man's land. They brought weapons to a peaceful continent where arms are banned, and you want us to play by some shitty rule book that someone wrote without even thinking that a situation like this could arise? Grow up, man. Either be a soldier or hand back your uniform.' Willis stood in front of the window, looking out into the white landscape. His hands twitched and his lips trembled. Had he gone too far?

Boris and Anton stared at him, apparently stunned into silence.

'Whatever you plan to do with the information you've gained, you won't get any help from me.'

'How can you say that? You haven't even heard what the information is.'

Boris moved forward as though tempted to intervene, but stopped. Willis was doing well enough on his own.

'I don't want to know what knowledge you have acquired; you got it illegally.'

'There's that word again – a word that you imagine lets you off the bloody hook. Yes, we collected it by force. But we *got* it.' Willis took a deep breath. 'We didn't need someone to carry us to bed as pissed as farts. What sort of rule covers that action by a UN major?' Willis knew he had gone too far.

Lars stamped out of the room, slamming the door.

'You made no friend there,' Boris said.

'I don't want friends like that. We will manage without him.'

'I can contact Zhongshan Station to speak to the leader. I ask permission to visit. We have good relations with Zhongshan and the Australian bases. Because Zhongshan is less than a mile away, we are the best of friends.'

'Then contact them both, please.' Willis was relieved. 'Don't tell them why we want to call. But let me talk to the lead scientist at Davis. I'd like to keep this as international as possible.'

Anton contacted Zhongshan and got permission to arrive with a delegation from Progress and Davis bases. Zhongshan's leader was nonplussed when Anton asked him not to broadcast their arrival in advance.

Willis spoke to Lucas Taylor, the Station Leader at Davis Base, requesting him to come to Progress and to bring half a dozen of his most trusted men. He asked Taylor to trust him. When he saw him, he would explain. Taylor wasn't happy, but Willis convinced him it was important. After Willis told him they already had permission to visit Zhongshan Station, he became more relaxed.

'Taylor should be here later today,' he told Boris and Anton. 'We will brief him before setting off tomorrow morning.'

***

That evening three genuine American Sno-Cats drove in, displaying the Australian flag. When the men had all eaten, Willis showed Lucas and his party to their quarters. Later that evening, both groups assembled in the largest room that Anton could provide. Also present were Taylor's six guys and Anton's trusted team. Leo sat in. Although his injury would prevent him from going with them, he could help fill in the details during the briefing.

As Willis rose to address the group, the door opened and Lars joined them. 'I am here as an observer. I intend to go with you in a supervisory capacity.'

'Only if you swear not to interfere will we agree you can come.'

Lars agreed, then selected a seat near the back. Willis stared at him, wondering if he could trust him.

To project a united front, Willis, Boris, Anton and Leo took centre stage. Willis kicked off by doing the introductions. 'This is Lucas Taylor; he runs Davis for Australia.' Taylor was a tall, bulky man with a full black beard but a bald head. Willis estimated him to be about two hundred and fifty pounds. Despite his weight, he looked athletic and fit. Taylor nodded. Willis repeated the procedure for Lars Andersen and the rest of his unit.

'The reason for Lars's UN squad being here will soon become clear.' Willis cleared his throat. 'Mike Reilly of MI6 contacted me in the UK in early January, asking me to investigate mysterious radio surges that had been felt in Antarctica. They were strong enough to affect electricity supplies.' He continued by describing his near-death experience on his flight into McMurdo, then brought them up to speed on the arrest of Dr Franck, but admitted that Franck's involvement was still a mystery to him. Willis described their visit to the laboratory and told them about their close-up exposure to the surge, then about their narrow escape when the site exploded.

'The UK requested the UN to send a peacekeeping force here. Lars came to assist and thankfully rescued us from the team of mercenaries who had attempted to extract their accomplices from Progress Station, using weapons. Lars now controls their ship.' Then Willis introduced Anton and Boris to tell Taylor and his men about Shan Cia's interrogation, but they took care to leave out the finer details of how they conducted the questioning.

Anton gave his contribution. 'Origin Electronics is based in Baltimore. Other than that, we know little about them. It's owned by an American consortium, but everything else is a mystery. Chinese Americans infiltrated the scientists working at the Chinese laboratory and reported back to their masters, acting as spies and reporting on how the work was progressing. Their leader, Shan Cia, had the ability to blow up the facility were it ever to be compromised. It was he who triggered the explosion, almost killing us all. What we discovered from the leader of the mercenaries who attacked the base is that they have a support team of around a dozen men at Zhongshan Station. They carry out meteorological research and measurements as their cover. In addition, they supplied the Chinese lab with goods and materials. The group also controlled the ship that was based off the coast of the Amery Ice Shelf. This craft was the one that landed the soldiers who raided the base, and who Lars has since captured, as Dr Willis explained.'

Lucas Taylor stood up. 'We reported sightings of that ship. Every few days, it sails past all three bases. We also made enquiries about who owned it, but we got no replies. It's been around for over a year.'

'Thank you,' Willis said. 'During their patrols, they, no doubt, assessed the capabilities of the three nearby bases. We have no reason to suspect that the Origin Electronics employees at Zhongshan Station know that we know about them. They communicated with the laboratory every three or four weeks. We believe the last time they were in touch was four days before the explosion that destroyed the site. They did, however, receive email messages from here – I allowed the scientists access to the email system, hoping they might let something slip. That's how we got hold of the name Origin Electronics. They must know we brought the team from the lab to Progress. Because the mercenaries haven't confirmed that the extraction was successful, we must assume they know it failed. But they won't know that we have interrogated their leader, or that we have discovered they are at Zhongshan. And it's unlikely that they will possess weapons – the security on any Antarctic base won't allow it.'

Boris took over. 'The men at Zhongshan Station are Chinese Americans. They work for Origin Electronics, but higher up the command chain than those who were at workshop. We will find out more about Origin Electronics from them. The company pays the Chinese government to host them on the base. China has informed us that it has no idea what they are up to; however, the Chinese scientists from the destroyed laboratory believed they were research team working for the Hōng Corporation in Shenzhen. The Hōng Corporation doesn't exist. The company's a cover for Origin Electronics.'

Willis stepped forward. 'Since Lars, working for the UN, doesn't have the authority to act in this case, I suggest that we send in an international consortium from our three bases. Once Zhongshan Station realises that these men are there under false pretences, I assume it will join forces with us, allowing us to repatriate the imposters to the USA. Although I realise that the shield they fitted in the laboratory prevented the surges from affecting you, I hope you will still help.'

'I'm in,' Taylor said.

'And I'll be there to supervise,' Lars said. 'If the Chinese give me permission, I will act.'

'Great. We're pleased to have you on-side.'

Leo, favouring his injured leg, stood up beside Willis. 'Just in case they know that we have discovered them, we ought to take as many tools with us as we can, to use as weapons. As many as we can carry, that is.'

'Our Sno-Cats are well equipped,' Taylor said. 'Your invite here was so cryptic that we brought a few goodies with us, just in case. I'm glad we did.'

'I will bring the confiscated armaments, but they'll remain in the Sno-Cats until we need them.' Lars's words were defiant.

That's an improvement, thought Willis. 'Great. I suggest we get an early night tonight. We'll set off first thing tomorrow. If we can arrive at Zhongshan before most of the site has been for breakfast, that will reduce the chances that the renegade Chinese team discovers we are visiting. There will be an element of surprise.'

***

They retired to the dining room. Boris offered Lars a glass of brandy and was told in very few words what he could do with it. Lucas and his men were less reticent about accepting Boris's hospitality.

The evening was going well, when one of Anton's guys came and whispered something in his ear. They conversed for several minutes. 'Bring them in here,' Anton finally said. 'I forgot about them.' Anton turned to Willis and the others. 'Our team has returned from the laboratory site with some boxes of papers they recovered. The fire that occurred after the explosion burnt most of the papers, and those remaining were blown to the four winds. The team did a tremendous job finding them, as the snow had hidden most of them. They don't think they recovered all the paperwork, but they searched an area of over several hundred feet around the lab, using a snow blower to shift the snow and reveal the papers.'

Six men marched into the room and placed half a dozen large boxes of documents on the table. Willis called on Shan Cheng to assist, and he helped sort the sheets into piles. Those with common headings, they put to one side. Shan recognised some as progress reports on the experiments. They were of no use to Willis. Others were invoices. Willis insisted they were stacked separately, since they might contain clues to the parent company. The sheer volume of stationery was daunting. They made twelve, then fifteen heaps. The papers spilled onto a second table. Most papers fitted into simple categories, some of which were of no interest. They made a much smaller pile, containing sheets of paper that didn't seem to fit into any category.

Willis said, 'This one is useful – it's a list of the names of everyone who worked at the lab. We can compare this with the names we already have.'

Shan's group helped to sort the papers. By the time they had completed the first pass, it was past midnight. They put the papers back into the boxes, with a box dedicated to each pile.

Willis had almost finished for the night when a sheet of paper attracted his attention. Written in biro at the bottom right-hand corner were two names. He struggled to make out the writing. The words were partly illegible, as the snow had made the ink run. Was it 'Senor' something? No – it was just 'Sen' something. The name that followed looked like it might say 'Barry Govern', but Willis wasn't sure.

'Do you have an ultraviolet light on the base?'

'There's one in the medical department.' Anton stood to lead the way.

'Let's look at this under UV light.'

In the medical department, Anton switched on the lamp. The filament took a minute to warm up. Willis thrust the paper under its blue glow. The ink fluoresced and showed up what was indistinct in normal lighting. The name was definitely Barry Govern.

'Isn't there a Senator Barry Govern in the USA?' Willis asked.

'I have no idea.' Anton looked at Willis, confused.

'It says "Sen Barry Govern". I need to email Reilly. This could be the breakthrough that we were hoping for. There's another name here too, but it's Chinese.' Both men looked stunned. Willis didn't believe what he had discovered. 'Let's go back to the dining room. I want to check that list of Chinese names.'

Willis went straight to the pile to the right of where he had been sitting. Leo was in his seat, sorting through more pages. Willis frowned. 'I put it here. I know I did.' He searched through the other boxes. The note had been on yellow-tinted paper, so it should be easy to spot, but he failed to find it.

'Has anyone taken any papers from this box?'

Everyone shook their heads.

'The list's gone – someone in this room has taken the list of names. Someone has something to hide.'

CHAPTER 34

The following morning, Willis was up before the others so he could call into the comms room and update Reilly. Willis told him about the name he'd found. The rest of his report was to tell Reilly about their trip to Zhongshan, where he intended to arrest the Americans posing as Chinese researchers. For good measure, he told Reilly about the missing sheet of names from the laboratory.

Willis went to breakfast. By the time Taylor and the others arrived, he had finished. Willis listened to the five Sno-Cats revving their engines outside. The drivers did this to warm the cabs, ready for them to set off on their trip.

'It's less than a mile from Progress to Zhongshan,' Willis said. 'It shouldn't take us long to cover the distance. We could almost walk it. But we should get going soon.'

'I've already told my guys to load the trucks. When we've finished eating, they will be ready to go.' Taylor pushed his empty plate into the centre of the table.

Taylor and his team boarded three of the transporters. Willis, Boris, Anton, Lars and their men climbed into the remaining two. Willis spotted the Tucker logo on the side of Taylor's orange Sno-Cats, confirming that the US supplied them. Boris, Anton and Willis were in the same Russian vehicle. 'We ought to discuss how we're going to approach Zhongshan,' Willis said. 'Once they hear our story, I hope they will hand over the men with little resistance. If I could rely on Lars to help, I'd feel a lot more confident.'

'I imagine that when the Chinese discover that the men are American and are using a false cover story, they'll be happy to get rid of them.' Boris's voice trembled in time with the Sno-Cat bouncing over the uneven surface.

'First, we will need to convince them that our version is true,' Anton added. 'Why should they believe us over the Americans?'

The journey continued in silence. Only a smattering of snow covered some areas of the soil. Apart from at McMurdo, this was the only bare earth Willis had seen since he landed at Pole.

***

Zhongshan was much smaller than the Amundsen–Scott Station. Its buildings were on shorter stilts than the ones at the South Pole, and they had been built on a slightly raised piece of ground. Willis imagined the summer sun would melt some of the snow each year, reducing the need for the stilts to be as high. On the left, they passed a row of what he assumed were containers for heating oil. The drums were cylindrical, and amusing faces of what Willis thought were Chinese dragons were painted on their ends. Obviously, it was an attempt to brighten up the pale landscape – and it worked.

When they reached the front of what looked like the main building, the vehicles slithered to a halt. A group of men stood outside. When they saw the visitors, they hurried indoors, and a few seconds later a figure clad in a red parka appeared.

Anton jumped down from the cab and waved to him. 'Hi, Li.' He walked over to join him. He gave a traditional Chinese greeting then turned to introduce Boris, Willis, Taylor and Lars. 'This is Li Dong. Meet your close neighbours.'

'Hello, Li.' Taylor shook his hand. 'We know each other very well. We all co-operate on this side of the continent.'

Li looked a little bewildered. 'I didn't expect this many visitors. Hi, Lucas.'

Anton finished introducing his colleagues. 'Boris is staying at our base. This is Dr Brad Willis, a visiting astronomer from Amundsen–Scott.'

'I am very pleased to meet you.' Li offered Willis a gloved hand, which he took and gave a hearty shake. Li's diction was excellent. He displayed no sign of a Chinese accent.

'Li's name is very appropriate. In Chinese, "Dong" means "someone who supervises", and he does that very well,' Anton said.

'What does your name mean, Dr Willis?'

'I have no idea – it probably has no meaning at all,' Willis said.

But Willis knew his name meant a well-respected person or family that is intelligent and kind. Although Willis was clearly too modest to tell them, he believed every word of its meaning. Willis smiled to himself. Maybe he wasn't as humble as he pretended to be.

'Come and get something warm to drink.' Li gestured for them to follow him.

Anton took Li aside and explained that it would be better if they met in his office first. Li led the way, and the five men followed. The rest of the men were led to the dining area. As usual it was the largest room on the base.

'I'm not sure that my office will be big enough to hold this many people.'

Willis nudged Lars's arm. 'Don't forget, you're only supervising.'

Lars ignored the comment.

Once they had settled in Li Dong's office, Li turned to Willis. 'This is all very mysterious. What is this meeting about?'

Willis began. 'I believe that you have a Chinese team here from the Hōng Corporation in Shenzhen?'

Li Dong nodded.

'I'm afraid that the Hōng Corporation doesn't exist. It's a cover for a company called Origin Electronics. The men are here under false pretences. The group is assisting illegal research in Antarctica, helping with the development of weapons.'

'Every quarter, we get a regular payment from the Hōng Corporation for housing the men – the company must exist.'

'It's what we call a shell company – it does no trading. Its only purpose is to transfer money to buy goods and services to help with its illegal research.'

'But the men came with proper Chinese IDs.'

'Although that might be true, they're probably first or second-generation immigrants to the US. They're all US citizens. We have arrested their colleagues, and Anton is holding them at Progress. But I am jumping ahead of myself. Allow me to explain everything we know about them.'

Willis repeated the full story, from his arrival in Antarctica to the explosion at the laboratory. Although he was adept at telling it, the repetition was becoming tedious, and he hoped it didn't show in his voice. He told Li about the plane crash and the other near crashes, and how powerful radio frequency transmissions from the lab had disrupted the power, making the planes fall from the sky.

This seemed to switch a lamp on in Li's memory. 'We had unreliable connections with our communication satellites.'

'I bet that stopped in the last few days?' Willis waited for a reaction.

Li nodded slowly, but he looked unconvinced. 'Because these men sailed in by ship from China, I can't hand them over without proper authority. I will need to send them back the way they came.'

'Unless we stop them, more murders will happen.'

'I hear what you say, but I have responsibilities—'

The door to Li's office burst open, and an agitated young man ran in and blurted something in Mandarin.

'Now do you believe us?' Boris asked. His knowledge of Chinese had allowed him to understand the message. He turned to the others. 'This young man says that the meteorological team are causing problems – they have taken a hostage. Unless they give the team safe transport away from the base, they are threatening to kill him.'

Li Dong followed the young man along the corridor.

'They're in here.' The young man indicated a steel door.

'That's the supply room.' Li's voice dropped to a whisper. 'There's plenty of food in there. They could stay in there for weeks.'

'How did they know the combination of the lock to get in?' Willis asked. He pointed to a keypad at the side of the door.

'You're a genius, Dr Willis. That's not a keypad; it's the temperature control for the cool room. We need to keep meat cold, even in Antarctica.' Li punched half a dozen keys and stood back. 'Either they'll be out in sixty minutes, or in an hour and a half they will be asleep.' He stopped and pressed one last key. 'Oops, I forgot to lock it.'

'Won't they simply cut the cables?' Willis put his hand on the door to check its strength.

'All the wires run under the floor. They won't kill the hostage either; it would be stupid of them.'

Willis drew cold air in through his teeth. Even Willis wouldn't be foolhardy enough to take a risk like that.

Li caught his expression. 'Believe it, they're Chinese. I know how the Chinese think.'

'But they're not Chinese, they're American.'

Li smiled. 'Once Chinese, always Chinese. Let's have that drink I offered you. We'll return in ninety minutes when they are well asleep. There's no point in taking unnecessary risks.' Li was grinning from ear to ear.

Remind me never to play poker with this guy, thought Willis. Then he remembered: the Chinese are among the best gamblers in the world.

***

Willis couldn't believe his eyes – or his ears. This was surreal. While a group of men froze in a huge icebox, they sat in a cafeteria and drank coffee and hot chocolate. After an

297

hour, he prompted Li, but Li was determined to delay for the full ninety minutes.

'I'll let you into a little secret.' Li leaned over and grinned. 'We have been listening through the metal door. After we hear all speech and movements stop, we will wait ten minutes, then open it.'

No sooner had he finished the sentence when a young man came and whispered in his ear.

'The ten minutes start now. Coming, Dr Willis?'

When the door opened, they saw the men lying motionless on the floor. To Willis's great relief, they were alive – just. Li withdrew his man first and rushed him to the medical department. The others they tied up, took them out of the icebox, then secured them in beds in separate rooms.

'It will be a few hours before they are mobile enough to cause trouble.' Li grinned at Willis. 'You didn't think I'd risk their lives, did you?'

Willis shook his head. Li had already gambled on them not killing his man. He shuddered.

'So will you let them come with us, so we can return them to the US?' Anton said.

'I'm afraid not. I still need to send them home to China. Sorry – my hands are tied.'

'What if I were to make a special request?' Lars Andersen leaned forward and showed Li Dong his ID card.

'That … might make a difference, Major Andersen. Whenever our paths cross, I have orders to co-operate with the United Nations.'

'I will accept full responsibility for returning the criminals to their host country. I anchored my UN ship offshore from Progress Station. There are already prisoners I need to collect from there, and I can secure them on board within a few hours.'

298

'Okay. If you're happy to take the liability, you can take them, but I will require your request in writing.'

'Consider it done.' Lars gave Willis a discreet grin.

'Can you speed up the recovery of the prisoners?' Lars asked. 'If they're in a fragile state of health, I wouldn't want to move them.'

Li shouted in Chinese to one of his men who stood guard along the corridor, then gestured to Lars. 'In an hour, you can ship them. You might as well relax a little until then.'

***

Chinese hospitality turned out to be much better than Willis had expected. They sat down to a sumptuous meal. The food was Chinese in name only. It was high in calories, like the cuisine at Amundsen–Scott, to help people cope with the cold, but it tasted delicious. Willis got stuck into the rice bowl as though it was his last meal, then asked for seconds. This endeared him to Li, who took great pleasure in replenishing his plate. His bowl was full of chicken, meat pieces and shredded vegetables covered in a spicy sauce. Li told him what it was called but the Chinese eluded him.

Li presented a bottle of Huangjiu and explained that its name meant 'yellow wine'. He said it was made with rice and other grains, but that it shouldn't be confused with Japanese saké. The recipe was completely different, he insisted, and far superior. 'I know it's still early in the day but we have captured our American imposters.' He handed the cups around the group. Even Lars risked a sip, but declined a second cup. He was clearly still smarting from his last experience with alcohol.

'You don't like it?' Li asked. Undeterred, he produced another bottle, this time of Shaoxing wine. 'Try this one, it might be more to your liking.'

Lars reluctantly accepted another cup.

'I also make my own brew,' Li volunteered. 'A stock of qū arrives every season. Before the winter comes, I have it delivered. Qū is a dried fermentation starter. I prefer Chinese wines because they're delicious when warmed. What else could one drink in this climate?'

Willis would have loved to try some of Li's home brew, but decided that it might be wiser to call it a day after two cups. Since he had no idea how much alcohol this wine contained, he settled for another cup of Chinese coffee. Its aroma rivalled his favourite Brazilian blend.

Over an hour passed before they heard that they could move the prisoners. Li instructed them to shackle the prisoners' ankles with rope. Li was taking no chances that they might resist.

Willis appreciated Li's foresight in keeping the detainees mobile. When they attempted to load the captives into the Sno-Cats, it helped. The cabs were hardly big enough for the original passengers, let alone extra men. As they crowded them into the cabins, it reminded Willis of the trip back from the laboratory, when they had been rushing to escape the explosion. Even with six transporters, they had to cram in uncomfortably. Willis considered their discomfort for a second, but only for a second. He decided that any discomfort he could inflict on them was only what they deserved.

They said their goodbyes to Li and his men and told them their help was much appreciated. Willis hoped that he might have the opportunity to return their hospitality in the future. They fired up the engines and began the drive to the coast, and Lars's ship. The Sno-Cats shuddered, rattled and lumbered over the rocky surface. Soon the base was behind them, and everyone settled down for the brief trip to the sea.

'Settled' might not be the right word; as the cab shook, the prisoners kept rolling off the shelf above the seats and falling. The sooner they reached the coast, the better, Willis thought. The vehicle Willis was in trailed behind the others. Eventually, they reached a flat snow-covered plain, which reduced the shaking to an acceptable level.

Then a bright light caught Willis's eye. He looked out the rear of the transporter and could see a red flare in the sky behind them. He nudged Anton, then ordered the driver to radio the leading vehicles to stop. The driver turned the Sno-Cat and drove back in the direction from where they'd come. A second flare appeared. Anton dug his arm between two prisoners and produced a flare gun. He opened the cab window and released a green flare in response. 'That will let them know we're on our way.' The other Sno-Cats followed Anton's lead and swung around.

After a few minutes, Willis made out the outline of a Sno-Cat – or at least, of its Chinese equivalent. The vehicle was travelling fast. This was urgent. As it approached, a dark foreboding engulfed Willis. What could have caused this amount of panic?

The vehicle drew alongside Willis and Li jumped out, flustered. 'I'm sorry. When we were cleaning the freezer after the prisoners left, we found this.' He handed Willis a sheet of paper. On it was a printout of an email sent from Progress to Zhongshan. Willis didn't recognise the address; it must have been from one of their prisoners. Willis read it, then showed it to Boris and Anton. The message read:

We take over base. Email me when you ready. We come collect you with transporter, then we will head for ship. We will retake ship and get off this damn continent.

It was signed, Shan Cheng.

CHAPTER 35

Willis shouted over the noise of the Sno-Cats. 'Lars, we need to send a message to your ship. Give Li Dong the ship's frequency. He will go back to Zhongshan and radio them to warn them we're coming. And tell them to have a landing craft ready at Prydz Bay to secure the prisoners and take them to the patrol boat. As soon as the captives are off our hands, we'll return to Progress.'

Lars gave Li Dong the frequency. Within minutes their convoy had turned and begun to head towards the ice shelf. But this time they were racing. The top speeds of the transporters varied, and the smoother ground let them spread out. Willis's Sno-Cat, which was at the rear when they left Zhongshan, was the fastest and soon took the lead.

'I shouldn't have trusted Cheng,' Willis said. 'Cheng must have taken the list of names from the table last night.'

For a moment, he remained silent, then he pushed his fingers through his dark hair. 'When I get my hands on him, I'll kill him.'

'You'd better not let Lars hear you say that.' Boris punched him playfully on the arm.

But things were no longer playful. The enemy controlled the base. Willis was worried. How many of the people might be injured?

'Leo will certainly have been hurt. Anton left him in charge, and he won't give up without a fight.' He put the negative thoughts out of his mind, clenched his teeth, and stared straight ahead.

Even although the transporters were travelling at almost fifty miles per hour, the journey seemed to last forever. It should only take a few minutes to reach their destination, but Boris kept checking the time as though that might help them arrive sooner. An expanse of snow and rock stretched ahead of them. Each machine drove through a tunnel of snow thrown up by the caterpillar tracks of the truck in front. Only the lead vehicle, Willis's, could see where it was heading. They dismissed all thoughts of crevasses and cracks in the ice. None was expected this close to the sea, because it was mainly bare stone between Zhongshan and the bay. The Sno-Cats continued to hurtle towards the sea.

'They will only wait so long for a reply from their friends at Zhongshan,' Willis said. 'When it doesn't arrive, they will set off either for Zhongshan or the ship. We need to intercept them.'

***

When they got to the coast, Prydz Bay stretched out before them. The bay was ice-free and a barge was waiting. It took two trips to get all the suspects aboard and secured. Eight of Lars's men joined them, armed.

They got back in the Sno-Cats and sped towards Progress. Willis dreaded what they might find there. So as not to alert the Chinese to their presence, the plan was to stop short of the base and proceed the last hundred yards on foot.

But events were taken out of his hands. When they got closer, one of the Russian Sno-Cats was ticking over, ready for action. A cloud of condensation from its exhaust filled the icy air. Before they took their hostage, the men from Zhongshan must have replied to Shan Cheng's email. Willis's transporter drove in front of the revving vehicle and stopped, blocking its path. Lars did the same to the rear. Several scientists got out and ran into the main building, securing the door.

Willis and Lars stood facing the door.

'They will have arms,' Lars said. 'My men had some of their weapons with them, and if they've been overcome, they will have automatic rifles. This will be a standoff.'

Then an answer came. The main door opened several inches and a burst of automatic gunfire spewed into the snow in front of where they stood. Urgently, Willis pointed to the protection of the transporters, and everyone ran to safety behind the giant vehicles. Lars crouched behind the furthest caterpillar track.

'We need to do a recce around the building,' Willis said. 'There must be a weak point somewhere. This facility wasn't built to be defended, so there has to be a way in. First, move your men out of sight to the ends of the base. That will unnerve Cheng. He will assume we are planning something devious. Not being able to see us will make them stressed. Leave two guys with walkie-talkies, one at the front and one at the rear. They will stay out of range, protected by the Sno-

305

Cats. They can report any movement they see. You and I will creep behind the building and search for a weakness. There's got to be a way in.'

Willis and Lars kept their heads down and moved closer to the wall. They inspected the floor of the structure under its low stilts. Nothing was visible; they could detect no easy access. To see in, Willis jumped up as he passed each of the small, high windows on the ground level, but he could find nothing there, either. Alongside the building stood two blue cargo containers. If they could get on top of them, it might be possible to look through some higher windows. A flight of steps led to an emergency door at the side of the containers. That could be a potential entry point.

'If I can reach the top of the stairs, I can jump onto the container. I would then have access to the first-floor windows. Let's go back for Anton. He will tell us which room these windows look into.'

Anton closed his eyes to help him recall which room aligned with which window. His lips moved, and he pointed silently at each pane. 'The two on the left are the main dining area, the pair on the right is the infirmary, and the two central ones face into the comms centre.'

Willis tried to memorise the building's layout. 'I'm going to look.'

He climbed the steps by the container, trying to make as little noise as possible, but it was difficult. With each step he took, the stairs rang and the railings shuddered. He grasped the handrail to deaden the sound, but it was only partly successful. Drat, he thought, Anton didn't tell me which room the skylight at the top of the stairway faces into, and I'll need to pass it to get to the top of the container. It was a low, square window, and Willis wouldn't be able to pass it without being visible to anyone in the room.

Willis stopped a few rungs down from the top of the stairs and swung over onto the wrong side of the railing. He was now standing on a narrow ledge that was an extension of the top platform of the stairs. He could hang on to the handrail and lower himself below the level of the glass. With luck, he would go unnoticed. He turned and, with his hands behind his back, gripped the hand railing. Willis flexed his knees, let go of the rail and allowed himself to fall forward, then pushed his legs straight as quickly as he could. He careered over the five-foot gap and crashed with a thunderous clatter onto the top of the container. The noise resounded through the empty metal box. Surely someone must have heard. He froze in the position he'd landed, legs bent, and listened for any shouts.

All was silent.

Willis rose and peered into the first room. It was brightly lit. Thank God. His silhouette would be less prominent. Inside the room, an armed man stood waving his rifle at the crowd of Progress personnel who filled the dining room. In the far corner he saw Lars's men, tied and bound. Only one man thought Willis, but he has a rifle. We need to distract him. He shuffled along to the comms centre. A man sat at the console, staring at an inactive screen, no doubt waiting for the email from Zhongshan that would never arrive to tell him that their friends were ready to be picked up. Although he was unarmed, it was still too risky, Willis thought, with a man with a gun in the next room.

He moved along and looked into the infirmary. This looked more promising. Leo lay on a bed, a doctor tending to his wounded leg. Since they were the only two in the room, Willis stood in front of the window and allowed his shadow to fall over the bed. Leo spotted him and waved the surgeon to leave him, then he hopped up to the triple-glazed window.

No sound could ever filter through it. Leo took a pen and a page from the doctor's pad. After scribbling on it for a few seconds, he held it up to the glass. It read:

No one is guarding the end door of the corridor. I can run there and open it. It's the side under the 'PROGRESS' sign and the Russian flag.

Willis breathed on the window. Luckily, because of the triple glazing, it was still cold enough to condense his breath. He wrote, in mirror writing, by drawing his finger through the condensation:

Do nothing until I cause a diversion.

Both gave a thumbs-up. Willis turned back towards the gangway. Although it had been easy to drop six feet onto the container, now he needed to do the same thing in reverse. He could reach the ledge he'd dropped from with about four inches to spare, but there was the five-foot gap to negotiate. Thank goodness for his six-foot two-inch height – and for the diagonal strut that supported the top landing of the stairs. If he jumped and put his feet— he shook his head. He wasn't thinking. The container was only eight feet tall, so he would lower himself off it to the ground.

'Right, Lars, Leo is going to open the door at the side of the complex with the "PROGRESS" sign. As soon as he does, you get your men ready to enter. Boris, take a Sno-Cat and drive to under the window on the left above the freight container. Anton, you take another Sno-Cat and pretend to ram the other side of the building. Knock some of the access steps away and cause a lot of noise and chaos. Collect a couple of Lars's men and have them fire on a door – aim for the one furthest from the "PROGRESS" sign. Keep firing intermittently for about five minutes – that will provide a diversion to ensure the door closest to the "PROGRESS" sign remains unguarded. Boris, about five minutes' firing should be sufficient for your guys, too. Before any of us gets hurt, we'll break in and disarm these bastards. And Boris, if you get killed this time, I won't believe you, so take extreme care, my Russian friend.'

Willis stood at the end of the block, far enough away to see both Boris and Anton. He raised his hand, then dropped it. The cacophony began. Bullets peppered the window of the galley area, crazing the reinforced glass and turning it translucent. Anton attacked the front of the building. The caterpillar tracks ploughed into the lower part of the steps, then reversed and drove over the middle level. The Sno-Cat couldn't reach the top of the stairs, but Anton's men sprayed bullets over the doors. Two doors opened, one immediately to the left of the dining room, and the one that Anton's men were shooting at. Automatic weapons protruded, and a return bout of fire rattled against the skins of the Sno-Cats.

Willis watched the door below the 'GR' of the 'PROGRESS' sign. He frowned. Leo should have opened the door by now. *Come on, Leo. What's keeping you?* Five of Lars's men lined the steps, ready for a quick entry. The door swung open, but it wasn't Leo. The figure shot at the five men on the stairs. They fell at awkward angles, some over the railing, others rolling down the walkway, blood gushing from their limp bodies.

Willis began to sweat. The taste of salt flooded his mouth. His heart thumped in his chest. His face flushed as adrenalin pumped through his veins. He recognised the symptoms: there was no point ignoring them, since he needed to act. Willis ran under the steps, using the corpses as cover, and grabbed an automatic weapon from one of the dead men. He raced up the steps, spraying rounds at the suspects coming out. They landed on top of each other, panicking as they got in each other's way. Willis continued to run towards the door. Soon he was inside, shooting down the corridor. The escapees abandoned the other doors and ran aimlessly into Willis's line of fire. The echoes of gunshots ricocheted off the walls. They came from Leo. He was firing from behind the group. He and Willis surrounded the men. Those in the centre held their hands up. Willis released the trigger, but it was too late to stop firing. Bullets thudded into the men's chests and they dropped like dolls. Willis stared at Leo over the pile of corpses. They were the only two left standing. Leo smiled at Willis and was about to say something when a shot rang out.

Leo coughed out a mouthful of blood and fell to his knees. Willis saw Shan Cheng standing with a pistol by his side. Willis fired at him, aiming at Cheng's legs. He sank to the floor in agony, clutching his thighs. Willis stood over him, raised his gun, pointed it at Cheng's forehead, then cocked the gun. Cheng whimpered and closed his eyes. Willis released a burst of shots into the wall next to Cheng's head. Cheng looked up, his lips trembling, vomit dripping from his open mouth. Willis ground his heels into the bullet wounds on Cheng's thighs.

'You ought to be grateful that I'm cured.'

Cheng stared at him, looking puzzled and confused.

Willis walked into the infirmary, fell into a chair and wrapped his hands around his head.

CHAPTER 36

'Gregori told me you were cured?' Boris stood with his hand on Willis's shoulder. 'He said he took you to St Petersburg to see a specialist. He said he'd fixed your PTSD.'

'Apparently not completely.'

'It's a good thing he didn't. We'd be in a right mess if you hadn't reacted as you did. You were in the same situation you found yourself in at the Baikonur Cosmodrome in Kazakhstan where you shot Klaus Fauler – but here you spared Shan Cheng, so something has improved.'

'Maybe so, but it was my fault that Leo was killed.' Willis's shoulders sagged. 'If I had reacted faster, I might have rescued him.'

'You didn't cause Leo's death. When he went to open the door for us, they fired at him. Before Cheng opened fire, there were already three bullets in his back. But Leo knew he was dying. Cheng's shot was the final straw.'

'He saved my life. I didn't have enough ammunition to stop everyone in the corridor, so I would have been a goner for sure. Sadly, I needed his help.'

'Leo was a good man, but he died bravely. Exactly as he lived.'

Willis looked up from between his hands. 'Where's that bastard Cheng?'

'He's in the infirmary. The doctor is removing the bullets from his legs, but Lars is chafing at the bit to take him into custody.'

'We can't let Lars have him yet. Boris, ask Anton to instruct the doctor that he can't be moved for some time. Before he's allowed to go anywhere, I need to question him, because he knows exactly what's going on and who paid for this whole damned project.'

'Lars won't agree to that. He has lost a lot of men and wants to see Cheng brought to justice.'

'Don't worry, we'll bring him to justice ... but after I'm finished with him. Lars won't work against a doctor's orders.'

At that moment, Anton walked into the room. Willis jumped to his feet. 'Anton, go and tell your doctor that Lars can't move Cheng for a couple of days. I need to be alone with him for a while before Lars takes him into custody. Let's go now.' Willis took Anton by the arm. They headed for the infirmary.

'Mad bastard, that's what you are.' Cheng looked up at Willis. 'You crazy. Almost single-handed, you wipe out all my men.'

'Good – remember that. You and I need to have a little chat.' Willis pulled a chair to the side of the bed and sat by Cheng's knees. 'Now tell me who masterminded this murderous plan. Who bankrolled it?'

'I tell you nothing. I have shit all to lose. Go fuck yourself.'

Willis turned to the surgeon. 'Please, will you leave us alone for a few minutes?'

'I haven't finished with his legs.'

'For a little while, his legs will be fine. Please leave us – now.' He spat out the last word, and the physician hurried off. Once he had disappeared, Willis faced Boris and Anton with his brow furrowed. 'Before I begin, would either of you gentlemen like to leave too?'

'I need to check on the base,' Anton said. 'It needs sorting out.'

When Anton left, Willis turned to Boris. 'There's a man who knows when to withdraw.'

Boris pulled up a chair on the opposite side of the bed to Willis's. 'He was always a little squeamish, was Anton.'

'Now, you bastard, I'll ask you again. Who bankrolled this project?'

Cheng spat in Willis's face.

'You ought not to have done that.' Boris raised his eyebrows to emphasise his point.

'Mr Cheng must have met us before, Boris,' Willis said, wiping the spit from his chin. 'Is this the spot where the bullet entered?' he asked Boris, pointing at one of Cheng's wounds.

'Maybe you'd better check, but I think so.'

Willis held his forefinger upright, tapped his nose, twisted the finger in the air, inserted it into the wound in Cheng's leg, and slowly twisted it. Cheng's scream bounced off the walls. 'We'd better close the door, Boris. I don't want to disturb the neighbours.'

313

Boris rose and opened and slammed the door.

'What's the other thigh like?' Willis put his finger in the other bullet wound and gave it a wiggle. Again, Cheng's cry tore through the air.

'Boris, I fancy a coffee. A really hot cup of coffee would be nice. Would you fetch me one from the machine?'

When Boris walked out into the corridor, another blood-curdling scream filled the surgery. Sweat dripped from Cheng's face. It ran down his neck. In an act of defiance, he shook his head. Willis repeated the procedure with two fingers at once. This time Cheng gritted his teeth. Although blood now poured from the three bullet wounds in his legs, he was becoming accustomed to the pain, so Willis pressed against the flesh surrounding the wounds. Cheng screeched. Clearly, his suffering wasn't severe enough to numb the nerves to the muscle around his wounds. Willis pressed again and again. He didn't ask Cheng any more questions. He wanted to make him think he was a genuine sadist. Willis wondered if he might be. No, he wasn't enjoying this at all. As Boris returned with the espresso, more screams filled the room.

Willis took a sip. Steam rose from his cup. 'Ouch, that is hot.' He leaned over Cheng and poured the boiling coffee into one of his wounds. He gave another deafening screech. 'Want to talk to me yet? No, I know you don't.' He tipped the coffee into all three wounds in turn. 'You can make it stop. Just say stop. I will stop if you ask me.'

Once again, Cheng shook his head and spat at Willis.

'You're not going to break him,' Boris said. 'Let's kill him for shooting Leo. Let's get it over with.'

'I fear you might be right, my dear friend. But let's have some fun. Anyway, I'm getting bored with this.'

Cheng took a deep breath and let his shoulders relax on his pillow for the first time in fifteen minutes.

'Where's that old Russian revolver you carry?'

Boris handed Willis a pistol. After Willis made a play of removing all the rounds, he showed Cheng the empty cylinder, then replaced one bullet, making sure that Cheng watched his every move. He held the barrel over Cheng's face. Willis slammed the gun closed, pointed it at Cheng's forehead, then squeezed the trigger.

Click.

Cheng let out a long, slow breath. Willis spun the cylinder, took aim again, and pulled. Zilch. Sweat was flowing freely down Cheng's face. 'If you kill me, they arrest you for murder.'

'Don't you think I've already thought of that? But no. You'll have committed suicide, ashamed after failing in your mission. They will find this ancient gun in your hand. This revolver is antique, so it's untraceable. Though you do have a good point. I'd better aim at the side of your head – that's where most suicides shoot themselves.' Willis spun the cylinder and pulled the trigger. 'My Chinese friend, you're running out of luck.'

'I'm not Chinese, I am American.'

'Oh perfect, you can call your friendly senator. He's Senator Govern and we know all about him. It's plain stupid to die to protect someone who's being arrested as we speak.'

The blood drained from Cheng's face. Willis saw his eyes flicker. A sign of weakness, he thought.

'I'm bored now,' Willis said. He spun the cylinder and pulled the trigger three more times. On the fourth spin, Cheng shouted, 'Stop. I'll tell you everything you want to know.'

He started to talk. 'Barry Govern is senator who masterminded project. He get help from David Morse, another senator. They bankroll it through Govern's company, which is based in Texas. I can prove it owns Origin Electronics. The original research started as offshoot of Origin Electronics, then they export it to Antarctica to cover up tests. But it is never anyone's intention to kill people. Govern upgraded the strength of components on his own, without checking with researchers.'

'What about the ship in the Ross Sea?' Willis asked.

'That was Govern. He impatient to see results. He planned to weaponise the device then sell to the US government, but that can't happen now because I destroy the drawings and notes on experiment that you rescue from our lab. Then, when they sink Ross Sea ship, all the other research was lost, along with some of Nikola Tesla's so-called missing files. We used them as basis for our work.'

Willis brought Cheng some sheets of paper and a thick pencil then said, 'I want you to write down everything you've just told us. If you do, we might tell the authorities that you co-operated. You never know.'

Willis turned to walk away, then stopped. 'Doctor, it's time to finish sorting this man's legs.'

The surgeon appeared and got to work. Willis leaned over the bed and opened the cylinder of the revolver. Making sure that Cheng could see what he was doing, he rotated it until the bullet came into view, then he tipped out the cartridge and turned it towards Cheng, letting him see the hollow casing. Willis carefully balanced the spent shell on Cheng's chest, then left.

He headed straight for the comms room, where he composed a detailed email to Reilly, asking him to send a copy to Admiral Jamie Wilson and Brigadier-General Joshua

S. Baker. Reilly knew both men from Willis's mission to Kazakhstan. They were both associated with US intelligence. Since two US senators had been accused of several murders, Willis told Reilly that Wilson and Baker would need to take action. After he hit Send, he went for a drink.

***

Anton brought Willis a brandy. 'After the mess you made of my stairs and windows, you don't deserve this. I'll have a helluva job getting it fixed before the winter comes.' He pushed the cognac in front of Willis.

'A helluva job?' Willis teased him. 'Your English is improving all the time. And *you* smashed your stairs. I just asked you to do it. You didn't need to comply.' Willis grinned and sipped the alcohol.

'I've learned some words I could do with unlearning.'

'That's impossible – once learned always learned, especially with the more choice phrases.'

Willis took another slug of his brandy and held it up to Anton. 'Cheers.' Willis looked at Lars. 'Here's to the good men you lost today. They didn't deserve to go that way.'

All four raised their glasses, and they sipped their drinks in silence. After several minutes, Boris broke the silence. 'I will recommend that we recognise their bravery.'

'Likewise,' Willis and Anton said.

'With a special mention for Leo,' Willis added. The others nodded and drank more brandy.

Then a tall, grey-haired man tapped Anton on the shoulder and gave him a thick pile of papers. 'These are the notes written out by Shan Cheng.'

Anton handed out the papers to the other men. 'There are four copies, one for each of us.'

Without commenting, they read the confession.

317

After Willis had convinced him to talk, it was incredible how much detail Cheng had supplied. 'These notes will be enough to put the senators away for life.'

'I hate to contradict you, my dear Willis, but Texas has the death penalty so they will face execution, not go away for life,' Lars said.

'Of course – I keep forgetting they still practise the death penalty in many US states. And both the senators are from Texas.'

'They are for sure. They're also on the board of Origin Electronics' mother company, according to Cheng's notes.'

'Texas keeps turning up all the way through this saga.' Willis stared into space, as was his habit when trying to concentrate. 'It seems to be the common thread connecting the various elements.'

'Drink your cognac,' Boris said. 'Try to relax. When you least expect it, the answer will come to you.'

'I suppose so.' Willis wasn't happy. He wouldn't let it rest. He took another sip from his drink, and allowed his mind to go blank. 'I still haven't explained Franz Franck's role. Or how he fits into the bigger picture.'

'There's no mention of a Franz Franck in Cheng's notes,' Boris said. 'Maybe he just forgot to add him. We can ask him in the morn—'

'I've got it!' Willis got to his feet. 'I know why Texas stands out. I must get back to the Amundsen–Scott Station ASAP. Is your plane available?' He looked at Boris.

'No, they haven't repaired yet, but there's more than one plane at Progress Station. They use this base to supply Vostok Station and some others. That's why Anton and I already know each other.'

'Anton, can you get the aircraft ready for immediate take-off? I must get back to my base as soon as possible. Lars, Boris, you ought to come with me.'

'It's late evening,' Anton said. 'By the time you get to Amundsen–Scott, it will be early morning. Everyone will be asleep.'

'Not everyone, I fear, my dear Anton, not everyone.'

CHAPTER 37

Anton did them proud. Within half an hour, the plane was ready. In thirty minutes, it had been refuelled and the engines were warmed and revving. At Willis's request, Lars brought six of his best men. 'Are you sure six will be enough?' he asked.

Willis nodded and climbed into the aircraft. 'This is going to be a long flight. We'd better get some sleep. At least we can relax – there won't be any surges trying to force us out of the sky.'

'Surely you're planning to tell us what this is all about? My men will need to prepare.' Lars raised his voice to Willis for the second time that night.

'I'm not one hundred per cent sure yet. I fear I might be making a mistake, and I hope I am.'

The lights dimmed. They shifted in their seats in an attempt to get comfortable, but it was likely that sleep would evade them.

***

About an hour out from the Amundsen–Scott Station, the pilot radioed his intention to land. On Willis's instructions, he deliberately sounded bored. He engaged in small talk and joked with the control guy. He told him that their boss was coming home and that Willis was looking forward to a big fry-up for breakfast.

Earlier, Willis had explained he wanted no one to suspect that this was anything other than a routine flight bringing him back to the base. He wanted everything to be relaxed. The last thing he wanted was for the comms team to chat about it in the galley. 'When we land, I'd like everyone to go for breakfast and act as normally as possible. Bring your handguns with you but keep them concealed. I will go to the comms centre and check for an email reply that I'm expecting from Reilly. I emailed him last night.'

Although Willis's actions puzzled Boris, he was sure that his friend would say what he was up to when he was ready.

An hour later, the group braced themselves for touchdown. The plane gave a single bounce then, surprisingly, made a smooth landing. They piled out of the plane and marched upstairs to the galley. Willis followed them, but turned left into the comms room. After five minutes, he joined the men in the galley, having read Reilly's reply.

They ate breakfast and chatted. McGregor, Sophie, Linda and Gabi came in and sat opposite Willis. Sophie looked at Willis. He was gazing into the distance, unblinking. Something was wrong. She put her hands on Linda and

Gabi's thighs and gave a minuscule shake of her head intimating that they shouldn't speak.

'Right, I need to learn all the news. What happened at Progress Station?' McGregor wiggled in his chair, impatient for an answer.

'You'll get to hear it,' Willis said. 'Is that Justin I can see over at the counter? I'll be straight back. Give me a minute.'

Willis returned with Justin and offered him a seat beside McGregor and opposite Lars. 'I'd like to introduce Major Lars Andersen. He's part of the UN and has joined to help us solve our problem.'

McGregor leaned across the table and shook Lars's hand. 'Before you leave, I hope we can spend some time together. I'm very pleased to meet you.'

'You'll get your wish. Callum McGregor, Major Andersen has come here to arrest you for murder. Lars, please read Mr McGregor his rights.'

McGregor jumped up, then stopped when he saw Lars's pistol pointing at his crotch. Sophie and Gabi screamed. McGregor sank back into his chair and sighed. 'How did you find out?'

'I checked out your history.' Willis turned and spoke to Lars. 'Mr McGregor told me that he was a member of the CIA. He even recognised some of my CIA contacts, so I believed him. For example, he knew that Admiral Jamie Wilson was a heavy drinker. He fooled me. But last night I asked for a background check on Mr McGregor. I found out that yes, he used to work for the CIA, but he'd left under a cloud. Meanwhile, McGregor had been doing some black ops work for – would you believe – Senator Barry Govern. Lars, may I introduce you to Justin Rowe, McGregor's assistant? How much Mr Rowe knew and was involved, is not clear yet, but I'm sure that will all come out in due course. If we check, we'll find that Mr Rowe's boots are the right size for the big treads we found leading to and from the telescope. Mr Justin Rowe, you are under arrest too.'

Lars nodded to two of his men, who secured McGregor's and Rowe's hands behind their backs and read them their rights.

'What made you suspicious?' McGregor glared at Willis.

'Only a few minor things. You faked a Glaswegian accent, but your real Texan accent kept appearing. You support the Dallas Cowboys – who are from the city where Govern lives. I had dismissed the thought on the basis that they were a bandwagon team – until I remembered that you'd said you visited Arlington for home games. You changed from being unco-operative when we first met to becoming my best buddy. Miraculous. They're all trivial details, but when you put them together, they add up. When we uncovered Senator Govern's involvement, I checked up on your background.'

Willis turned and looked at Justin.

'You, Mr Rowe, a potential PhD student, should have had a little more focus on what your study plans were. And you didn't volunteer any information about your university. I thought that was odd. Lars, take them away and lock them up until you're ready to leave.'

'Well, that was a revelation and a half,' Boris said.

'I know, but I wished I'd been wrong. I liked both of them. I find it surprising how easy it is to be led astray by friendship.'

'Now do you think you've finished, or are there more revelations to come?' Boris looked at Willis in disbelief.

'It's finished. Franz Franck puzzled me, but McGregor turned him in to cover for himself. Dr Franck sacrificed himself for the cause. If I hadn't caught on to McGregor, Franck would have got off due to lack of evidence. I even suspected Anton might have been involved at one time. The many delays with him getting the papers from site of the explosion lead me astray but only for a very short while.'

'What about John Connor?' asked Sophie.

'John was a sad man, torn apart by the death of his wife. He blamed the base for her death – things all got too much for him. John had nothing to do with the illegal goings-on. He was a very sick guy. Had we known in time, we might have saved him.'

'While I know it's very early, my English friend, let's have a vodka,' suggested Boris. 'This is truly a cause for celebration.'

'Yes, let's drink to me not having to bury you again on this occasion.'

'I'll still need to disappear … somehow.' Boris gave a cheesy grin and walked over to fetch the vodka.

'So, what are your plans now that the mystery is over, Star Man?' Sophie snuggled into his arm.

'That will depend on whether I can hang on here. They're looking for a new Station Leader so my role here is only temporary.'

'Would you like to stay?'

'Would you like me to stay?'

'Listen, you two lovebirds, give us a break. Why don't you just marry and get it over with?' Linda asked.

'I wouldn't want to marry you then leave you at the bottom of the world to go home.' He kissed Sophie on the cheek.

'The SPT needs another team member,' volunteered Linda. 'And I could recommend that you come and join us. If you did, you would likely stay on as Station Leader as well. After lunch, I'll email and make enquiries. But only if you want me to.' She grinned mischievously.

Willis turned to Sophie. She raised her eyebrows and tilted her head to one side.

'I think that's a yes. Thank you, Linda.'

Within minutes, Boris was back with vodka and wine for the ladies. 'Why do you never offer us girls a vodka?' Linda asked.

'If I had any chance of chatting you up, I would,' Boris said.

'Shut up, you old flirt.'

'Less of the old. Unfortunately, I will need to say goodbye to you wonderful people and return to Progress Station. Maybe Lars might give me a bunk on his ship back to civilisation. I'll miss you, comrade Brad Willis. It's always a pleasure to work with you.'

'And with you, my good Russian friend. What do you think the chances are of us ever bumping into each other again?'

'Probably very good. After this, anything is possible. The probability of meeting you at the South Pole was near zero. In this adventure, comrade, we had a very short shave.'

After a slight delay, Willis said, 'You mean we had a very close shave, but I understand what you mean.'

'That's what I said.' Boris looked at Willis quizzically.

Willis took Boris's hand, held it in both of his, and gave it a mighty shake. 'I'm glad you're not dead after all.'

'Funny you should say that. So am I.' He threw back his vodka and set off to meet Lars, who was leading his two prisoners onto the plane. He raised his arm and gave Willis a slow wave.

'There are tears in your eyes, Dr Willis.' Sophie handed him a tissue. 'I like that in a man.' She leaned over and kissed him on the lips.

'Boris is off with a box of hamburgers, and I hope he enjoys them. Let's have an early lunch,' Gabi said.

'I'm sure I can eat this food all winter.' For the umpteenth time, Willis cut the meat on his plate and took a delicious mouthful.

***

'I received an email from Reilly. Brigadier-General Joshua S. Baker sends his regards and thanks us for our help. Senator Barry Govern and his accomplice Senator Morse are both in custody and helping the CIA with their enquiries. There's a feud taking place between them and the Feds about who has jurisdiction over the case. Somehow I think Antarctica being involved will help Baker win the argument.'

Sophie looked at Willis, unimpressed.

'Reilly wants me back in the UK. He has another job for me, but I've sent my apologies. I've told him we're snowed in.'

'We soon will be,' Sophie said. 'The last flights will leave this week. The weather is about to take a turn for the worse. If you're not off the base by Friday, you'll need to stay all winter.'

'Glen Mason's plane will land soon and he will tell us who the replacement Station Leader is to be.' Willis sounded disappointed.

Linda cut in. 'I have approval for Dr Willis to join our team. Congratulations, Doctor.'

'Many thanks, Dr Foreman.'

'And congratulations from me.' Glen Mason walked up and patted Willis on the back. 'Welcome, Dr Willis, our new Station Leader.'

'It's all happening. I'm being set up.' Willis smiled and shook Glen's hand.

'It's traditional, or at least it should be, to hold a massive welcoming celebratory dinner for our new Station Leader.'

'We're sure we can arrange that.' Linda and Gabi spoke in unison. 'Let's get it organised.'

***

It was the party to end all parties. Willis was a hero to everyone on the base. Alcohol flowed like it was going out of fashion, and musicians emerged from everywhere: guitarists, trombonists, accordionists, flautists and singers. A spinning globe hung in the centre of the room, projecting five-pointed stars onto the ceiling and walls. A vast selection of cocktails was shaken, stirred, and served. They vanished as quickly as they appeared.

They danced until the small hours of the morning. If he didn't cut down on the free-flowing alcohol, Willis was sure that he would experience a cracker of a hangover, so he slowed down and sat in a corner with Sophie. He stared into her eyes. 'Do you think we will get through the winter together, or will one of us murder the other?'

'Of course we'll survive the cold, but that will only happen if we keep each other warm. There have been enough murders here to last a few years.'

Then a dark silhouette sauntered in front of them. Stars from the spinning globe reflected off the shiny panel behind them, illuminating the figure's face. Willis screwed up his eyes to see more clearly. The silhouette spoke. It was Glen.

'These two ladies have told me you are planning to get married?' Clearly expecting a reply, he spread out his hands, palms up.

'This is Antarctica,' Willis said. 'How can we get married?'

'I can marry you. I'm a celebrant. Even in Antarctica, I can arrange it. All you need to do is ask.'

'We don't have the paperwork.' Willis turned and winked at Sophie.

'No problem. I can have it sent over by satellite, overnight.'

'We'll think about it.' Willis smiled. He winked again at Sophie, but this time she looked away. Until Glen had re-joined Linda and Gabi, he bit his tongue. Once Glen was out of earshot, he took Sophie in his arms. 'If I asked, would you marry me?'

'Are you asking?'

'Will you marry me?'

'I've always wanted a white wedding.'

'You can't get any whiter than this.'

'In that case, yes, I will marry you.'

Willis was breathless. He sank onto one knee. 'I will ask you again. Please will you marry me?'

Sophie took him by the hand. 'Yes, my darling Dr Brad Willis, I will marry you.'

Willis leapt to his feet and dashed over to Linda and Gabi. 'She's going to marry me! She said she would marry me!'

'It's about time,' Linda said, then walked over and put her arms around Sophie. 'Congratulations. That's splendid news.' She kissed Sophie on the cheek. 'If we were to suggest a double wedding, what would you say?'

'Have you proposed to Gabi?'

'Not yet.'

Linda disappeared over to the other side of the room. Soon Sophie saw Linda and Gabi in a tight embrace. She smiled.

'We can be each other's witnesses.' Linda looked at Mason.

'It's a pity we couldn't be the other's best man and maid of honour,' Sophie added.

'You can do whatever you want,' Glen said. 'I'll go and arrange the paperwork.'

'It's already too late for us not to see the brides before the big day.' Willis laughed and made a joke of covering his eyes.

Gabi and Sophie said, 'We're not superstitious.'

'That means yet another party, tomorrow after the wedding,' Glen said. 'I'll announce the good news.'

***

The next day was a holiday on the base. Nearly everyone was present at noon, the time they had chosen for the ceremony.

As each of the couples repeated 'I do', an enormous cheer went up. No one took notice of the chunky sweaters that Sophie and Gabi wore.

It was Antarctica, after all.

CHAPTER 38

It wasn't until the end of November that Sophie and Willis returned to Willis's cottage in Madingley. Staying over the winter hadn't been as challenging as Willis had imagined it to be. They were now feeling the effects of post-South Pole blues. Everything about their lives felt unreal, as though they were visitors in their own lives. The long months in Antarctica seemed a long way off, even if it had only been three weeks since they'd left McMurdo on the C-17.

Willis made a point of carrying Sophie over the threshold. 'Unless I carry you in, we don't count as married.'

Willis's cottage was cold. Mrs Burns wouldn't have expected him home, so she hadn't put the heating on, but they remarked that the temperature in the little front room was like summer. Their bodies were still acclimatised to Antarctica.

'Here we are.' Willis threw his jacket on the sofa and switched on the lights to brighten the dull November day. 'I'll make a cup of coffee.'

'Who's there?' a Glaswegian accent asked from behind the back door. 'Who's th-th- there?'

'Don't worry, Mrs Burns, it's just us.'

'My goodness me, I thought for a moment we were being burgled.'

'People don't get burgled in Madingley, Mrs Burns,' Willis said.

'Oh aye, they do. Mr Mohammed across from the pub had his shed broken into last year and his spade stolen.'

'How have you been, Mrs Burns?' Willis asked, in an attempt to change the subject.

'If ye'd told me ye were coming, I'd be a lot better. I would have put on the heating and made ye a bite to eat.'

'That's unnecessary, Mrs Burns. All we need is a wee rest and a nice cup of coffee,' Sophie said.

'You've met Sophie?' Willis asked.

'Of course I have. I've no' got that dementia thing yet.'

'She's Mrs Willis now.'

'Mrs Willis, it's splendid to meet you again.'

Mrs Burns's face fell. She looked at the floor and walked to the door.

'Where are you off to, Mrs Burns? Are you not going to make us a nice cup of coffee?'

'Ye'll no' be needin' me any more. Ye've gone and got yourself a wife.'

'Of course we'll need you! Sophie and I will each do our separate projects and visit each other when we can. When I'm working at Cambridge and Sophie has nothing on, she will stay here. She will return to Switzerland, to CERN. But because her job needs a load of electricity to drive the experiments, they close down in the winter, so as not to deprive the local residents of power. As a result, Sophie won't have a lot to do between November and March, so she'll live here.'

'That's braw.' Mrs Burns was smiling again. 'Ptolemy will be happy to see you, no doubt. I've made a pile o' your letters over there, on the sideboard, but I don't suppose any are urgent after a' this time. I'll go and make ye a lovely cup of coffee. Oh, and I bought some of yon Brazilian stuff ye're fond of. I prefer the Italian blend myself.

'This is a delightful cottage and you'll love living here. This is a grand wee village too. But you'd better keep the doctor in his place – he has a few bad habits.' When she spoke to Sophie, Willis noticed that Mrs Burns's accent had all but disappeared. She used her posh voice when speaking to folk she didn't know too well. That will change shortly, he thought.

'I'll certainly do that, Mrs Burns, and I would appreciate any advice you can give me about Brad's bad habits.'

Mrs Burns walked over to put on the percolator. Soon the aroma of freshly brewed Brazilian coffee percolated throughout the house.

'How's Rabbie doing?' Willis said. Rabbie was her husband; his real name was John. Willis called him Rabbie because he enjoyed making him smile. He took it in good spirits. Since he was confined to a wheelchair and seldom got out, that was just as well.

Whenever he travelled, Willis brought him something back. On this trip, he'd bought him a sweater with 'SOUTH POLE STATION' printed on it that he'd bought at the store at Amundsen–Scott Station. Willis draped the shirt over the shelf in the sitting room. Mrs Burns knew he left his gifts for John there.

'He's well, thank you.'

'How's his poetry coming along?'

As always, Mrs Burns knew when to ignore Willis's silly questions.

Meow.

'Hello, Ptolemy.' Willis bent down to stroke his cat, but Ptolemy dived past him onto Sophie's lap. 'That's me told off by both of my friends. I know my place.'

The coffee was most welcome. Willis had introduced Sophie to several blends at Amundsen–Scott, but this tasted far superior. Sophie nodded in agreement, and Ptolemy curled up on her knee and purred loudly.

Mrs Burns called goodbye and made to leave. The door was almost closed behind her when Mrs Burns called back, 'Ye'll need to put more money in the cat's tin.'

Willis looked at the old tea caddy on the dresser shelf, then walked over to check it. It was empty. That meant Mrs Burns had been financing the cat from her pension. Tomorrow he would transfer funds into her bank. He knew Mrs Burns's savings account details and used them to send her money when he was away. In Antarctica, he had been too preoccupied to think about transferring cash.

Willis picked up the pile of letters from the sideboard and turned to Sophie. 'She's saved everything, even junk mail.'

It was an enormous bundle of correspondence, but soon it was down to a quarter of its original size. Willis opened the door of the log burner and threw all the adverts inside. After this, he tossed in another twenty per cent of the mail. If a letter was important, it was easy to tell, but if he made an error, he was sure they'd send a follow-up. Once he'd reduced the load to a three-inch-thick wad, he seriously got down to tackling them.

The first two inches were all bills. Those he regularly paid by direct debit, he discarded. The others would take more time. A plain brown letter stood out from the rest: he recognised the handwriting. Reilly always handwrote any communications he sent to Willis. Willis ripped the envelope open. He was right. It was from Reilly.

Willis couldn't believe his eyes. Inside were two sheets of paper covered with registration numbers for Triumph TR3s. As was usual for Reilly, there was no name or signature on the message, just the two pieces of printed stationery.

He said to Sophie, 'Reilly has substituted every letter on the partial plate that I remembered with every possible combination of letters and numbers. He's then run them against the information in the DVLA database. That's exactly what I intended to do when we got back, but Mike has saved me the time and effort. One number stands out from the rest. It's the one I planned to check first. HN 3.'

Under hypnosis, Willis had recalled the partial number as MN 3. But he reasoned that he could have misread the 'H' as an 'M'. Beside it was the owner's name and address. It was in north Essex: he could get there in just over an hour.

Now all he needed to do was persuade Sophie to come with him, to help him investigate. He knew she would want to help. She knew how significant this discovery was to him. Sophie had been with him in St Petersburg when Professor Sidorov gave him the disc with the information on it, and she'd seen the look on his face as the evidence came to light. Willis wouldn't have to convince her that it was still important to him to find Carole's killer, even now that he and Sophie were married.

He would book a meal at their favourite restaurant and, over dinner, ask her to come with him. Meanwhile, he prayed that Reilly wouldn't ask him to take on a project. This needed his undivided attention. He folded the letter and put it in his shirt pocket, leaving the remaining letters unopened.

He had other things on his mind.

If you enjoyed this story, please consider leaving a review on Amazon. Reviews help attract readers' attentions to books and promote sales.

Thank You.

ACKNOWLEDGEMENTS

I would like to thank my editor Jane Hammett for keeping me on the straight and narrow and for her encouragement and useful suggestions.

To Dr Jonathon Shanklin, Emeritus Fellow, British Antarctic Survey for his advice on living on the world's remotest continent.

To Joe Phillips - 2014 South Pole Winter Over - for taking the time to read my original manuscript and advise on the finer details of life on Antarctica.

To Dr Amy Bender of the Argonne National Laboratory and the South Pole Telescope collaboration for her advice on the specifications and use of the South Pole Telescope.

About The Author

Tom Boles has discovered more supernovae than any other person in history. Tom is a Fellow of the Royal Astronomical Society and a past President of The British Astronomical Association. He was awarded the Merlin Medal and the Walter Goodacre Award for his  contribution to astronomy. The International Astronomical Union named main-belt asteroid 7648, Tomboles in his honour. He has published many scientific papers on supernovae and written numerous articles for popular astronomy magazines. He has made many television appearances ranging from BBC's Tomorrow's World to The Sky at Night. During recent years he has given Enrichment Lectures on astronomy aboard Cunard liners, mainly their flagship Queen Mary 2. During these trips he had designed and presented shows using the ship's onboard planetarium. His experience as an astronomer inspired this story. His first novel- DARK ENERGY was published in June 2021. He lives in rural Suffolk where he enjoys dark skies free from light-pollution.

BOOKS BY THIS AUTHOR

DARK ENERGY

The first book in the Brad Willis series

When renowned scientists start dying, the scientific community is on full alert. The explosions appear to be unrelated. Their only connection is that they happened in scientific centres of excellence in Switzerland and the United States. Brad Willis knows that he must uncover the secret to save more lives from being lost. MI6 calls on Willis to use his background as a renowned astronomer to infiltrate the scientists to discover the truth behind the deaths. When Willis starts to uncover the facts, everyone is under suspicion... until they start dying. The situation gets more dangerous as two hired assassins hunt him down.

COMING SOON

The third book in the Brad Willis series

Brad and Sophie trace the red Triumph sports car involved in the hit and run that caused his late wife's death. His investigations reveal many facts about Carole's life that neither Brad nor Carole knew. This leads him into a world of crime and deception putting both his and Sophie's lives in danger.

Printed in Great Britain
by Amazon

70204700R00200